TEAMMATES

I0689830

Edited By
Eric Summers

Herndon, VA

Published in the United States by STARbooks Press
PO Box 711612, Herndon, VA 20171

Many thanks to graphic artist John Nail for the cover design. Mr. Nail may be reached at: tojonail@bellsouth.net.

Cover Model: BLADE BYRON
Cover Photo: www.PhotosbyJAE.com

Printed in the United States

Herndon, VA

STARbooks Press Titles by Eric Summers

Can't Get Enough – More Erotica Written by John Patrick

Don't Ask, Don't Tie Me Up

Love in a Lock-Up

Muscle Worshipers

Never Enough – The Lost Writings of John Patrick

Ride Me Cowboy

Service with a Smile

Teammates

Unmasked – Erotic Tales of Gay Superheroes

Unmasked II – More Erotic Tales of Gay Superheroes

Unwrapped – Erotic Holiday Tales

CONTENTS

THE CENTER OF ATTENTION
By Milton Stern

Billy played center for as long as he played football, beginning with peewee, then middle school, high school, and now, college. For some reason, coaches automatically put him in that position, bent over with a quarterback's hands up his crotch. Was it his size? He was always the tallest – and widest – kid with the ability to run over anyone headed for the quarterback like a steam roller? Or, was it his round muscular butt, which was so tantalizing in that position. He never thought it was his butt. After all, he had a talent for hiking the ball and immediately knocking down at least three defensive linemen before they knew what hit them. Years of playing football in his hometown of Newport News gave him a reputation, and many a lineman would try to challenge Billy, but by the end of the game, the quarterback on Billy's team would never have a scratch on him.

He entered college with a full scholarship. By eighteen, his frame had filled out quite nicely, and now in his senior year at age twenty-one, he was, as one of the cheerleaders called him, 'hunkalicious.' Billy was over six-foot-five, weighing more than 280 pounds, with a chest that measured at least fifty-four inches, biceps that approached twenty inches, a waist that although thirty-eight inches was tight and ripped, quads that measured over thirty inches and of course, that big round muscular butt. While many of his teammates were using steroids and other 'enhancements,' Billy had no desire to do anything that wasn't natural. He didn't have to as he was one of the lucky few who could get more muscular just from looking at a dumbbell. To make his teammates more

1

jealous, Billy had inherited the best of both his Russian and Moroccan genes – smooth dark skin, strong facial features, green eyes, thick curly hair and bright white teeth. His hands and feet were huge, and he could palm a football with no problem.

Their first two seasons were highly successful with few losses, so the team was quite surprised when their coach resigned under pressure, and a new coach from a Southern university was brought in. And along with that new coach, arrived a new quarterback. The new quarterback was not unexpected as Jerry Garrison had graduated the prior year and was playing pro-ball now. Billy wasn't envious, for he was not looking forward to a pro football career. He was a straight-A pre-med student, and he was actually looking forward to ending his football days. After all, he had been playing center since he was six years old, and all the practices were getting old.

The team entered the locker room silently the day after the announcement of their new coach and quarterback. As they changed into their practice uniforms, there was grumbling about the new coach's reputation, rumors and gossip that Billy didn't care to hear. The advantage to playing center was that all he had to do was remember when to hike the ball, plow forward and hope he hadn't hurt a defensive lineman – too badly.

After changing, they ran out to the field and lined up, awaiting the introductions.

Billy looked to his right and spotted a tall, black man with an almost equally tall, but younger, black man beside him. The older man looked to be in his mid-thirties, around six-foot-three and muscular. Billy guessed he played football in his youth and maintained his athletic physique. He was wearing a tight white polo shirt that accentuated his large chest and bulging biceps and blue coaching shorts that did little to hide his full basket. He was wearing a cap, but Billy could tell the man had a

2

shaved head, and the hat did not hide the fact that he was perhaps the most handsome man he had ever seen with dark smooth skin and a bright smile surrounded by thick sexy lips. The younger of the two looked to be about Billy's age and maybe only an inch shorter if that much. He was muscular but leaner than the older man. His hair was cut short, and he had high cheek bones, a wide sexy mouth and big dark eyes. He was wearing a green practice jersey and matching sweat pants, but they weren't nearly as tight as the coaches, which is why he probably didn't look as muscular at the moment.

The two men approached.

"I'm Coach Clifford Montgomery, and this young man is your new quarterback, Karl Johnston," the older man said with a bit of a Southern twang Billy recognized, for they were from the same part of Virginia that he was. "Assistant Coach Frase will run you through your drills today ... Which one of you is Greenberg?"

"I am," Billy answered.

"You come with Karl and me," Coach Montgomery said as he signaled for Billy to follow.

As Billy left his teammates, he shrugged his shoulders but did as he was told and caught up with the new coach and quarterback.

"I think it's important that a center and quarterback get to know each other intimately. You two will have to work closer than anyone else on the team, you understand, Greenberg?" the coach asked.

"Yes, sir," Bill responded.

"Good."

Karl just looked back at Billy and smiled.

They continued walking in silence until they reached the locker room then went back to the room that

3

was usually used for rehabilitation with its massage tables, whirlpool and other useful equipment. Billy notice the coach had moved some things around and created a large area in the middle of the room with a section of workout mats. Needless to say, Billy was a little confused. After playing football in the same position for over fifteen years, he was used to new coaches, but never had been brought into a situation with just the coach and quarterback.

"I hear you aren't heading for the pros after college? They say you're going to medical school," Coach Montgomery said.

"Yes, sir, I've always wanted to be a doctor. Playing football was a way of getting scholarship money, and what I didn't spend on undergrad, I can use for medical school," Billy answered expecting the coach to give him the same spiel he always got about how with his talents he should go pro and all.

"Good for you," the coach said, surprising Billy. "You'll have a longer career as a doctor and be able to walk without pain after thirty as well."

"Wow," Billy responded. "You're the first coach to give me that response."

"Johnston here is also pre-med, and the sexy fucker wants to be a surgeon, so I need for you to protect him, so he doesn't injure those hands," Coach Montgomery informed him. "I am not all that keen on playing pro unless you're too stupid to become something else. All that money and a broken body never make for a good combination."

Karl smiled, while Billy wondered if he actually heard the coach call him a 'sexy-fucker.' This wouldn't be too shocking, for coaches and players usually referred to each other with sexual innuendoes and pet names all the time. It was a male-bonding thing, yet there was

4

something about how he said it and the fact that Karl smiled and still had not said a word.

"Damn, a surgeon. Cool. I'm going to become an OBGYN," Billy said directly to Karl.

"All that pussy? Can you handle it?" Karl finally spoke, and what a deep, sexy voice he had, Billy thought as he smiled back at his new quarterback.

"OK, enough of this flirting, love birds, let's get to work," the coach said. He then handed Billy a football. "Greenberg, I want you to practice hiking to Johnston. I don't want any fumbles, none. You hear me?"

They both nodded as Billy bent over to hike the ball. The room was particularly hot, and Billy was dressed in all his pads. He was thankful he had not put on his helmet or he would have passed out.

"Aren't you curious what it's on?" Karl asked.

"Oh yeah," Billy said. "It's just that this is strange for me. I've played center for as long as I can remember, and I never had to practice hiking like this in a room away from everyone."

"You'll find I have new ways of doing everything," Coach Montgomery said. "Before we get started, why don't you get out of those pads; it's hot as fuck in here, and I don't want your parents crying to me when you die of heat exhaustion."

Billy turned to leave the room, when the coach stopped him. "Where the hell are you going?"

"To put on some sweats," Billy said.

"Forget the sweats," the coach said. "Just take off the pads. We're all men here. Hell, you've seen parts of your teammates they've never seen themselves every time you girls shower together."

5

Billy turned around and took off his practice jersey then his shoulder pads. He was wearing a white T-shirt underneath that was soaked with sweat and clinging to every muscular inch of his torso, but he decided to leave it on. He then took off his shoes and his football pants. Now he was just standing there in a jockstrap that did little to contain his huge basket. His teammates had teased him for years about his big balls and thick swinging dick, so he waited for the usual comments. None came. The coach and new quarterback sort of looked but were all business, and Billy was grateful.

"On thirty-two," Karl said as Billy bent over once again. Karl placed the back of his hand against Billy's balls and formed a cup with the other facing up, waiting for the ball, and began, "Twelve, sixteen, thirty-two ..." and before he could say hike, Billy had launched the ball between his legs, into Karl's hands and was propelling forward before Karl knew what hit him, dropping the ball.

"They said he was the quickest center ever, Johnston," Coach Montgomery said with a chuckle as Karl picked up the ball. "He's already knocked down three guys, and a fourth is gonna grab *that* ball ... Coach Phillips already warned me about you, Greenberg."

Billy smiled, but he was not the cocky type, so he felt a little sorry for Karl. "Sorry about that. Let's try it again."

"You're gonna take a little getting used to," Karl said as he wiped some sweat off his brow. "This one on three."

He bent over again, and Karl began, "Seven, four, twenty-two, three ..." and again he dropped the ball as Billy hiked with lightning speed and lurched forward, but this time the coach was standing right in front of him, so he stopped just short of knocking him over.

"Fuck!" Karl said frustrated.

6

"Greenberg, bend over," the Coach said. "Watch, Johnston." And the coach took the quarterback's position behind Billy. "You gotta slam the back of your hand up there," and he firmly 'slammed' the back of his right hand against Billy's balls, then formed a cup with the other hand below it waiting for the hike. It wasn't enough to hurt, just enough to send a shiver up Billy's spine. "And hold them there. You should place them in just the right position to lift this big sexy ass off the ground." And with that, he lifted Billy off his feet, leaving the center to use the ball as a support to keep from falling flat on his face. The coach then gently put him back down. "That way, no matter when he hikes the ball, you won't drop it. Now you try."

When the coach removed his hands, Billy actually missed them; then, he realized his dick was starting to swell a bit, and some precum was leaking out. Now, he wished he had gone to get those sweat pants. He hoped that if he continued to sweat as much as he was now, his jock might be too wet for anyone to notice.

"On twenty-three." Karl resumed his position, this time slamming the back of his hand up Billy's crotch, then forming a cup with the other hand. He then attempted to lift Billy up, but he couldn't, so he just began, "Twelve, twenty, sixteen, twenty-three ..." and this time he held onto the ball, but not before almost dropping it again.

"You're getting it ... again," the Coach said.

Billy quickly assumed the position before they could notice the precum or the fact that his dick was starting to grow.

He really wished he could get his sweats.

"On seventeen this time," Karl said. "Wait a minute; it's too fucking hot in here." Then Karl kicked off his shoes, pulled off his sweat pants and removed his shirt, wearing nothing but a jockstrap himself. Billy could see all

7

this when he looked through his legs. Now he knew he was in trouble, for Karl was a brown-skinned god. He then slammed his hand against Billy's balls, but this time he slid them up and down just a tiny bit. "Damn, your butt is all sweaty," Karl complained.

"Just get to it," Coach Montgomery said.

"Thirteen, four, fifty-six, forty-two, forty-three, sixteen, seventeen ..."

Billy hiked and lurched forward, and when he turned around, Karl had the ball firmly in his hand and a big smile on his face. He looked over at the coach who had taken off his shirt, and he really worried about that wet spot on his jock.

"Again," the coach said.

Billy assumed the position for three more hikes. By now, both Billy and Karl were covered in sweat, and he had finally removed his wet T-shirt. On the fourth try, Billy waited for the familiar 'slam' of Karl's hand, but it didn't come.

Instead, he felt something soft and realized it was Karl's tongue on his ass!

"Oh man, I just couldn't help myself," Karl said between licks. "I couldn't stare at this beautiful butt a minute longer."

Billy looked up and saw the coach's bare feet in front of him. With his hands still on the ball, he looked further up, and Coach Montgomery was standing there wearing nothing, not even a jock, and his long thick, dark brown cock was pointing straight out above Billy's head. The coach then squatted down, looked the surprised center in the eyes, and said, "You are one beautiful man." Then, he planted his thick full lips on Billy's, and they made out swapping spit and encircling each other's tongues. He never took his hands off the ball, and he no

8

longer worried about the wet spot as his jock was one sticky mess with the coach's tongue in his mouth and Karl's tongue all over his ass.

Karl reached up and grabbed the waist band of Billy's jock to pull it off, or at least he tried for the center's dick was so big and hard, it was making it difficult. Karl reached between Billy's thighs and freed the obstruction, giving the sweat and precum coated dick a nice stroking while he removed the jock with the other hand, never letting his tongue leave that hot ass in front of him.

The coach continued to make out with him, and Billy didn't want him to stop, but the coach left the center's mouth for just a second, and replaced his tongue with his long, thick cock. Billy finally let go of the ball and grabbed the backs of Coach Montgomery's thighs.

No one said a word. There were slurps and moans of satisfaction, but nothing needed to be said.

Billy's ass suddenly felt cool as Karl stopped licking it, slid between the center's thighs and flipped over on his back. He then grabbed Billy's butt and pulled him toward him until the center's enormous cock was aiming at his mouth, and Billy did as directed until he felt the warmth of the quarterback's mouth on his dick. But this position didn't quite work, so Karl slid from between his legs, stood up and guided Billy over to one of the massage tables. He made Billy lie down on his back. The quarterback then bent over and with easy access gave Billy the wettest, most sensual blowjob of his young life, and it was a good thing he had a wide mouth to accommodate Billy's legendary cock. The coach stood near Billy's head and stuck his cock back into the center's mouth.

Karl was stroking his dick and about to blow, when he announced, "Who wants it?"

"I do," the coach said, and with that he bent over just in time for the quarterback to stroke his cock one

9

more time, aiming it at the coach's mouth. Coach Montgomery then took Karl's dick gladly and swallowed every bit of the young quarterback's tasty load.

"My turn. Take it, Greenberg," and the coach blew his huge load into Billy's mouth, which brought him closer to the edge. Billy made sure to get every drop, and the coach did not deny him any.

"Who gets mine?" Billy panted as he let the coach's cock slip from his mouth. Neither the coach nor the quarterback said a word; they just both went down on his throbbing cock, swapping spit between them, and when he shot, one mouth was on it, then the other, and back and forth until he was spent.

The coach looked down at Billy and said, "This is how I like for my center and quarterback to know each other intimately."

A PASS
THROUGH THE MOUNTAINS
By Justin Shepherd

It had been a long flight from New York, but on landing at Marco Polo Airport in Venice, I felt a surge of energy as I anticipated ten days of hard training and racing through the Italian Dolomites that lay ahead. I was one of ten road cyclists selected from across the United States to participate in this event and was looking forward to meeting the other members of the squad. It was a relief to see my bike case being rolled into the oversized baggage area, and after claiming it, I was easily identified by the team officials who were there to meet us.

"Team America?" an athletic-looking man asked me as I left the baggage claim area pulling my bike case behind me.

"Yep, Jason Esperson from New York," I answered with a firm handshake.

"Great, you're the last one we're picking up on this run, so we're ready to head off. The van's parked just outside."

We exited the airport into the crisp morning air, and after loading my bike and suitcase into the already stuffed van, I climbed into the one remaining seat, and we set off for Trento, some 50 miles northwest, where our event was to begin. There were eight of us in the van, all males in our early twenties, and the sight of their defined, fit bodies shown to good advantage in scant summer apparel, sent tingling sensations into the head of my cock, and it was all I could do to keep from getting hard. Beside

11

me was probably the hottest of all the passengers, an African-American man whose body and face combined to create an expression of male beauty that might've made Michelangelo want to recreate his famous David.

"Hey, wassup man? Tyler Davis," he said as our hands clasped in a firm handshake.

"Jason Esperson, nice to meet you man," I responded. As the journey proceeded, the animated and unfocused conversation of the passengers, mostly geared toward breaking the ice and establishing our worthiness as warriors of the road, gave way to more meaningful conversations usually with neighboring passengers.

"So where you from?" I asked Tyler, eager to begin such a conversation myself.

"Philly," he answered. "You?" he continued, almost as if to deflect the conversation away from himself.

"Brooklyn," I responded. "Tried to leave the place a few times, I always end up going back there. And always to Bay Ridge. Remember *Saturday Night Fever*? Well, that's my 'hood.' How about you, been in Philly a while?"

"Yeah, I guess I'd call it home, for better or worse. Like you, been away now and then, always seem to end up back there."

Tyler was rather short on details, and by the end of our conversation, which had often been interrupted by banter with other passengers, I learned little more than that he had an engineering degree from Penn State University and that he'd raced for the university cycling team. As the drive continued, the countryside growing increasingly hillier as we moved inland from the coast, I noticed my right leg moving closer to Tyler's left, whether from the movement of the van or my strong impulses to move closer to him, I couldn't be sure. One thing was certain though, he was not moving his leg away; in fact I soon began to feel what I thought was slight pressure from

12

his left leg. Through the vineyards and olive groves, our legs pressed more firmly together, this signal of our identity and our mutual interest confirmed by Tyler's left hand caressing my right, the gesture discreetly concealed by a copy of *Cycle Sport America* which had been passed around the van earlier.

Arriving in Trento, the van wound its way through its ancient streets, and I knew we'd soon be arriving at the hotel, so I thought I'd better act quickly.

"Got any plans who you're bunking with?" I asked Tyler.

"No, no plans about that," he responded.

"Same with me. Wanna be roommates?"

"Sure, sounds cool."

"Great. I'll text the guy looking after all that and let him know," I said as my thumbs went to work on my Blackberry.

The hotel was modest and functional, exactly like all the other hotels I'd ever stayed with a racing team, but I'd never before shared a room with a man this hot and with so much potential for off-bike action.

"Any preference for which bed you want?" I asked as we entered the room, wanting to start things off on a good footing.

"Doesn't make much difference. We may only need one," Tyler answered, resting his arms on my shoulders and losing no time in continuing what had begun in the van.

"Works for me," I said, draping my arms similarly across his shoulders as we exchanged a lingering kiss on the lips.

"This isn't what I expected when I got off the plane," I remarked, "but I'm lovin' it."

13

Before long the two of us were on one of the beds, slowly undressing each other. I've always had a weakness for a man's chest and torso, and Tyler's were possibly the most perfect I'd ever seen, with a six-pack as hard as granite, his chocolate brown muscular shoulders encasing a chest that made my cock as hard as his six-pack. Tyler seemed to be as impressed with my body as I was with his, as he ran his hands up and down my chest and torso whispering words like "nice" as his hands did their dance on my upper body.

Before unbuttoning his 501s, I did a similar dance with both my hands, feeling the outline of his erect member against the denim, and following the contours of his ass as my hands continued their exploration. Finally, I could hold off no longer, and I ran my finger down his fly causing the metal buttons to be released from their well-worn buttonholes. I opened his jeans, and his erect, musky cock sprang out before me. I held it in my hand for a brief while, then licked his shaft hungrily from top to bottom before taking the magnificent piece in my mouth. He was uncut, and the moist head of his dick felt especially tantalizing as it met my tongue. I pulled his jeans off leaving him naked except for his socks, and only seconds later, my jeans also were on the floor, and we locked in a tight embrace. I was surprised at the intimacy I felt with Tyler, having met him only just hours ago. It usually took me a while to reach a comfort level such as this one, and it had never before happened with a teammate on an important competitive event. But, there was an electricity with Tyler that drew me closer to him and left me wanting to go deeper.

# # # # #

After four days of riding through beautiful but exhausting terrain, we were making our way in a perfect pace line into the city of Bolzano. Tomorrow would be our rest day, and even the most driven members of the team were ready for a day off the bike. In addition to the torturous *Passo di Stelvio,* we had traversed the grueling *Passo di Gavia* and the even more grueling *Passo di Mortirolo,* with the steep climbs and dizzying descents of the *Madonna di Campiglio* and the *Passo di Tonale* thrown in to keep the pressure on. The cerebral scenery of the Dolomites together with the unearthly crisp cool air at high elevations provided at least as much fuel as the loads of pasta and other high carb foods that were the staples of our diet. As a climber, my skills were put to the test and all boundaries pushed to their breaking points, as I and the other climbers drafted the sprinters up the hills and around the switchbacks, preserving their energy for later when the power in the legs would propel them forward to cross the day's finish line first. Tyler was a sprinter, and never did I feel more energized than when drafting him up a hill, no matter how cruel its gradient. Evenings were spent reviewing the day's performance with the rest of the team and our coaches and planning for the next day's ride, followed by carousing with teammates, visits to local bars, or simply sleeping, especially when climbs like the *Mortirolo* loomed before us the next day.

Tyler and I had developed a close bond, which was not unnoticed by the rest of the team, but that was of no concern to us. I didn't know much about love, as I hadn't much experience of it, but I was beginning to wonder if it had cast its spell over me in the person of Tyler. I didn't let myself go too far down that road, for it occurred to me that there were aspects of Tyler that I found a bit mysterious; but I didn't want to ask a lot of questions because I was discovering that Tyler was a man of few words, especially when talking about himself. I liked his quietness, even though sometimes it troubled me. There was a softness, a sadness to him that worked as a foil to his rugged, hard body, his superb masculinity and his phenomenal bike-handling skills.

Awakening to the sound of church bells, as so often happens in Italy, we kissed each other tenderly and our

15

hands explored wherever they could reach as the bells chimed out hymn tunes or simply rang randomly in their towers.

"Bolzano's a great place to spend a rest day, but we're not far from Innsbruck," I said with more than a hint of suggestion in my voice. "Might be cool to check out Austria. The train station's just up the way. I checked the schedule. There's lots of trains there and back, through the Brenner Pass. Supposed to be beautiful. And so is Innsbruck. How about it?"

"You're thinkin' we should head up there?"

"Why not? Get away from these hammerheads for a while, be on our own for a bit."

"You're bad, bro, very bad." Flipping me over on my stomach, feeling the contours of his light, sinewy body on top of me, he added, "That's why I hang out with you, man. I'd be up for a trip to Innsbruck. But first let's get this day started right." I felt the weight of his warm, manly body on my back and closed my eyes in ecstasy.

After breakfast, we told the team director of our plans for the day. "Today is yours to spend however you like," he consented. "Just make sure you know what the plan is for tomorrow's ride to Corvara, and don't be gettin' back here at some crazy hour."

"You got it," we assured him.

The next train to Innsbruck was a sleek all first-class train with a hefty premium added to the price of the ticket.

"Damn, maybe we should take a different train," Tyler said. "That's a hell of a price."

"Let's just do it. After those climbs, we deserve some pampering."

With precision that was more like the Swiss than the Italian railways, the train arrived exactly on schedule. It was clear on boarding and making our way to our luxurious assigned seats that this was no ordinary train. Soon after we departed, Tyler and I decided to check out the dining car, where we would spend most of the journey drinking coffee and eating sandwiches and snacks that our coach would not likely have approved. The stunning good looks of the young Italian dining car attendant did not escape our attention. A cyclist himself, he soon figured out that we were bike racers and engaged us in lively conversation. He spoke perfect English with an Italian accent, which only added to his appeal, as also did the complementary espressos he made for us. Before long, we knew that cycling wasn't the only thing he had in common with us.

"This is a cool idea you had, Bro," Tyler said admiring the beauty of the Brenner Pass as we headed toward the Austrian border. "At first, I thought it was a bit crazy, now I'm glad we did it."

"Me, too. Makes me glad to be alive."

"Bein' alive's what it's all about," he responded. "Gotta make every minute count. You never know what can happen, and it all changes."

I was puzzled by this response, which wasn't the first such reference that Tyler had made in the short time I'd known him.

"Especially racing a bike through these mountains," I added. "Talk about livin' on the edge. We've already got one busted collarbone in the squad. Would've been a lot worse if the dude hadn't been wearing a helmet."

"Injuries ain't never pretty, busted collarbone or busted head." A doleful look came over Tyler's face, and his deep brown eyes seemed to be viewing something more than the mountain scenery, something only his eyes could see. Our legs touched lightly under the table. I wondered what he might have going on in his mind, but was reluctant to probe any further.

"The only time I feel really alive is when I'm on my bike, especially when I'm riding hard over this kinda terrain. And also when I'm in bed with a hot man," I added with a smile, trying to bring Tyler back to the moment. "Or on a train with one."

"Or on a train with one," Tyler added, his gaze directed now at me rather than out the window. "I wonder if this train has sleeping compartments."

"Ooo, I like you how think. Bet it does. It came overnight from Monaco. Our waiter here would know. Should we ask him?"

"How else we gonna find out?"

We were the only ones in the dining car, so eye contact with the waiter, whose name we now knew was Ottavio, was all it took to bring him to our table.

"How's everything, my friends?" Ottavio asked in a dolce voice.

"Couldn't be better," I answered. "We were just wondering if there are sleeping cars on this train."

"Of course. This is The Blue Train, first-class service from the French Riviera to Vienna. Ever heard of the Orient Express? The Blue Train is its sister, and has even more stories. It's all about knowing the conductor. I learned that a long time ago. I could get you a sleeping car compartment, but only until the Austrian border. That's where we change crews. You'd only have about half an hour."

"That's all we'd need," Tyler said with a mischievous smile, as my cock began to strain behind the denim of my jeans as it became apparent that the Ottavio wasn't joking. He called the conductor on a cell phone, and after

18

speaking to him in Italian said to us, "Car number 5641, three back from this one. Stephano – he's the conductor – says I can close up here since my shift's almost over and take you back to car number 5641. He's going to open up compartment 7 for you."

Compartment 7 was a tight squeeze, but had everything we needed. We invited Ottavio to stay, and my hand feeling the outline of his massive cock was all the coaxing he needed. In minutes the three of us were naked, our bodies pulsating to the gentle purr of the fast-moving train, our cocks as hard as the rails we rode on. Ottavio's skills extended far beyond that of the barista and his versatility in the pleasures of manhood, both giving and receiving, amazed both Tyler and me. After about twenty minutes of an octopus-like union of dancing limbs in flavors of vanilla, chocolate and olive, all three of us shot our loads into the condoms we were wearing, and the three of us lay breathless on the bed as our heart rates began slowly to decelerate as our hands continued to explore our sweaty bodies.

The train stopped at Brenner, the border point between Italy and Austria. Ottavio was again dressed in his dining car uniform and prepared to leave the train with the rest of the FS crew, who would now be replaced with a crew from the Austrian State Railways, the OBB.

"Have fun in Innsbruck, and good luck with your racing. Maybe I'll see you in the *Giro d'Italia* one day!" Tyler and I returned to the seats printed on our tickets. By the time the train pulled out of the Brenner station, the all-male Italian crew had changed into jeans and T-shirts or polos and were talking casually among themselves on the platform. They seemed at once aware and unaware of the intense virility and masculinity they possessed, set in bold relief against the powerful train that was now leaving the station. Ottavio waved to us with a broad smile as our car passed the former train crew. Tyler seemed to be deep in thought as we waved back, his face no longer

19

passionate and dreamlike as it was in the sleeping car compartment; rather the look of sadness that had puzzled me since we first met had returned. We spent a pleasant day in Innsbruck, returning to Bolzano late that evening on a much more ordinary train than the first one. Our teammates welcomed us back, and we joined them in the hotel lounge for a nightcap. They were intrigued by our excursion to Innsbruck, but our encounter with Ottavio took its place in the library of untold stories aboard The Blue Train.

# # # # #

It was now the last day of our time together in the Alto Adige region of Italy, the day of a much anticipated one-day competition against teams from Italy, France and Spain. The usual peacefulness of the town of Corvara was nowhere to be found amid the spectators, bike racers, support vans, team busses, police motorcycles and all the excitement of a race start point. All the riders from Team America were primed and ready for the event, which included the dreaded *Passo di Fedaia*, better known as the *Marmolada*, the highest mountain of the Dolomites. Over the past nine days we had bonded well as a team, and each of us knew what we had to do to make today the success we all wanted it to be. Tyler had been particularly quiet ever since returning from a ride he went on alone last night, but our minds were focused on today's race, so nothing was talked about. From the moment the clock started, all of us were giving it all we had. After several hours of hard racing, we were now at the steepest, most relentless part of the climb, and I was drafting Tyler up this segment. My whole body ached, but he kept saying, "Faster Jason, faster," and I dived deep into myself to find more strength to go faster, though I had no idea where the strength was coming from. There was a passion, even a fury, in Tyler's voice that I had never before heard. I thought my body would burst and my guts would spew out over the road, so intense was the pain as I turned the crank harder and harder, allowing Tyler to make the climb in my updraft, conserving his energy for later in the race. I could practically feel his breath on my back, he was that close behind me. I only hoped the wheels of our bikes wouldn't touch, which would send us both to the pavement. At last, we reached the summit, my heart rate at 190 beats per minute, my lungs gasping like a bellows gone mad.

I knew the hardest part of my work was over, and I moved left allowing Tyler to pass. He then began what was to be a magnificently controlled descent, followed by a breakaway and a neck-and-neck sprint to the finish line between Tyler and a ferociously strong and determined Spanish cyclist. Tyler was the first to cross the finish line by only a fraction of a second, his hands raised skyward in the traditional V as he decelerated and came to a stop amid the cheers of the spectators.

All of Team America, and many hopefuls and contenders from the European teams, were stunned by Tyler's performance and in awe of his unexpected achievement of first place on the podium. Race officials, pro team scouts, cycling press and spectators swarmed around the Team America bus where Tyler was receiving his post-race massage and a briefing from the team director as to what to expect. He was not accustomed to attention on this scale and was visibly uncomfortable with it, despite his best efforts to appear to be taking it all in his stride. He mentioned to a journalist that he couldn't have done it without having been pulled through the *Fedaia* pass by "the best climber I've ever drafted with," which left me feeling both humbled and exalted.

"What the hell happened today? Where did the power come from?" I asked when at last we were back in our hotel room in Corvara, naked, showered, tired, and beside each other.

"We'll talk about it tomorrow," Tyler answered, the familiar look of sadness slowly returning to his face. "Let's get some sleep now." We fell asleep in each other's arms.

The next morning, we packed up for the last time, since today's destination point – to be reached by team bus rather than by bike – was Trento, where we'd started ten days earlier. From there, we'd be taken to the Venice airport, some this evening and the rest of us tomorrow depending on our flight arrangements.

"Jason and I are going for a little spin," Tyler said to the team director after breakfast. "We'll leave our bikes with the mechanics when we get back."

"Don't be long. We gotta be on our way before eleven."

Tyler and I headed out of town on our bikes, this time with me following Tyler as I wasn't sure where we were going. We left the town of Corvara and started up a hill along a road we'd not ridden with the rest of the team. A few miles up the hill, with the massive slate-colored elevations of the Dolomites surrounding us beneath a canopy of a deep blue sky with billowing white clouds, we came to a church that had probably been on that site for at least 500 years. Beside the church was a striking monument to the men from that region who had lost their lives in World War I. A column of granite on which was affixed local stone rose into the air, with helmets and bayonets at the top of it suggesting that the granite column was meant to represent the infamous trenches. Beside the column, possibly within the trench, was an angel cast from bronze, strong and powerful-looking, but with a grief-stricken look on its face. In its arms, the angel gently carried the lifeless body of a young soldier, also cast in bronze, his naked torso and arms revealing the health and youthfulness of his life now lost.

22

Engraved on the monument was the inscription: *PREMADIO AL SUOI GLORIOSI FIGLI SOLDATI EROICAMENTE PER LA PATRIA.*

"Remember the night before yesterday's race I went out on my bike after dinner? Well, for some reason I ended up here, and I couldn't take my eyes off this monument."

"It's powerful," I said, not wanting to add anything more but sensing more was to come.

"I used to be in the U.S. Army. I did three extended tours of duty in Iraq during our worst years over there. I saw stuff that no man should ever have to see. Only thing that kept me going, only thing that kept me from turning a gun on myself, was my friend Tony Wilson. He was a brother. Best friend a man could ever have. He was gay, like you and me. But it was don't-ask-don't-tell, and that's how it was at home for him, too. Southern Baptist family and all, you know how it is with that. He was an athlete, Tony was, and bike racing was in his blood. Used to say to me, I wonder if a brother will ever wear the Yellow Jersey. I told him, why not? He said he wanted to give it a shot after he got back home. Tony never got back home. He was killed in a bomb attack. I was there when it happened, with him when he died. I've relived it a thousand times. That monument right there, with those colors and that soldier's face, that's Tony there, Jason. That's Tony. It's like that angel brought him here, so I could see him again and carry on his dream."

"Holy God," I said. "Now it all makes sense. I always knew there was something on your mind."

"When we were on the train the other day," Tyler continued, "you said something about the only time you feel happy is on the bike, riding hard, and when you're in bed with another guy. Strangest damn thing, that coulda been me saying those words. Truth is, only time I feel free is when I'm on my bike, only time I'm happy is when I'm close to another man. Everything else just kinda scares

23

the shit outta me. I've kept quiet about being in the army cuz I don't wanna talk about it. I can't talk about it. At least not yet. All that talk the politicians give about bravery and honor and all, they don't know shit about any of that. They ain't seen what I seen." Tyler paused a second, looking at the monument. "This angel here, he knows the story. You can tell by the look on his face." Again, Tyler paused, and I respected the silence and said nothing. "Anyway," he continued, "with that win yesterday it won't be long and everyone's gonna know I was over there. Not sure how I'm gonna handle it. Doesn't matter. I'll figure it out. But yesterday goin' up the Marmolada, it was like Tony was right there, next to me, maybe even helping me somehow. It was weird, man, but that's where the power came from yesterday. I was riding for Tony."

"Thanks for bringing me here, Tyler, and for telling me all this" I said, not knowing quite how to respond. "It's not every day stuff like this happens in the world of bike-racing, or any competitive sports. That's a lot you just told me. As for don't-ask-don't-tell, it needs to disappear from sports as much as it needs to end in the army."

"Wouldn't wanna hold my breath waitin' for it to happen in either case," Tyler responded.

"But then, who'd have thought anyone could ride a bike over terrain like this," I added with a sweeping gesture of my arm toward the surrounding landscape. "Someone had to build a pass through the mountains. Maybe it'll be up to us to start clearing the way for a pass through another kind of mountain that's just as big as any of these. Think Tony would like that?"

"Yeah, I do. I think he'd be real proud."

"We better head back to Corvara," I said. "Otherwise we'll be riding our bikes to Trento."

"Thanks for everything, man," Tony said looking deep into my eyes. "Been quite a trip."

24

"I'm the one who should be saying thanks," I replied as we embraced with a lingering kiss, which we knew would be the last one until we met again on the other side of the Atlantic.

JOCKS & COCKS
By R. Talent

"Bring that sweet candied ass into my office ... now!" Coach Leavenworth snarled, standing in the door of his basement office, across from the showers and locker room that I was exiting.

I knew it was coming. I felt it. I went off his script. Off of his plan. And although we won the game based on my defiance, in his eyes it was still defiance.

He knew I knew. He thought he was getting under my skin, knowing how badly I hated Sweet Candied Ass, so I looked at him dead on. I tried to contain the anger that was boiling inside of me, along with the clouding fear that one of my teammates might have heard him. I tried, but I couldn't stop myself from cutting my eyes and mean-mugging the short bastard with the Napoleon complex.

"I don't give a shit! Roll them fucking eyes all you fucking want! Because the next place they will be rolling is out your head and on the floor!"

I limped into his office, fully understanding that if he had to repeat himself it wasn't going to be good for me.

"What kind of shit was that, Wes?"

I could have easily thrown it up in his face that we, as a team, were victorious because of my move. I could have reiterated that the pitcher was weak. And that we were scoring homeruns off him as if he was a bitch in heat with everybody taking a turn at it. So, there was absolutely no point to hit as sorry as he pitched, being a bunt or any other sort of weak swing.

"Leadership," I paused. "Leadership you taught me, coach. A decision I stand by," I said, remembering his infinite speeches that if anybody went off script that it better be a good and winnable move.

I knew though, no matter what I said to him, what I did, his way or my way, he was going to find some kind of fault with it.

Like the saying goes, we were at the end of our road together.

I bet that our story plays out on college campuses everywhere, every year:

Small town boy starts out as a big fish in his small town pond, soon discovers that as a freshman at a big university he is nothing more than a guppy swimming in an ocean. As a freshman, he is the rookie of the bunch. He receives little, if no love on campus. Because his regiment is so strict to keep his scholarship, he is restricted to study and playing ball. He has no room to fraternize. His books and his playbooks become his frat buddies. His coach begins noticing his eagerness and puts him in when another player is out. He is good, but not great. He has potential, but lacks practice and advance skill. The coach takes him under his wing and gives him the tools. The player lives for this. The coach becomes the mentor he needs, learning the ins and outs of his players, their strengths, their weaknesses, and their intricacies. He comes across the golden nugget that his player is lonely, very lonely, and homesick. He is lonely because he is at the bottom of the totem pole and hasn't quite learned, naïve rather, that in order to come up that it costs to play to be the boss.

A couple of congrats here and there. A pat on the shoulder, from time to time, moves from the broad back down to the lower back mixed that in with a couple of in-your-face pleasantries. Warm breaths kissing his sweet young face, gives him something to think about for a few nights alone in his dorm tossing and turning with an incredible hard-on in his hand. The coach makes his move pressing close against his pupil, holds him in a way that a coach shouldn't hold a player with his long thick erection jabbing right there at his inner thigh.

'I'm not gay,' his naïve player says or tries telling himself.

The coach says something to the effect like 'nobody had to know' or 'I'm not either' or 'if you're secure with your sexuality you can't be gay.'

He reaches out and touches the nervous scared eighteen-year-old dick before him, trapped in a denim-clad prison.

The coach goes for broke. Touching and feeling, groping and caressing that doesn't feel like anything that has ever been felt before – not even when he jerks off. The feelings are so strong, so raw, that it is all an ecstatic blur overcome with automatic orgasms.

He knows that his subordinate is got, ready to be had.

He wants his reciprocations.

He somehow talks his player onto his knees to face the enormous monster that belongs to neither human nor beast, attacking from his groin. He tells his player that for now he needs not to worry about anything but the tip, the head, the technical term, the glans.

His player nervously, but enthusiastically, obliges, taking instruction well, licking it as if it was a cool flavored Popsicle. Round and round. Back and forth, as if he's got an unscratched-able itch at the roof of his mouth.

His player goes at it.

The coach comes.

No warning.

He wants the thrill of watching his player try and spit it out. He knows a drizzle will seep down the back of his throat. What excites him most, however, is that regardless of how much he tries to get it off his tongue, there is always the hidden knowledge that he came in his mouth.

His is the first to have him there.

He will be remembered.

His player is highly confused. What the hell just happened?

In that day or that night or a week or two or a month later, the coach convinces his curious player it is only fair that they go all the way. It is only fair. He knows the tricks, suck and then finger fuck. Eat him out to unleash his inner bitch and finger fuck him again. A condom and some lube happen to be nearby, ass up face down in the soft suffocating pillows. Pow! Stuck him right in his sweet tender ass! It feels a mighty python is snaking up the unforgiving tubing of guts as the coach tells him that once he gets it all in that 'it'll feel real good.' But all that is there, at first, is a head-busting headache and the inescapable feeling of being clipped in two.

He hurts, yet he starts to feel good. Pleasure and pain and pleasure again. He stays in the player like this, for a really long time, being that he wants to be the one remembered as the one that unequivocally shatters his cherry.

He grabs his player by the waist, spends him on his meat and onto his back. He wants his player to watch him; because of age and inexperience, he wants to watch him do the number three after he loses himself after a few hefty strokes in this new position. He moves faster, almost in demon force. Sweat pours from him, thrusting hard and more deliberate, letting his player know that he belongs to him, body and soul and butthole. Their breaths and

30

screams are manic. His player groans. He grunts, pulls out, pulls off and uses the hard stomach below him as a cobblestone cumdump.

The virgin, the virgin-tight hole is sloppy and open and sounds like its farting when it is not deliberately. He looks at his player, fascinated by his country-boy naivety. He loves that he could talk him on to his big dick, without even knowing that it was incredibly huge by standards.

I was so turned out by the experience, needing him inside of me, that I allowed him to fuck me almost every day for the past four years since we met. And now that I was on the verge of graduating, he was certain that our rendezvous was coming to an end, and he was angered by it.

I sat there, listening to Coach Leavenworth, my first, rant about my defiance. He was hoping to coax out some sort of rouse out of me. After four years, I knew the routine. It had been awhile since the last time we fought and fucked. It was my sad attempt to wean myself off the potent drug that was him. Even when he flipped the script and became the sweet-talking man that knew he could get this young country ass anytime he thought about it.

But things changed. I was no longer that naïve freshman. I was a cock of the walk senior that quickly discovered the semester before last that while I love stuffing my ass with his big boner, I loved poking my dick in between some tight oven-warm buns.

Coach Leavenworth gave up after an hour and allowed me to go about my day.

Not a moment after I came up the stairs to cut through the gymnasium to get back to my dorm was there Tuck, a sophomore, sitting in the stands.

Tuck was a teammate of mine and was very much lovesick. He was drawn to me like a moth to a flame, believing every word that came out of my mouth was like

31

gold gifts from the gods. He looked to me as I probably did to coach in the beginning – except I was the full package from head to skills to toe.

I'm not saying that Tuck was an ugly mofo. He was one of those kinds of dudes that just by looking at him at first sight that 'good-looking' wasn't a phrase that came easily to mind. Yet, he was attractive in a masculine way with his square head, long face, big lips, and hard-lined jaws that sandpaper could've smoothed out. Once you got to know him though, and his unwavering loyalty, it was hard for me not to fall. This made me feel both happy and sick the first time I got him on his back to call me Big Daddy.

But after taking one good look at his tight athletic body and his shelf-life phat round basketball-dribbling booty, I was hooked and still smiling.

"What did he say?" Tuck asked.

I looked at him. I had been telling him for weeks that the reason the coach was so preoccupied with me was because he was trying to transition me into the pros.

Tuck hadn't a clue that Coach Leavenworth and I were continuing fuck buddies. And, I didn't want him to think otherwise, as he was deeply in love with me with wild hopes of me giving up my dreams of going pro to settle down and build a life with him after he graduated.

Yeah, right.

I wrapped my powerful arm over his neck, leading him back to my dorm and said, "He told me if that boy is sucking your dick like that, that you're hitting homeruns like its water flowing freely, you need to find a way to always keep your dick in his mouth."

Defiant? Deceptive? Absolutely not!

It is how everyone learns their lessons at the university level.

THE END OF THE GAME
By Wayne Mansfield

Brad sprinted across the oval with the football. He dared not look behind him even though he knew he was being pursued by an opponent from the visiting team. He could hear him getting closer and closer. At the last minute, just as the opponent was about to tackle him, he handballed the ball to Greg, Number 27, and continued to run toward the goal posts.

"Over here," he called. "Over here!"

He could see that Greg was just about to be tackled. He kept calling out, desperate for Greg to kick the ball to him so that he could try for a goal. He was within reach. It would be a piece of cake.

"Over here, Greg!"

Greg lined the ball up with his foot and kicked it. Brad ran toward it, not taking his eyes of the oval-shaped leather ball, not noticing anything else on the field. If he marked the ball and didn't drop it, he would get a free kick, and being so close to the goal posts, he couldn't miss. He launched himself into the air; everything seemed to be in slow motion. He reached up to catch the ball knowing that he was just seconds from scoring his team a goal that could win the match for them.

His hand touched the ball. He smiled. But suddenly he felt a sharp pain in the small of his back, and he was knocked forward with an almighty force. A player from the opposing team, who had jumped up to knock the ball out of Brad's hands, had misjudged the height and distance between himself and Brad and had landed, studded boots first, in the small of Brad's back. Brad's eyes widened, shocked, and he put his arms out to break his fall, but as his hands touched the muddy grass of the football oval, the big guy from the other team came crashing down on top of him, jarring his arm and dislocating both shoulders and shattering the bones in his right arm.

When the rest of his body hit the ground, he was already writhing in agony and didn't notice the referee, his mother and several of his team mates rushing over to see if he was okay.

"Are you alright, love?" asked his mother, her eyes filled with tears.

But Brad couldn't answer. The pain in his shoulders was so excruciating it was all he could do to stop himself from screaming blue murder. He was aware of a small group of people gathering around him, but he didn't recognize any of the faces. Their words of comfort and sympathy were wasted on his ears. He could hear what they were saying, but the message wasn't registering. Finally, he blacked out.

That had been three years ago. He had been fifteen and playing on his school's football team. Football, or footy as it was known, had been his whole life. His heroes were all football players, and he followed his favorite teams, the West Coast Eagles and the Sydney Swans, religiously, travelling the two-hundred-thirty kilometers to the city with his father to see every match the Eagles played. His dream had been to become good enough to one day join the Eagles and play footy for his state. But, that was not to be.

As a result of the injuries he had sustained on that fateful day, his footy career had been nipped in the bud. Several months of depression had followed the announcement from his doctor, and not even a message from his favorite West Coast Eagle's player could pull him out of it. His parents were almost beside themselves with worry, wondering what they could do to get their happy, healthy son back from the dark place he was in.

34

After three years, Brad still hadn't come out from under the black cloud hanging over him, and it was about that time that his father, having had enough of his only son moping about the house, decided to take some action. He had been chatting to Bluey Peters down at the local pub, and he had mentioned there was a job going down at the football club. Brad's father had an idea. At first, he wasn't sure how effective it would be. It had the potential to backfire, but if he didn't give it a go, he would never know.

"Hey Bradley," he said one day after work. "Got some news for you."

Brad looked up from the couch, where he was sitting.

"What?" he asked, totally disinterested.

"I've been talking to Bluey Peters down at the footy club. He said they've got a job going down there. In the locker room."

Brad immediately switched off. He didn't want to know about it. As a teenager, he had spent a lot of time in that locker room, and he had a lot of memories of the old brick and cement building. It would also be too painful being around other guys who were able to play the sport he had loved so much while he waited in the wings to clean up after them.

His father didn't push the issue.

"Just thought I'd tell you," he said. "You might not be able to play footy any more, but you can still be a part of it. It's been three years now, and the guys would all like to see you again."

His father disappeared into the kitchen to say hello to his wife, who was busy preparing dinner, leaving Brad alone with the television and his thoughts.

Brad tried to forget about his father's news, tried to push it to the back of his mind, but the harder he tried, the more stubborn that little voice inside his head became, refusing to be silent. He wrestled with it for the rest of the night. It kept him awake when all he wanted to do was to go to sleep. Maybe his father was right. Just because he couldn't play, didn't mean he couldn't help out. His father had also been right about three years being long enough to get over his injuries and the ensuing problems. He had been depressed and disinterested in life for so long that it had become more of a habit than a genuine condition. Maybe he could go in for a trial run and see what happened.

The following day, Brad woke up in an uncharacteristically good mood. His parents suspected the reason for this sudden change but didn't mention it for fear that they might break whatever spell he was under.

"Might talk to Bluey today, Dad," he said.

"Great. So you're going to take the job then?"

Brad shrugged his shoulders. "Might ask him for a trial run. Don't know how I'm going to go."

"Good idea," his father agreed. "At least you're making an effort, and that's the main thing."

The meeting went well since Brad already knew the drill. He had played enough games and spent enough time in the locker room to know what his duties were to be. Chiefly, it would be to clean up the place after the players had showered and gone. It would also be his job to ensure that there was enough soap in the showers and clean towels for each of the players, then, when the players had finished their showers, to gather all the towels and jerseys and throw them in the washing machine. Lost property, things left behind by the players would be another responsibility.

36

On the first Saturday, he arrived half-way through the game. He didn't feel up to watching. He got out of his car and went straight into the locker room. Bluey was on the bleachers, yelling instructions, which couldn't possibly be heard from the sidelines. It didn't matter. Brad knew what he had to do.

By the time the players came off at the end of the game, Brad had done everything he had to. There was fresh soap in all the trays, clean towels on a table by the entrance to the group showers and two plastic clothes baskets where the players could throw their used towels and dirty jerseys.

"Hey Brad," a couple of the players cheered as they noticed him hovering by the clean towels. "How are you going, mate?"

These were old friends, guys who had been expecting him, guys who had encouraged his decision to come back and help on the team. In fact, Brad knew most of the players since he had gone to school with them, but there were a couple of new guys as well, men who had moved into the town from elsewhere.

As they began taking off their muddy jerseys and shorts, a strange feeling came over Brad. The sight of twelve sweaty, hairy bodies began to arouse him. He couldn't understand it. He'd always been attracted to girls, even though he hadn't had a girlfriend since the accident. He'd never thought about guys in a sexual way. Nevertheless, he could feel himself getting hard inside his shorts as the guys removed their shorts and peeled their sweaty jockstraps off, revealing a collection of cocks, all surrounded by thick bushes of pubic hair and some with low, hanging nuts, swinging as they were freed from their elastic restraints.

Over in the corner, Trevor, whom he had also gone to school with, was bent over his bag, fishing around for something inside. The sight of his ass cheeks, slightly

37

open to reveal a crack covered in black, curly hair, was almost too confronting for him. He took one last look at his mates butt then took the basket with the jerseys into the laundry. By the time he had loaded the three washing machines with the contents of the basket, his hard-on had disappeared, yet he was left contemplating what it all meant.

Unfortunately for him, he had to go back out into the main locker room and continue working. The guys were starting to finish their showers, and he had to go along and pick up the towels they were supposed to be putting in the plastic basket. As he walked along collecting the soggy, white towels and chatting to his mates, he noticed that a couple of the guys still under the showers were semi-hard. As their owners washed them, the cocks bounced up and down like they were spring loaded. He also noticed one of the guys surreptitiously stealing glances at the guys showering on either side of him. Brad averted his eyes and finished the job he was being paid to do.

"So mate, how was your first day?" Bluey asked as the last of the players filed out of the locker room to waiting girlfriends and spouses. "Not as easy as it looks, hey?"

"It's alright," he replied. "It's not that difficult."

"Good then. Here are the keys. You'll need to lock up after you've finished with the laundry. Remember to lock the cupboards after you've put the jerseys and towels in."

"No problem," replied Brad.

Over the following weeks, things got even easier. He was getting the jerseys in the wash within seconds of them having been removed, one machine load at a time. However, about four weeks after he'd started, after he'd put the last jersey into the washing machine, Ryan, the

38

guy he he'd noticed checking out his fellow teammates in the shower, came in late from the field. He undressed, dropping everything in pile on the floor where he stood before walking into the shower. As Brad walked over to collect the last remaining jersey, he thought he saw Ryan wink at him. He blushed but was not at all offended.

Ryan was six-feet tall, lean and well-defined. He didn't have much hair on his body, and he obviously clippered his pubic hair to enhance his rather average cock. It worked. His cock looked much larger than it was at first glance, but the truly noticeable thing about him was his sack. Brad had never seen such a pair of low swingers. Ryan wore a neat moustache and a small triangle of hair directly beneath his bottom lip, and the fact he had jet black hair meant he had a dark, five o'clock shadow. He was thirty-two.

Brad himself was not what anyone would call a 'looker,' but he was not without his charm. At eighteen, he had a body in reasonable shape. He was lucky he had good genes on his side. His once lean, athletic body was now not as firm as it once had been since his accident prevented him from playing most sports. But he had dark hair and piercing blue eyes, framed with thick black eyebrows, all of which gave him an exotic look.

As he bent down to collect Ryan's jersey, he noticed the twisted straps of his sweaty jockstrap lying just beneath it, and suddenly he had the strangest desire to take it. He looked up to see if anyone was watching, which of course they weren't, they were all too busy showering and congratulating each other on a game well played. Then, noticing he was unobserved, he wrapped them in the jersey then disappeared into the laundry room. He lifted the lid of one of the washing machines up and threw the jersey in, but kept the jockstrap. He rubbed the elasticized fabric between his fingers, noticing how damp it felt, then brought them up to his nose and breathed in the musty aroma of sweat with a small hint of urine, knowing that the fabric had been snugly holding Ryan's cock and nuts. He inhaled deeply enjoying the masculine smell and noticing that beneath his own shorts he was rock hard. It was then he got the notion to wrap his cock in the dirty jockstrap, only he was interrupted.

"Hey mate ..." Ryan stopped.

Brad dropped the jockstrap to the floor and blushed.

For a moment, they stood looking at each other, Brad dreading what Ryan was going to say next. Behind him, in the locker room, he could see that most of the men had finished their showers and knew that he should have been inside collecting the towels.

"I was just looking for my jockstrap," Ryan explained. "I see you've found it."

Brad bent down and picked it up. "I must have picked it up with your towel. Sorry."

Brad moved toward Ryan, holding the garment in question out in front of him.

"Here you go," said Brad. "Sorry about that."

"Don't worry about it," Ryan replied, grabbing the jockstrap and Brad's hand at the same time. "An easy mistake to make."

Ryan let go of Brad's hand and turned to leave, but before he did, he glanced down at Brad's crotch, which was still quite impressive even though his cock had only just started to go flaccid. He made it so obvious that Brad was instantly embarrassed.

That evening everyone left the locker room in a hurry. There was a big fund-raising dance in town, and everyone was excited about going. While the men had either been playing footy or watching it, the women had been getting their hair and nails done, and trying on frocks and shoes so that nothing was left to chance.

Brad was left alone to wait for the washing machines to finish, put the jerseys into the industrial size tumble dryer, then wash and dry the towels. He was in the middle of folding the dry jerseys when he heard a noise behind him. He turned.

"Hi mate."

It was Ryan. Brad immediately felt uncomfortable.

"Nearly finished?" Ryan asked as he walked toward Brad.

"Nearly," he replied.

Ryan walked up to Brad, standing over him and looking down at him.

"I caught you sniffing my jockstrap," he said accusingly. "What do you think I should do about it?"

Brad swallowed the lump that had formed in his throat.

"W-w-what do you mean?" he asked, gulping.

"Well you watch me walking around naked then I catch you with your nose buried in my underwear. What do you think I should do with you?"

Brad looked down at his feet.

"Take your clothes off."

Brad looked up at Ryan.

"W-w-what?"

"Get them off. Now!"

Brad didn't know what else to do. He looked around to make sure that everyone had gone, even though he knew they had, then removed his shirt, his sneakers and

41

socks, and finally his shorts and underwear. When he had finished, he stood there and stared Ryan in the eye.

Ryan looked him up and down, then reached down and grabbed Brad's cock.

"How big does this thing get?" he demanded to know.

"I don't know," Brad replied. "Never measured it."

"Well, get it hard, so I can see."

Brad couldn't believe what was happening to him. Who did this guy think he was treating him this way, telling him what to do and making him strip off? He could see where it was leading, after all he had seen Ryan checking out the other guys, and he had to admit he was at the very least curious.

Brad began to rub his cock against his pubic hair and pull it with his right hand.

"Is it getting hard?" Ryan asked. "Let me see. That's pathetic. Maybe you want to sniff something."

Ryan removed his tracksuit pants, revealing he was not wearing any underwear, bent over and pulled his ass cheeks apart.

"Sniff this," he said. "I want to hear you sniffing it."

That was all it took. Brad's cock grew from a floppy three inches to a raging seven and a half inches in the space of five seconds. As he put his face closer to Ryan's ass, he thought he would blow his load right away before anything had even happened.

"Sniff it!" Ryan demanded as he began jerking off.

Brad did as he was asked, breathing in the clean, musty smell of Ryan's smooth ass hole. He closed his eyes, enjoying the faint aroma trapped between his fleshy butt cheeks. Almost despite himself he stuck his tongue out and softly licked the pink, puckered skin surrounding the entrance to Ryan's anus.

"Yeah boy, lick that hole. Lick it real good. I want to feel that tongue going to work down there."

Brad didn't need to be told twice. He had never done anything like this before, but he was certainly showing a natural aptitude for it. Ryan was moaning with pleasure, and these noises were egging him on to go deeper into the hole, to try and lick the inside of his beautiful man cunt.

Suddenly, just as Brad was getting into it, Ryan spun around and blew a load of warm, sticky cum all over Brad's surprised face. It took him a moment to realize what had happened, to realize that Ryan had sprayed his man juice all over his face and that was what he could feel running down his cheeks, and dripping off his nose and onto his lips. He licked them, tasting Ryan's cum and enjoying the way Ryan was looking at him, watching him as he drained the last few drops of cream from his swollen cock.

Ryan leaned down and kissed Brad quickly on the lips before standing up again. Brad noticed a few drops of cum on Ryan's moustache. It looked sexy. The sight of him licking his own cum off his lips turned Brad on even more.

Ryan walked over to his bag and removed a couple of lengths of rope. Brad was not sure what Ryan intended to do with them, but he didn't have a good feeling about it.

"Get over there to the showers," Ryan ordered him. "Now! Quickly!"

Brad did as he was told, moving as fast as he could, his stiff man pole slapping against his legs as he ran, his nuts feeling heavy between his legs.

"Get up against the taps," Ryan said.

43

Brad obeyed.

Ryan walked over and tied Brad's hands loosely behind his back and then tethered them to the tap. With the second piece of rope, he tied Brad's ankles together.

"Can you move?" asked Ryan with a devilish look in his eyes.

Brad tried the ropes.

"Not really."

"Good."

Ryan looked Brad up and down, first from the left and then from the right. He reached out and slapped Brad's cock so that it bounced off the boy's stomach.

"Ouch!" he cried out

"If I do something like that you are not supposed to cry out," Ryan explained. "You're supposed to enjoy it."

Brad hung his head.

"Now squat."

Brad squatted.

Ryan squatted, too, only he was able to squat lower since Brad's restraints only allowed him to go so far until it became painful. Ryan then reached between Brad's legs and rubbed his ass hole with his middle finger.

"You ever had anyone fuck you?"

"No."

"Finger you?"

"No."

"You ever fingered yourself?"

"No."

Ryan stuck his finger into Brad's hole, but didn't get very far.

"Well you're not joking about that. You're as tight as a nun's nasty down there. Gonna have to loosen that up."

Ryan removed his finger then spat on it. He tried to slip his finger into Brad's hole again, massaging it until it relented slightly, letting Ryan's finger in up to the second knuckle before the muscles of the anus clenched down. Ryan removed it and spat on it again, replacing it into the hole and wriggling it in until the whole finger was in.

Apart from a small amount of discomfort, which he was getting used to, Brad was enjoying all the new sensations his body was experiencing. He wanted so much for Ryan to take his cock into his mouth or his hand and relieve the need welling up inside. He wanted to shoot his load, he could feel it building up, increasing in intensity but without enough stimulation to be freed.

"Play with my cock," Brad said finally.

"You want to blow?"

"Yes."

"No. I won't let you blow. Yet. I want you to really want it. I want you to beg me to blow."

"I beg you," he pleaded. "Wank me. Pull my cock. I can't stand it. I have to come."

Ryan laughed.

"You think you've been punished enough for sniffing my jockstrap?"

At that stage, Brad would have admitted to anything.

"Yes, Ryan. Yes, I am sorry," he said thrusting his cock toward Ryan's face, making it difficult for Ryan to keep his finger up Brad's ass.

Ryan chuckled to himself as he looked up at Brad and saw the desperation on his face.

"Actually, I should be getting dressed now. I have to go. Big dance on tonight."

"Please don't," Brad begged him. "I want to shoot my load. Don't leave me here."

Ryan looked at the boy and decided he had tortured him enough. Without any warning he swallowed Brad's throbbing member straight down his throat, sucking it firmly with his lips and his tongue, then deep-throating it, taking it right down the back of his gob. He enjoyed the sensation of having a nice big cock slipping halfway down his throat and back again. Meanwhile, his finger was sliding in and out of Brad's tight hole, massaging the prostate as he went, feeling it harden and knowing that at any moment Brad was going to empty a load of sweet boy juice into his gut.

He wasn't wrong. As Brad writhed against the cold, hard tiles of the communal shower recess, he could feel himself tensing up. He could feel Ryan's finger fucking him faster and faster and Ryan's mouth going faster and faster on his cock. His heart was racing, and sweat was dripping off his brow. Finally, he blew, his cock spewing a thick, creamy load down Ryan's open throat. He thrust his cock in deeper and harder, wanting to prolong the feeling, and nearly choking Ryan in the process.

"That was a nice way to end a game," Ryan said, wiping his lips then kissing Brad a second time, briefly on the lips. "Thanks mate."

Ryan walked into the main change room.

"Hey, what about me?" Brad called out after him.

46

But Ryan didn't reply.

A wave of panic swept over Brad, as he struggled against the ropes. His shoulders hurt, they weren't as flexible as they had been before the accident, in fact, they were hurting quite a lot from being tied up for so long. He tried the ropes around his feet, wriggling them until he'd loosened them enough to be able to slide his feet out of them. But that didn't help his wrists. He was stuck. There was no way he could get out of those ropes.

"Ryan," he called out. "Hey mate. You there?"

Silence.

Now he really began to panic. Not only was he tied to the showers of the place where he worked, but how would he explain it? Notwithstanding the fact his parents would be wondering where he was if he wasn't home soon. Shit! That was a thought. What if they were the ones to discover him?

"Ryan!" he screamed out. "Ryan!"

"What is it?" Ryan said reentering the room fully clothed.

"Are you going to untie me?" he snapped, getting angrier by the second.

"Well of course I'm going to untie you. Can't you let a man get dressed first?"

Brad didn't say anything. He waited for Ryan to untie him then stormed off to the small pile of clothing on the floor in the locker room. He pulled them on, putting his shirt on backwards in the process, knowing it but not caring.

"You want to catch up again?"

Brad looked up at him but was too angry to reply.

47

"Okay," said Ryan walking toward the door. "Have it your way."

Brad relented. He had had his first taste of something that seemed forbidden and dangerous and he had liked it. He wanted more.

"Okay," he called out. "When?"

"When I'm ready," replied Ryan. "Now don't forget the towels. I think the machines have stopped."

Brad gasped. He had completely forgotten about the towels, and he hadn't even finished folding the jerseys. When he looked back toward the door, Ryan had gone. He re-commenced folding the few remaining jerseys, but his mind wasn't on the job. His mind was on Ryan and on the feeling Ryan had awoken within him. Despite the fact Ryan had played a nasty joke on him at the end, it was the danger and the slight edge of fear that had gotten him hooked, and the masterful way with which Ryan had unfolded the scenario, peeling back the layers until they had got close to the core.

Half an hour later, Brad was startled by another noise at the front door.

"You're still here?"

It was his father.

"Your mother sent me down to see where you were. She's put your dinner in the oven. Did you forget about the big dance tonight?"

"No," he replied. "I just don't feel like going. I think I'll just go home and eat dinner and watch a bit of tellie."

His father looked at him, trying to decide if this was healthy for him or not. He didn't want his only son slipping back into the days of inactivity in front of the television.

48

"Are you sure, mate? You could meet a nice girl at the dance. It might change your life."

"I don't want to meet a nice girl, and if I did, I wouldn't need your help. You and Mum go ahead."

His father turned to leave realizing there was nothing more he could do.

Brad said goodbye to his Dad and returned to his duties in the locker room and his thoughts of Ryan. Imagine, he thought to himself, if he hadn't taken his father's advice and got the job; he would never have met Ryan and maybe never discovered that part of himself that Ryan had awakened.

It was true what they said, everything happens for a reason. All things are interconnected, and if one thing was to change, everything that follows would change, too. Life was mysterious and exciting all at the same time, and if he hadn't taken his father's advice, he may never have remembered that. Next Saturday couldn't come quickly enough.

LUMBER JACK-OFF
By Logan Zachary

The buzz of the chainsaw reminded him of the old horror movie he and his grandfather saw at the drive-in when he was thirteen. But instead of screaming women running through the Texas sage brush, tight, black pants clad asses and sleeveless team jerseys milled around the lake front park. LumberJack Days were in full swing in Stillwater, Minnesota.

The second to the last weekend of July blazed warm, but not as hot or humid as in past years. Stihl, the orange chainsaw sponsor, and Cabel's, the largest sporting goods store, hosted this annual event.

Lars Anderson left the cinderblock shower/restroom building and headed back to his team's trailer. The rig was a converter horse trailer pulled behind a pick-up. The overhang in the front was used for sleeping. Cabinets and storage lined the walls, and the center was open.

"Did the brothers show up yet?" Bruce asked as Lars pulled open the door. He pulled up his black pants and adjusted himself before zipping up the fly.

Lars' stare lingered on Bruce's hairy torso. Each line of muscle was well defined despite the thick pelt of hair that covered his body. Most men would shave themselves to have a smooth and well defined body, but Bruce liked the hair, and Lars did, too. He stepped up to him and gave him a long deep kiss. "Do we have a winning team this year?"

51

Bruce pulled Lars' pelvis to his and held him there, looking into his eyes. "I signed up two brothers sight unseen, and another guy answered my ad on Craigslist. This will be a re-building year for us."

Lars kissed him again. "I can feel myself re-building already." He rubbed his aroused flesh into Bruce's groin and felt the heat and swelling grow between them.

A knock on the trailer's door broke their embrace. Bruce stepped back to put on his shirt as Lars turned and stepped down to open the door.

Two blond Nordic gods stood at the door of the trailer. Lars shook his head trying to clear his vision. He was seeing double, but if he was seeing double, shouldn't he be seeing the same thing? One man had a smooth face while the other had a thick blond moustache.

"Hi, we're Erik and Derek Lindstrom. We grew up in the Iron Range." The twins wore tight Levi's that hugged their twenty-two year old bodies, their upper torsos triangled down like a bodybuilders. Muscles rippled across their shoulders as they extended their arms to shake hands.

"I'm not sure the uniforms will fit," Bruce said, as he stepped behind Lars. "They have huge arms."

Erik, the twin with the mustache leaned forward. "What size are they?"

Bruce picked up a team jersey from the counter and read the tag, "XL".

"I know we can make them fit." He unbuttoned his flannel shirt and exposed his blond fur covered chest.

Lars wanted to run his hands through the soft, thick pelt.

"I'm Erik, by the way." He nodded to his twin. "That's Derek, he's my younger brother."

"By five minutes," Derek said.

"He hasn't hit puberty yet, that's why he can't grow a stache."

"You split my lip open in third grade, I can't grow an even one now."

"Run to Mommy." Erik took the jersey and turned it inside out. He carefully pulled out his pocket knife and cut along the inside seam. He left it attached at the elastic bottom and quickly reversed the shirt and cut the other side open. Slipping it over his head, he pulled it over his broad chest. It fit him like a glove and gave Lars a peek-a-boo view of his sculpted furry chest.

We'll win points just for that, Bruce thought, as he tossed the other jersey to him.

Erik quickly modified his brother's jersey.

Lars and Bruce turned to wait for him to take off his shirt. They wanted to see if these guys were identical twins in all ways.

Derek looked at the trailer. "Is there enough room in there for us, too? Or would you like us to find a room for the night?"

Bruce and Lars looked at each other. "We hadn't ..."

"Money's tight, so we'll take whatever you got. We're willing to rough it if we have to," Erik said.

Derek nodded his head. "We can sleep on the floor. We brought sleeping bags and an air mattress, just in case."

Lars opened his mouth to speak, and nothing came out.

Derek's mouth took on a crooked grin. "We could play for positions. Whoever earned the most points in the day's competition would get to choose which bed they slept in for the night."

Lars gasped, and Bruce touched his shoulder to calm him.

Derek turned to Erik and shrugged his shoulders. "It'll save us money, and it's not as if we haven't bunked together before."

Images of underwear clad blond gods wrestling in bed gave a stirring in Lars' loins. He adjusted himself automatically. "Welcome aboard," he said.

Erik and Derek entered the camper and stowed their bags under the table. Derek removed his shirt and slipped on the team jersey. His body was perfect, too. Blond soft hair covered his sculpted chest.

Lars nodded to Bruce. Identical.

"Let's see if the pants fit," Erik said, as he unbuttoned his fly and started to pull down his jeans. Derek followed in a mirror motion.

"I'll turn on the air conditioner," Bruce said, and busied himself with the dials.

Another knock sounded on the door.

"I'll get that," Lars said and opened the door.

A small compact man with short wavy black hair stood looking in. His eyes widened as he saw the golden gods taking off their pants. "I ... I'm Tony."

Lars extended his hand, but the man's eyes were glued to the twins. Lars couldn't blame him. "Come on in and join the fun."

Tony bound up the steps without a hesitation.

"I think we have another one," Lars said to Bruce.

Erik and Derek wore tighty whities. The sheer cotton molded to their butts. The fabric stretched tight over the front, too. All held their breath at the sight.

"I think we'll have to draw straws to see where everyone sleeps, and then we can head over to the park. Our team has a demonstration this afternoon."

Tony stood staring at the brothers as they slowly stepped into their black pants. Their pants hugged their legs and asses like a second skin.

Bruce hoped the seams would hold for the competition, but then again ...

He picked up Tony's uniform and tossed it to him. It just bounced off Tony's chest. That seemed to shake him from his thoughts, and he bent over to pick them up.

All eyes turned to stare at him.

Tony dropped his duffle bag on the floor and pulled his T-shirt over his head. He looked like he was an extra from *The Lord of the Rings*, but as his body came into view, images of Viggo came to mind, just in a smaller version.

Tony looked up at the four pair of staring eyes and blushed. He unzipped his pants, but turned his back to them. His tight ass bent over to them as he slipped on the black pants. He turned to face them. "Ready."

The five men left the trailer parked in the main stage parking lot and drove into the campground, looking for their demonstration station. As they pulled into the parking spot, they saw a group of men and children in jeans and flannel shirts, many shirts were sleeveless to allow for freedom of arm movement and ventilation. Timberland boots covered woolen socks.

Sawdust covered the ground, and the scent of freshly cut wood hung in the air. Lars and Bruce's team showed how to perform the log toss. They showed the basic throw and demonstrated the proper body mechanics to prevent injury and maximize distance.

Erik, Derek, and Tony listened carefully and stepped alongside Lars and Bruce to help the audience practice their toss. Tony worked with the children, helping them throw smaller logs as their father's practiced their skills.

The other corporate sponsored teams wore similar uniforms, all had tight black pants with sleeveless shirts with side slits and big buckles. Each team demonstrated a different event or skill, from chainsaw carving to the axe toss, speed climbing to the underhand block chop, standing block chop, single and two-man bucking.

The sponsors provided an all you can eat barbecue. Beer flowed freely, and the first day of Lumberjack Days drew to a close. The men made their way to the truck and drove back to the camper in silence. All were exhausted.

Lars and Bruce unlocked the door, and the men filtered in. "So, what do you guys think?" Bruce asked.

Erik looked around. "You guys should take the bunk, and we'll hit the floor."

Lars walked to the overhang and picked up a cooler. "Oh no."

"What's wrong?" Bruce asked.

"The cooler sprung a leak and flooded the bed." His hand sloshed in the puddle.

"You're welcome to join us on the floor," Erik said. He pulled his shirt off and spread it out on the counter. He took off his pants and set them on top. He bent over and picked up the sleeping bags. He tossed the air mattress to Derek. "Blow."

The men quickly spread out blankets and sleeping bags across the floor. One by one they stripped down to their underwear and crawled under the covers. The twins cuddled together, as easily as their bodies allowed and Lars' leg brushed against Bruce's. They pressed against each other. Tony lay between the pairs, alone.

As the night cooled, the five men slowly moved closer and closer.

The next morning dawned cool and misty, a haze hung in the air. Slowly, the men woke and made their way to the shower and bathroom to get ready for the day.

Lars stepped out of one of the stalls and headed to a sink, when he noticed the curtain in one stall was partially open. One of the twins soaped up his tan body as water cascaded across his beautiful body. Lars' body responded instantly as the bubble butt bent over to wash legs and feet. A pair of low hanging balls swung freely, as the sight hypnotized Lars's eyes.

A smooth face revealed this twin was Derek. He worked his hand over his butt and soaped up his crease. Foam poured down his legs.

Lars wished his hands were helping him shower.

Erik's face peeked out of the next stall and smiled. "When's breakfast?" he asked.

Lars swallowed hard and squeaked out, "They're setting it up as we speak."

Erik turned off the water and stepped out of the stall with a towel loosely draped around his narrow hips. A massive bulge tented the front of the cotton towel. He pulled back his brother's curtain. "Hurry up, breakfast."

Derek pivoted just as Erik stepped in the way, blocking Lars' view.

Lars threw cold water on his face, pushed his pelvis against the sink, and hoped no one would notice his aroused state as he left.

A huge pancake breakfast with sausages, hash browns, biscuits and gravy waited for them as the first day of games began. Team Red was ready.

Brightly colored logos of water, beer, and pop bottlers, lumber companies, saw and hardware stores covered every inch around the elevated stage. A water tank dominated center stage, and behind it, two poles rose up for the climbing and chopping events. Logs, saws, and axes lined the back of the stage, waiting for their events.

The two-man bucking competition led off the morning. The twins nodded to each other as the countdown began.

"Three, two, one, go."

Erik and Derek moved in sync, one pushed the large two-man saw blade as the other one pulled. They knew each other's motion, how long each stroke would be back and forth, moving deeper and deeper into the log, cutting and sawing.

Some teams worked on force and speed, but lost momentum and power by working against each other. The twins worked well together, like an oiled machine, pumping back and forth. Powerful strokes made by bulging muscles.

Lars watched the brothers work. In his mind, he saw them sharing a bed. Blond, tan, fur covered muscular bodies working in unison as one. A mirror image looked into the eyes of the other, matching stroke for stroke. He swallowed hard, as the limbs intertwined, rolling over each other, sweat pouring off from their effort.

The other team grunted and groaned, swearing under their breath as they pulled on their blade.

Erik and Derek looked into each other's eyes as they worked, unaware of the crowd, the other team, the contest. They were only aware of each other.

Their blade sliced through the wood, sending a spray of sawdust and wood chips back and forth with each thrust and pull. Their slit team jerseys opened and closed over their torsos, rippling muscle and tan flesh flashed all who watched as the men worked.

Bruce nudged Lars. "Watching them is like viewing clothed porn."

"If it wasn't so beautiful, I would think it's obscene."

Their lats rose and fell as they fanned out over the twins' rib cages. Their tight butts and narrow pelvises rocked back and forth in a mating ritual, only a few would be honored to see.

Their blade neared the bottom of the log, and their pace quickened. Faster and faster, deeper and deeper, harder and harder.

Lars felt his balls rise up alongside his hard shaft, as if it was preparing to blow his load. His uniform fit tight, and he was glad the fabric was black and absorbent, afraid of the huge wet spot that was spreading over his inseam.

A sharp wood cracking sounded as the disk on the end dropped off and landed at their feet. The other team swore and pulled harder against each other, their blade pinched and wedged in the wood. They paused and started again, three more strokes and their disk dropped to the ground.

The brothers set down their saw and rushed to each other, they embraced, and the crowd cheered.

Lars wondered if the crowd cheered for the win or for the grace of the two men's athletic ability.

"Team Red, winner."

"Oh yeah," Lars said with a smile.

The Speed Pole Climbing events started after lunch. Bruce headed over to the poles and stepped into his harness. The straps framed his ass like a jock strap and cupped his package into a huge bulge in the front. He adjusted himself before he cinched the belt closed.

He dug the spikes on his boots into the wood to check their hold and readied himself with the strap, which wound around the pole. He tried a few take-offs as he prepared his climb.

His competitor followed suit, ten years younger, but about twenty pounds heavier.

One foot on the ground, both men prepared. The timer said, "Three, two, one, go."

Bruce kicked off the ground and scrambled up the pole. The gold bell dangled twelve inches from the end of the hundred foot post. He passed over the thirty foot mark and clawed his way to the sixty. The harness cut into his legs, his low hanging balls were pushed forward and out of his way as he kicked his leg up higher.

Sweat beaded across his brow and burned his eyes, as a stream ran down the small of his back and between his hairy butt cheeks. His gloved hands grabbed the rope, looped it up, and pulled back on it hard, propelling himself up and up. The bell swung back and forth, almost in reach.

His neared his goal and swung his arm and hit the bell. "Ding, ding."

As soon as it tolled, he let his leg drop, and he started his descent. They were only allowed to free fall fifteen feet, before a foot had to tap into the pole.

"Ding, ding," sounded a half a second later. He knew gravity would help his opponent on the way down. Sixty, thirty, and ground.

"Time," the timer called, as Bruce's foot hit earth.

Lars jumped up and down, as he looked at his stopwatch: 20.97 seconds, his best time ever.

The times appeared on the huge scoreboard that was a video screen used in most concerts. The camera crew was able to project the small details of the races in full glory for the audience to see.

Team scores flashed on, pushing the red team into second place. A replay in slow motion showed Bruce's butt rocking back and forth with each kick. Another camera caught his pelvis, showing his balls and cock swing from one side to the other.

Lars poked his shoulder as Bruce watched, "Bigger than life."

Bruce blushed.

"Big in life, too." Lars glanced at the twins who watched the replay with proud happy smiles. Tony adjusted himself as he watched.

"Tonight could be very interesting," Lars said to Bruce.

The last event of the day was the Springboard chopping.

"Three, two, one, go."

Tony's small and compact body shimmied up the pole, switching the springboard for springboard as he raced up the pole nine feet. When he reached his spot, he took his axe and started chopping the block firmly attached at the top. Chucks of wood flew out of the wedge as he hacked.

His competitor appeared to be twice his size, weighing in at over two-hundred-thirty pounds. His hands were the size of Christmas hams, and his legs looked like the logs they chopped.

Tony switched to the other side and started the same process there. Another deep wedge quickly formed and the top end of the pole started to lean. His sinewy arms worked harder and faster, like the wings of a hummingbird. A cracking of wood echoed over the stage area, and the end toppled over. One final chop and the end cleaved off and fell to the ground. Tony unhooked his boards and descended the pole.

"Team Red, winner."

The crowd left, and the men stood at the pool on stage. Lars was able to use it for an hour while he practiced log rolling. No one was allowed to watch another competitor practice before the event, so Team Red had the stage to themselves.

"Who wants to join me on the log?" Lars asked. "I could use the practice."

Erik and Derek stepped back. "That is one event, we don't even try," Erik laughed.

"Bruce can't stay on very long," Lars said as he used the pole to pull the log into place.

Tony stepped forward, took off his shirt, and picked up a long pole. "I'll try." His leprechaun body waited as Lars stepped onto the log. He used his pole to steady himself as he stepped on, and both men held the log.

"Throw your poles," Bruce said.

Lars and Tony released their poles to the twins, and they started rolling the log. Tony's little feet ran over the bark as Lars read the wood. The log rolled one way and then the other. Both men switched and stopped, continued and switched, trying to knock the other guy off.

Lars started one way and faked Tony out, sending him backward into the water. Tony popped up spitting water, and the twins clapped. Everyone gave Tony credit for working out with Lars.

Lars dropped into the water and hugged Tony. They walked to the edge of the pool and reached up to the twins. Erik and Derek offered their hands, but as they touched, Lars said, "Now."

Tony and Lars pulled hard, and the twins splashed into the water. Both stood up and looked at Bruce, who stood looking down at them.

"Why not?" Bruce said, and jumped into the water.

The five splashed around and dunked each other, enjoying the fun and ease of friendship.

"Ah hum," a man cleared his voice.

All eyes looked at Team Green. Lars waved. "We're done, just let us get out." He walked to the ladder and his teammates followed. The soggy crew walked back to the trailer and looked at the door.

"We'd better strip out here, so the bed doesn't get wet," Erik said. He pulled his jersey off and slipped out of his pants. Standing in only his underwear, the wet cotton did little to cover him. Feeling the other guys stare, his arousal swelled and grew.

Lars quickly stripped to his boxers and jumped inside for towels. He handed them out as the men dropped their pants, trying to save everyone embarrassment.

The men set their clothes to dry and entered the trailer. Once all were in, they stood in a circle and looked from one to another.

"Now what?" Bruce asked.

The men still stood in their wet underwear.

Lars grabbed his waistband and said, "Three."

The twins reached down and grabbed theirs.

"Two."

Tony and Bruce joined in.

"One, go."

And all the men pulled down their underwear and threw them into a corner.

Tony slipped off his underwear, and as he turned around, his cock looked as if it had been photo shopped onto his body, but he stood there in the flesh. His massive dick rose from his slender pelvis and arced gracefully with each step.

Lars was the only smooth man in the group. He and Bruce kissed to break the ice. As they finished, each one turned to a twin and kissed them as well. The couples opened their arms and Tony stepped into the center. All mouths kissed him. Hands explored and pulled them closer, making a tighter circle of five.

Erik moved in front of Tony, and Derek slipped behind. They wrapped their muscular arms around him. Their golden brown skin contrasted from his pale complexion making a human vanilla Oreo.

Each twin knelt and licked Tony along the way. Derek spread Tony's tight cheeks as Erik ran his tongue along the underside of his shaft. Four hands reached and fondled his testicles as they swung free. Erik kissed the tip of his cock and slowly swallowed the massive organ. Derek found his sweet hole and tongued him deep.

Tony bounced between the brothers' mouths like a ping pong ball.

Lars and Bruce watched, enjoying the view. Their erections rose fast and hard, each man grabbed the other one's cock and gently stroked. They admired the twins' asses and watched the muscles flex and relax, flex and relax. Their butts bounced back and forth, calling to be touched, tasted, and teased.

Tony moaned with pleasure as the twins double teamed him. His legs could barely hold him up as he was in Erik, and Derek was in him. He brought his hands to his nipples and pinched them, twisting them hard. His head fell back as a long, low moan grew from deep inside. He reached down and ran his fingers through their blond buzz cuts, enjoying the scratch and tickle.

Lars pulled Bruce forward by his dick and released him as they neared the dynamic trio. He caressed Derek's ass with both hands, his hard-on brushing the crest of his butt cheeks as Derek rocked back and forth, slipping his tongue into Tony's butt.

Bruce mirrored Lars on Erik's ass. He massaged the fleshy fur covered orbs, and kneaded them. He spread his cheeks and looked down the hairy crack, which begged to be explored, mined for a treasure that await deep down.

They slid their cocks over the cleft of the twins' asses, plowing the strip until their balls pressed against their bubble butts. The brothers pushed back against them, never slowing their work on Tony's tortured body.

Tony reached out in welcome, caressing Lars and Bruce's chest as they ground their hips against the brothers' bottoms. He worked lower and grasped their cocks, gripping them and stroking their length as pre-cum seeped out of their tips. He glided them down the twins' creases in search of their hot openings.

Bruce and Lars dropped down and licked the brothers' asses. They worked over the hard muscles and tenderly explored the crease. Lower, they worked down the curved slopes to a tight pucker. They licked and kissed, while their tongues sought entry.

Lars continued lower and licked over Derek's furry balls that swung free. Dangling low, he drew one into his mouth. His tongue rolled it around as he tried to swallow it.

Bruce flipped onto his back and licked along Erik's shaft. He licked to the tip and teased the oozing end with his lips, drawing it in and out. His tongue ran along the underside of his shaft, slowly he took the twin's thick eight-inch cock in to its hilt. He gagged at first, until his throat relaxed and was able to accommodate the whole length inside.

Derek pumped his butt up and down on Lars' tongue, trying to get him to take both balls into his mouth at the same time.

Erik humped Bruce's face, his balls slapping his chin with each thrust. More pre-cum oozed out, slid down his shaft, and pooling on Bruce's tongue.

Tony's cock sent out another wave of pre-cum, it ran over Erik's lips and down his chin. He swallowed what sweetness remained. His balls pulled up alongside his shaft. His butt relaxed, as he felt Derek's tongue enter.

Derek knew Tony was ready and slid one finger into his bottom. The tip pressed against his prostate and sent more pre-cum out and into Erik's waiting mouth. He pulled one out and slipped two fingers in.

Tony's tight butt stretched further, wanting more.

Derek tried three and slowed worked them in and out. He rose to his feet, pulling his balls out of Lars' mouth. He slipped on a condom, lubed up his cock with a bottle that seemed to appear out of nowhere, but which Lars had made available once the action started, and pressed his erection into Tony's wanting hole.

Lars rose and pressed his nose into Derek's crack and pulled his balls back into his mouth as Derek drilled into Tony. The tip of his nose pressed against the tender opening as he drew down hard on his balls. He could feel Derek's balls expand and his nut sack start to retract.

Lars stroked his cock as he sucked, he could feel his juices flow out of his uncut cock and run along his shaft.

Bruce grabbed Erik's balls and pulled down on them as he sucked on his cock. He felt another wave of pre-cum fill his mouth. He grabbed the bottle of lube, poured it into his hand and used it to grease up his pole. He stroked it a few times and felt an orgasm crest in his balls. He stopped so not to shoot too early.

Tony's cock was ready to shoot, and Erik's hot mouth milked him as his tongue hit the sweet spot underneath the tip. Tony erupted, spraying across Erik's face and lips, rope after rope of hot cum spilled out of him. His butt muscles clenched down hard, setting Derek's cock into orgasm.

Derek filled the condom as he pumped into Tony. Lars felt Derek's balls slip out of his mouth as this cock pulsated with each orgasm.

Tony and Derek collapsed into a heap as the other three looked down at their hard work.

Lars moved over and took Erik into his mouth as Bruce sucked on Erik's balls. Each man jacked their own cock as they worked on the twin's equipment.

Tony and Derek moaned and gently caressed Bruce and Lars legs as they worked.

Erik lay back and let the pleasure ride over him. His balls pulled up, and his cock spasmed as cum shot out of him. Lars swallowed and swallowed as each new spasm sent more cum into his waiting mouth.

Tony wiped himself off and watched as his cock swelled again.

The twins turned their back to Tony and made their way to Bruce and Lars' erections. They bent forward and licked along their lengths and teased their hairy balls with their tongues.

Lars moved parallel to Bruce, lying side by side so his hairy legs could rub against Bruce's. His hand reached over and caressed Bruce's hairy chest.

The twins straddled their legs as their mouths continued to work over Bruce and Lars' hard-ons. Derek looked over his shoulder and saw Tony's erection. He rose up onto his knees and offered his ass to him.

Erik saw Derek's motions. He moved over and lined up cheek to cheek with his brother. Four fleshy furry buns in a row.

Tony stepped between their legs and massaged the twin's asses. He explored their creases and found their tender openings with his fingers. He felt them moist and relaxed, ready to for use. Sheathed and lubed, he moved behind Derek and slowly entered him, slipping his massive cock into his waiting hole. He rode his tight butt for a few long, slow strokes.

He pulled out, moved over, and entered Erik. He pumped into him several times. His hands worked over the twin's back muscles. He pulled out and moved over to Derek. Wash, rinse, repeat. Erik, Derek, repeat.

Bruce and Lars lay back and watched as their leprechaun bounced from one brother's ass to the other. The twins' mouths, warm and welcoming, sucked on their swollen members. They closed their eyes to enjoy the sensation, but opened them so not to miss a single second of this sight.

The brothers pushed back as Tony entered them. Their bodies rocked with his as they pleasured their teammates. One hand helped them suck on their teammate's dick, as their other stroked their own erections.

Their rhythms increased, faster and faster, as the anticipation grew. Pre-cum and saliva ran down Bruce and Lars' balls as they slowly ascended to their respected shafts.

Tony sliced into Derek, deeper and harder. He could feel his orgasm start as he pulled out.

Lars and Bruce moved closer and kissed. Their tongues dueling as their balls released at the same time. A stream of cream shot over a smooth and a furry belly as the brothers rose up and frantically jacked their own cocks.

Two more twin eruptions added to the pools on their chests.

Tony stepped between the twins and emptied his balls, half on Bruce and half on Lars. His legs swayed as he knelt down. The twins caught him and pulled him close as they all landed on Lars and Bruce. They lay together as an exhausted heap. Slowly, their breathing and heart rate returned to normal.

One by one, they fell asleep in each other's arms.

The sun rose as the five men made their way back from the brick shower house and entered the camper single file. Their uniforms were still damp, and deep wrinkles refused to smooth out. A woody, sweaty scent clung to the fabric, despite their dip in the water.

They breathed in deeply, savoring the smells, the tastes, the sights and the feelings of the past few days.

"No matter what happens today," Lars started, "we gave it a great try. We made some wonderful friendships and memories."

The men looked from one to the other and smiled.

"A team is what happens when five men work together to become one. I feel we succeeded in that. The

69

scoreboard is close and may not go in our favor, but I hope we'll all be back next year."

Erik put his hand into the middle of the circle, followed by Derek. Tony slipped his small hand in, and Lars covered his. Bruce hesitated for a moment and put his on top. They pushed their hands down and brought them up with a whoop.

Champions, every last one of them, and their trophies at the competition's end proved it.

"I can't wait until next year," Erik said.

"Who says we need to wait? We may need to re-group the team for some intense practice throughout the year," Bruce warned. "Any problems with that?"

No one complained.

BALLS TO THE WALL
By Rob Rosen

We had a week to go until the big tournament. Regional racquetball title. Amateur, but still heavy competition. Jeff and I were practicing more than usual, three times a week, two hours a day, all the spare time we had; practiced until we were in sync, power hitters, the team to beat. Jeff had a wicked backhand; my serves were practically un-returnable. Lightening fast.

Too fast, in fact, if you got smashed in the nuts by one of them. Poor Jeff never knew what hit him. The doctor recommended ice, lots of ice. And no physical exertion for at least a week. Meaning, no tournament. At least not for the two of us.

"Go find another partner," he told me. "Just for this one competition. Shame to waste all that effort."

"But it's too late. How will I find someone on such short notice?" I asked, not even sure I wanted to play with anyone else.

"Post it at the club. See what turns up. Worth a try, anyway."

I nodded. I hated to admit it, but he was right; it would've been a shame to see all that practice go to waste. "Fine," I relented. "I'll give it a try. You rest your nuts. There's always next time."

He shot me a wry frown. "Fucker. I probably won't be able to have kids now."

"You hate kids," I reminded him.

"Not the point."

71

In any case, I left him with his iced-up groin and went back to the racquetball club to post my partner-wanted sign. I made it there with an hour to spare, tacking up my last-ditch effort and then turning around to head on home.

I almost made it back outside before I heard someone hollering for me from the down the hall. "Dude, wait up!" I turned and saw him running toward me, my sign held in his hand. "Did you just stick this up?" he asked, almost out of breath. "Are you the Steve that's looking for a partner for the tournament?"

He stopped a few inches away, his startling blue eyes boring a hole right on through me. And then it was I that was almost out of breath. "Oh, um, yeah. You interested?"

He smiled, revealing a dazzling array of pearly whites, blinding beneath the overhead fluorescent lighting. "Yeah, my own partner had to go out of town suddenly. Emergency business trip. Name's Pete, by the way." He paused and nodded. "And, your note was perfect timing."

Indeed, I thought, giving him the once over – twice. "Are you any good?"

He winked, sending a flush through my belly that caused my cock to stir. "So I've been told. We still have an hour. Wanna see for yourself?"

I coughed, imagining what else we could do in that hour. "Sure. Why not?"

His smile widened. Intoxicating. He turned, and I followed him downstairs, my eyes zooming in on his rock-solid ass as he took the steps two at a time. Place was nearly empty. We had our pick of the courts and chose the one without a viewing railing. "To keep the fans at bay," he joked.

I shrugged. Fine by me. Hell, we could play naked for all I cared.

We entered the court, locking the door behind us. Click.

I handed him a ball, my finger brushing his, flesh on flesh. Again he flashed me that smile, his eyes locking on to mine for the briefest of seconds. "Let's just volley for a bit," he suggested.

"Sure," I managed, stepping back to let him serve.

Dude hit a power shot, the ball zinging an inch off the ground. I caught it with my racket and sent it careening back, also an inch above the floor. He dove, tripped, landed on his butt, his legs up, apart. I stared down, my eyes zeroing in on his hefty balls, now in sight within the gap between shorts and thigh. Fuckin-A, I thought, running to help him up. Guys playing commando.

"Sorry," he said. "I'll do better."

And, he did. In fact, he was almost as good as Jeff. Certainly hotter, at any rate. Meaning, the rest of the week should prove interesting.

An hour later, both of us dripping with sweat, we exited the court. "Two hours tomorrow?" I asked.

He grinned, the smile spreading from east to west. "So I'm hired?"

I laughed. "For this tournament, yes. Then back to our original partners. Deal?"

We shook on it, a million jolts of electricity shooting up my arm and then through the rest of my body. "Deal," he replied, his hand lingering, much to my throbbing cock's lament.

We headed to the locker room, the last two guys left in the place. His locker was down the aisle from mine. I watched him get undressed out of the corner of my eye. His drenched shirt came up and off, revealing a densely muscled torso covered in a brown matting of fur. Sneakers next, then socks. I stopped my own undressing, waiting for the crescendo. He turned around and slid his shorts down, his perfect ass coming into sight, hairy like the rest of him, his balls hanging down low in between parted legs. I gulped at the sight of him, putting my jeans back on before he could turn around and glimpse my arcing cock.

He was dressed and out the door a few minutes later. "Tomorrow, dude," he said.

"Tomorrow," I yelled after him, watching his exit, longing for his return.

I walked over and snatched up his towel, sniffing the sweet smell of his funk, my prick pulsing at the heady aroma. I took it to a stall and dropped my pants, breathing in his scent as I beat my meat. It only took a few quick strokes, my balls rising, my cock spewing, splat, splat, splat on the tiled floor as I moaned and groaned, my knees trembling, my body twitching.

"Damn," I said. "This is gonna be a hard fuckin' week."

And, man, was it ever.

We practiced two more times, getting accustomed to each other's game play, our strengths, our weaknesses, his tight shorts, no jockstrap, intoxicating aroma. Fuck. Fuck, fuck, fuck.

Then it was the day before the tournament. Meaning, our last time alone together. Meaning, I had to up the ante. It was now or never.

We met an hour before they closed, as we had done the first time, again choosing the private court. I breathed in, deeply, upon entering, trying to calm myself down. We

74

walked inside, locking the door behind us as we smiled and nodded. "Last chance," he said.

"Don't I know it," I replied.

"New shorts?" he noticed.

"Um, everything else is in the laundry. I, um, dug these up out of the closet."

He shrugged and served, the ball slamming against the front wall and coming back my way like a bullet. I returned it, hitting it off three walls, forcing him to zig and then zag across the court, my body getting in his way. On purpose, of course.

Down I went, tumbling over for effect, the stitching I'd sewn into the rear coming undone, as planned. I sat there, the wind seemingly knocked out of me. "Sorry," I said. "Nice serve."

He smiled, chuckled, and pointed. "Um, you're shorts. They, um, ripped."

I lifted my rump and looked down. "Fuck. Guess that's why they were in the back of the closet. Now what?" The ball, as they say, was in his court.

A slight blush appeared on his face, his voice suddenly hoarse. "Guess we play. Tournament's tomorrow."

I stood up, my ass hanging out, the white of my jockstrap in plain sight. "Guess so." I smiled and bade him to serve, the plan going as, well, planned. Of course, with each serve and volley, my shorts tore and separated some more until they were barely hanging on by a thread. "Damn it," I soon said. "Can't play this way." I slid them off and threw them in the corner, standing there in my sneakers and jock and sweat-soaked t-shirt. "That's better."

"If not a bit distracting," he commented, with a nervous chuckle.

"Well," I said, returning his verbal serve with a fast-ball response. "If you were a good teammate, you'd play the same way."

He volleyed back with, "I'm, um, not wearing any underwear, dude."

I shrugged. "Not my problem."

He hesitated, then unbuttoned his shorts, sliding the zipper down just a touch, his black bush now visible. He stopped and looked up. "Mind if I ask you a question, dude?"

My pulse quickened, my heart nearly leaping out of my chest. "Shoot," I managed.

"You planned this, didn't you?"

Fuck. Fuck, fuck, fuck. "Um, sort of. Do you, um, mind?" I stepped a foot away, in case I had to make a hasty retreat.

"Mind? Why do you think I don't wear any underwear when we play?"

I laughed. "Bait?"

He touched finger to nose. "Bingo. I took my jock off before we met that first day."

I moved back in, close, closer still. "Risky play."

Now it was his turn to shrug. "And yet you're in your jockstrap and I'm about to take off my shorts."

I closed the gap, my face in front of his, my lips brushing against his lips. "Guess it was worth the risk then." I reached my hands around his waist and pulled him in, mashing my mouth into his, swapping some heavy spit, then saying, "But why are you still in your shorts?"

76

"Dude, I think you're trying to seduce me."

"Is it working?"

He reached for my hand and placed it over his crotch, which was now tenting, steely hard. "What do you think?"

I looked down, admiring my results. "I think I'd like a bird's eye view." He backed away as I lay on the cold floor. Quickly understanding what I was getting at, he stood above me, feet on either side of my head, then slowly, seductively started to lower his shorts, lifting a foot to get out of them, until he was bare-assed above me.

"Well?" he asked.

"Tweet, tweet," I replied.

He chuckled and crouched down, his hairy asshole lowering to my face, the musk of his crotch filling up my sinus cavity. I breathed in, jutted my tongue out, the first taste like heaven. He mashed his hairy ass into my mouth. I sucked and slurped on his hole, tongue-fucking him while he stroked his thick prick, his moans and groans reverberating around the four white walls.

"Mmm, what else can you stick up there?" he asked.

"Let's. Find. Out." I said, in between licks and laps.

He hopped off my face and got on his back, his hirsute body laid out before me like a veritable buffet; I jumped up and dug in. My hands traversed his peaks and valleys as I kissed his neck and shoulder, my mouth working its way ever southward. He put his hands behind his head and watched my progress. "Getting warmer," he quipped. I looked up and winked, my tongue making a bee-line from ab to ab, circling around his belly-button, moving still downward. "Warmer," he sighed. I kissed a straight line through his trimmed bush and then up, up, up his ramrod-stiff woodie, engulfing the slick

77

mushroomed head in one quick gulp. "Fucking hot," he groaned.

I sucked his cock, a happy gagging tear streaming down my cheek, while he bucked his ass upwards, filling my mouth and throat will all that glorious meat. I reached up and tickled his balls, giving an appraising tug and then a sharp yank. He moaned, softly, his back arching. I pulled hard, harder still, his face in a grimace of both pleasure and pain. "Fuck yeah," he spat, raising his legs up and out as I heaved and hauled. "Now eat my hole."

Naturally, he didn't have to tell me twice. I pushed his legs farther back, his knees to his chest, his perfect hair-covered ass glinting in the overhead lights. I gave each cheek a slap, the sound pinging around us, the spank seconded and thirded, the white turning to hot pink. He pushed his prick up, his hole and his cock now both in clear view, which meant I could alternate between the two, lapping at his portal while I jacked on his cock and then sucking on his prick while I slid a wetted finger up and in and back.

"Your turn," he told me, beckoning me with a flick of his index finger.

I hopped up and slid out of my jock, my cock bouncing as I flipped around, knees on either side of his head, my cock gliding down his throat, while I again buried my face in his ass and jacked his massive prick. "Best practice I had all week," I told him, in between slurps.

He popped my prick out of his mouth. "Dude, you so don't need the practice. On this court, you're already a winner."

"Sweet talker," I said, slipping one, then two fingers up his chute, feeling the smooth muscled interior of him. "Still, practice makes perfect."

He laughed. "Agreed," he said, now assaulting my ass with his double digits, until we were both finger-fucking and cock-jacking one another, finding a steady matching rhythm, the sound of our workout filling the small rectangular space.

Soon enough, my balls began their gradual rise and my fingers were butting up against granite. "Close," he groaned.

"Closer," I panted, each of us piston-fucking and jacking the other.

His asshole clenched around my fingers, his cock pulsed in my grasp, and then he shot, ropes and ropes of man-sap that drenched his defined belly, dense with muscle and hair. The sight and the smell of it sent my cock into overdrive, my white-hot load raining down on his face, dripping down his chin before splashing across his broad chest. And all the while, our bodies bucked and shuddered, our growls and groans like a symphony to my ears.

I collapsed on top of him, out of breath, my fingers still teasing his pretty, pink hole as his legs at last came down. He continued to play with my now-sensitive cock, my body twitching with each cruel stroke. "Play nice," I told him.

"Nice guys finish last," he replied.

"Dude," I said. "Judging from all this cum, I'd say finishing is not a problem for you."

He laughed. "And if you play half as good as you fuck, we'll be unbeatable tomorrow."

Though winning an amateur racquetball tournament wasn't nearly as easy as getting him off, or even almost as fun. It was a round-robin, you won, you stayed in the game, you lost, and you were out. There were twelve teams. You can do the math, but it only adds up to one thing: a hard fucking day of competition.

Hours later, we were sopping wet, completely exhausted, and sore all over. Fortunately, we were in better mental shape than the last remaining team, both guys younger than us, with even bigger builds, but obviously not looking forward to a victory fuck as much as we were.

We kicked there asses, twenty-one to sixteen.

And then, as planned, sucked and bucked and fucked the night away, our trophies on either side of the bed.

"Shame," he said, the next morning, his body spooning mine in a naked embrace.

"What?" I moaned, his hand already stroking my stiff prick.

"To have to break up such a successful partnering so soon."

I laughed, rolled over, and planted a warm wet one on his perfect lips. "Only on the court," I told him. "Off it, dude, we've only just begun to play."

THE GYMNASTS
By Donald Webb

I'm at my desk, concentrating on college-required paperwork, when a deep male voice interrupts.

Tyler, a gymnast, stands in the doorway. He's naked from the waist up, and he's wiping his chest with his balled up T-shirt. Muscular quads and calf muscles spring from the legs of his gym shorts. His massive deltoids, biceps, and forearms look out of place on his small frame. Dark-blond hair – cut in punk style points – sticks up from his scalp. His masculine aroma permeates the air.

"Do you have time to give me a massage, Brad," he asks.

I'd kill to make time for him.

"Sure, what's up ... you aching?"

"Yeah. I guess I must've been practicing too hard. Josh says that you know how to get rid of the stiffness."

Do I ever.

"Josh is right," I say. "Go behind the curtain and lie down on the table."

"Shouldn't I shower first? I'm all sweaty."

What would he say if I told him I liked my men sweaty?

"No, you're fine the way you are."

I close the door and join him. He's removed his gym shoes and is lying on his stomach. I should've told him to strip.

81

I pour oil onto my palms and start kneading his muscles. The skin over his biceps is smooth and pliable, but I know this is only at rest. In the poster I have tacked up on my bedroom wall showing him performing the iron cross – looking as if he's been crucified – the veins on his arms are standing out as though ready to burst from his skin.

I work on his arms and shoulders until I feel him relax, and then I move my hands to his back.

When I'm finished massaging his legs and back, I say, "How does that feel? Have I got all the kinks out?"

He rolls over onto his back. "Well ... um ... there's one place still sore."

"Where?"

He places his hand between his legs. "Here. My hand slipped off the pommel, and I landed hard."

My heart races. Am I hearing correctly? Is he asking me to check between his legs?

"Can you see if I'm okay? I need to make sure I'll be alright for the match on Saturday."

"Sure. Let's have a look."

He pulls his shorts and jock off, falls back on the table, and spreads his legs. His dick and balls hang to the table.

"I think I'll be able to see better if you're on your stomach."

He rolls over. I place a couple of pillows under his hips, making sure his dick and nuts are on display. His butt is big and muscular, like two over-inflated white balloons laid side-by-side. The fringe of dark-blond hair on each side of his perineum, and in the deep rift between his cheeks, emphasizes his white skin. His low hanging nuts frame his substantial uncut dick.

Lying there, in that position, he looks defenseless and vulnerable.

I bend over him and inhale deeply. His sweaty muscular aroma acts like an aphrodisiac on me. My leaking dick is leaving a telltale wet spot on the front of my shorts, so I put my hand in my briefs and adjust my hard-on. It would be so easy for me to lose control. If he said, "Fuck me," I'd be on him in a second.

His butt quivers when my fingers probe his perineum. "Is this where it hurts?" I ask.

"Yeah, that's the spot."

"You need to spread your legs further."

He follows my directions.

I massage his perineum until I feel him relax. "What about your testicles? Did you injure them?"

"They're kinda achy."

I hold his nuts in my hands and roll them around checking for injury. They're big and loose in his smooth pink pouch. The kind I like to suck. I take my time examining them. I want this to last forever.

"They seem hard and full of cum," I say. "When was the last time you shot your load?"

He squirms around, like a fish caught in a net. "Um … it's been a while."

I gently squeeze the hard spheres. He whimpers.

"Does that hurt?"

"Uh-uh," he says and pushes back against my hands.

I've got him where I want him.

"You're leaking as if you're horny," I say.

He doesn't respond.

83

I take his rapidly expanding dick in my hand and run a finger down the shaft toward the head. Precum oozing from the meatus covers my palm.

He's so excited he's having trouble controlling his impulses. He pushes his hardening dick through my clamped hand and lets out a groan.

"What's the matter? You have pain in your penis?"

"No ... it's just ... it's just ... no one's ever touched my dick before."

I find it hard to believe that such a hunk's still a virgin.

I hold onto his dick with one hand and probe the area around his anus with my other hand. My hand slips up and down his shaft when he moves. I'm slowly jerking him off.

"I hope you didn't bruise your prostate gland. Maybe it should be checked?"

I hold my breath. How will he react to my suggestion?

"How do you do that?" he asks.

I explain the procedure to him.

"Does it hurt?"

"No, not if you relax."

"You really think I need it?"

"It's up to you, but if it were me, I would have it done."

"Should I see a doctor?"

"If you want to ... but I know how to do it if you want me to have a go."

Please, say yes, I'm thinking.

84

He's quiet for a few moments then says, "Maybe you should give it a try."

"Try and relax," I say as I spread his tight sphincter with my thumbs.

His face is buried in a pillow, and his fantastic butt is spread to the max. I can't stop myself. I have to taste him, so I lean over and lick his smooth slit. The manly taste and aroma of his hole stimulates my desire for him. He doesn't move, so I keep licking. I want to chew on his asshole, but I'm scared he might lift his head and see me.

I keep rimming until his hole dilates, then I lubricate my middle finger and slip it into his rectum.

He groans.

"What's wrong? Am I hurting you?" I ask.

"No, it's just ... weird to have someone doing that to me."

"Let's try it with you on your back. It might be easier," I say.

When he rolls over, I push his legs up to his chest. He covers his eyes with his forearms, exposing surprisingly hairy armpits. The head of his dick pops out of his foreskin when his shaft becomes fully hard.

I lubricate his hole and penetrate him with two fingers. The hot smooth lining of his chute clings to my fingers as I push upward and contact his prostate.

He pushes against my fingers and lets out a long groan.

I clench my ass-cheeks in sympathy. I remember when I lost my cherry.

"Is that painful?" I ask.

He shakes his head.

As I massage his prostate, my other hand raises his dick into an upright position.

I keep massaging until his manhole is completely relaxed. "Your semen is clear, so it looks like your prostate is okay," I say.

He lets out another groan and bites his bottom lip when I slip a third finger into his dilated chute. "Maybe we should check to see if you have any pain when you shoot your load?"

"You're kidding!"

"No, I'm serious. Sometimes that's the only way to see if you've been injured."

My fingers keep sliding in and out of his chute while he thinks about it.

"You want me to go in the restroom and jerk-off?"

"No, it'll be better if I do it. That way I'll be able to tell if there's an obstruction, and anyway, I should continue to massage your prostate while I'm doing it."

"You won't tell anyone, will you?"

"Why would I do that? What happens in here stays in here."

"You better do it then."

He groans when, in earnest, I start stroking his shaft.

He's thrashing about on the table when I ask, "Did you ever get a blow-job?"

He shakes his head.

"Want me to show you what it feels like?"

He doesn't answer, he is too far gone to object, so I lick his piss-hole and slurp his semen into my mouth. He shudders when I slip my lips over his dick-head, lock them around the collar, and run my tongue around the smooth surface. He raises his hips, and I sink his rod in my throat. When my lips contact his silky pubes he holds my head and grinds his pelvis against my face.

His prostate hardens against my fingers.

A cry of anguish rises from his lips. "Fuck, dude, stop. I'll cum in your mouth!"

"Does my buddy's cock taste good?" a different voice says.

Josh, another gymnast, stands at the foot of the table. Josh and I frequently have sex, so I'm not bothered by his sudden appearance. He often sends me athletes for my special treatment. He's naked, and he's stroking his big salami. Josh is a little taller than Tyler, but he still possesses a typical gymnast's body. A thin line of dark hair connects the pelt of hair on his chest to his pubic bush. The dark hair on his head is closely shorn.

"Oh, man," Tyler says, "what are you doing in here? It's not the way it looks ... he's just ... checking my prostate."

"I know what he's doing. Why do you think I sent you in here? He's good ... isn't he?"

Tyler gapes at him. "You mean ... you mean ... he's done it to you?"

"Yeah, but I've done it to him, too."

Before Tyler can react, Josh climbs onto the table and straddles him in a sixty-nine position. His mouth engulfs Tyler's dick.

"Fuck, Josh ... we can't do this, we're not homos," Tyler says.

I lock the door, and then move to the head of the table. I pull Josh's long uncut dick back between his legs and pump up and down. I want to suck him, but his dick

87

is too stiff. I hold Tyler's head in place and rub Josh's dick-head over Tyler's tightly closed lips.

"Suck him," I whisper in his ear.

He tries to turn his head away, but I won't let him.

I hold Josh's dick at his lips. "Just lick it. It's no big deal," I say. "He's doing you."

The point of his tongue tentatively licks Josh's dick-head.

"That's the way," I say. "Open your mouth."

He opens up, so I lift his head and push Josh's cock into his mouth. He starts sucking like a babe suckling at his mother's breast.

"There we go ... that's the way," I say.

Josh spreads his knees and lowers his shaft into Tyler's mouth.

Josh's anus is partially hidden in the lush growth of hair between his legs. I part the damp hair with my hands, and run my tongue over his sweet-tasting pucker. I hold him open with my thumbs and fuck him with my tongue. He's tight, very tight. I try to insert a finger, but he won't let me in. I lick his ball sack and suck his nuts into my mouth.

Tyler is doing fine, so I move to the other end of the table and disrobe.

Josh is an accomplished cocksucker. In one lunge, his mouth sinks all the way down to the hilt of Tyler's dick, and then slowly rises up again to the crown. Each time he hits bottom, he buries his nose in Tyler's nut sac. His head rises and falls like a rocking pump jack out in an oil field.

Tyler groans when Josh pushes two fingers into his asshole.

Josh winks at me.

"You like that, Ty? You wanna get fucked?" Josh asks.

"No fucking way ... I'm no fag!"

"Don't my fingers feel good, Ty?" Josh says as he pushes a third finger into Tyler. "Imagine how good a dick'll feel."

I watch Tyler's face as he thinks it over. "Yeah, I gotta admit, they feel good. If I let you do it, can I fuck you, too?"

"Sure," Josh says, but I know that's not going to happen. One finger is all I've ever had in him.

I gather up some condoms and lube from my desk drawer, place them on the table, and then probe Tyler's chute with two lubed fingers. When he's open, and receptive, I climb onto my knees on the table. Before I can roll a condom down my shaft, Josh grabs me by the nuts and deep-throats me.

His mouth is hot and moist. His tongue licks my nuts when he has me fully imbedded.

"Fuck, that feels good. You sure know how to suck cock," I say.

Josh sucks me until I'm on the brink of shooting. I pull his mouth off my dick. He rolls a safe down my rod, lubes it, and then rubs the head of my dick over Tyler's primed hole.

"Fuck him with that big cock," he says.

Tyler's tight sphincter tries to keeps me out, but I bear down until my knob pops inside. I sit back on my haunches and wait for him to relax. When his hole starts milking my dick-head, I rise up and throw it into him. I can't believe that my dick is sliding into the hole that I have lusted after for so long. His channel is hot and juicy.

89

Just like I knew it would be. I pull out – all the way, and slap his dilated hole with my hard-on, and then pound back in, right to his very core.

I can hear Tyler whimpering around the dick in his throat when I pick up speed and long pole him.

Josh jumps off the table and watches us fucking. He moves behind me, slaps my ass a few times, and then spreads my cheeks. When his tongue touches my hole, I jerk into Tyler and rest on his hard body. I lock my mouth on Tyler's mouth. He resists. I raises my ass and drive back in. His mouth opens in a groan. I slip him my tongue. He grabs my head and holds my mouth to his. I've tamed the wild mustang. He'll never be the same again.

I take a big breath when I feel Josh's sheathed knob at the entrance to my channel. With one shove, he's balls deep in my chute, and I'm in heaven. He fucks me hard and fast for a few minutes, and then he backs off – until just the head of his dick remains in my ass, so that I can move between them.

Their huge arms engulf me when I resume fucking Tyler. The double stimulation is fantastic. I feel as if I've been skewered on a rigid pole. On the forward stroke, I sink into Tyler's incredible ass, and on the backstroke, I impale myself on Josh's huge rod.

I'm in the home stretch, when Tyler suddenly says to me, "Can I do it to you? I want to see what it's like."

"You got it," I say.

We decide to do it standing up, so I bend over the table and spread my cheeks. Tyler's condom encased dick slips into my well-primed hole. His body slams into mine when Josh throws it into him. The table legs screech on the floor as it moves toward the wall. I grab my dick and jerk-off as my rear-end receives the workout it needs.

Tyler licks my ear. He's hyperventilating. His hot breath makes me shiver. I turn my head and kiss him. He probes my mouth with his tongue.

"I'm coming," Josh yells.

"Oh yeah," Tyler says, "me, too."

I milk Tyler's dick with my ass muscles as I shoot my load over the floor

There's a pounding on the door.

"Oh, fuck," I whisper. "Who the hell is that?"

We dress quickly. The smell of sex is in the air. I can feel lube oozing from my hole when I go to the door.

It's the coach.

"Sorry, coach," I say. "I didn't realize the door was locked."

"Is Tyler in there?" he asks.

My heart misses a beat. I nod.

"Is he okay?"

"Sure. He was stiff when he came in, but I've managed to get rid of the stiffness."

"Good. I've got a new routine for him to try in the morning. You may have to work on him again tomorrow."

"I'll be ready for him," I say.

"I know it's late, but do you think you can make sure that Kevin's okay before you leave? He thinks he's pulled a muscle in his groin."

Kevin, another gymnast, is sitting on a bench outside my door.

"No problem, coach, I'm not going anywhere."

"Good. See you in the morning, Tyler," he calls out as he leaves.

91

Josh winks at me as he and Tyler depart.

"Do you want me to take a shower?" Kevin asks.

"No, you're fine the way you are. Go behind the curtain and strip."

I lock the door.

IN THE ZONE
By R. W. Clinger

My goal is simple: to confirm the rumors true that Cade Lewis likes dick. Can a beefy jock suck cock? And if so, how can he pull it off without the Razors rugby team knowing? This is my mission. This is what I intend to find out. Ready or not, Cade is going to come ...

Yattamere Rugby Field has its own gym, locker room, and showers that The Razor's staff can use at freewill. No monthly fees. No major rules. We just have to show our press passes if asked, and the place is for the taking.

Cade Lewis, our team's hooker, is said to be for the taking, too, if you're into a rough and tumbly jock with a five-eleven frame, 190 pounds, broad shoulders, and a hairy chest that tapers down to a narrow waist. Cade has silver bars through his nipples, and rumors say that he doesn't mind a dude's tongue exploring them. I do a once-over of his ripped bod in the locker room: white towel snug around his middle, outlined six inches of soft cock under the cotton, hairy navel, massively ripped chest, shoulders like a jungle gym, and almost-aqua blue eyes. The sports journalist is twenty-nine, takes care of his body, face, and can't keep his gaze off me. He asks, "Zack, you getting a shower with the team?"

We are The Razors. The number one rugby team in our division for the past three years, sponsored by *The Razor*, a daily newspaper we bust our asses at. I'm new to the job, just six weeks old, and new to the team.

Following a Saturday practice, we are comfy in the underground locker room: red lockers to the right and left, benches down the middle, office and supply room in the rear, which are always empty, and the shower area to the left, beyond the lockers.

I peel off my mud-caked cleats and uniform, ready for an afternoon shower with the hottest jocks in the newspaper business, and the roughest rugby players in the east. "I'll be there in a second. Start without me." I'm down to my skin in seconds, showing of my goods and ...

Cade doesn't move. He shares a sexy once-over with me; something he has never done before. He sums up my suntanned bod from head to toe: blond buzz cut, six-two structure, 200 pounds, five inches of drooping cock, fresh out of Alabama looks that are cute to the core, twenty-eight years old and ready to be naughty with the toughest dimple-cheeked man on the team.

I grab my white towel and say, "The last one to the showers is a fag."

Cade tries to bolt past me, jumping over the bench. My size stops him, and we end up face to face. Our chests touch and nipples kiss. No one is around. It's just the two of us. The rest of the team is in the showers, scrubbing down after a muddy practice. Cade breathes heavily into my face, winks, and says, "What, Flyhalf?" with enough sexy attitude to make me pop a joint between my firm legs.

My view shifts down to his block of hairy chest. The towel around his waist has fallen to the floor and his uncut crank is exposed, which looks absolutely irresistible. I reach out and roll a palm around it, and whisper, "We're a team. We work together. If you suck my cock, I have to suck yours."

Cade's meat starts to grow firm in my palm. We are no longer playing "the fag" game all The Razors play. This is real. Guy with guy stuff. This is the bomb.

"You game?" I ask.

94

"Suit yourself, Zack. Let me show you what I'm made of. I can't let the team down." The star player drops to his knees, laps at my already-hard dick with his sloppy mouth, hungry for my man-beef. Once he gets a good taste of me, he pulls off, studies my smooth torso, and says, "You're not playing with the boys anymore."

"We've got a few minutes before the guys get out of the showers, so prove it," I challenge, and push his head down to my swollen stick, which is ready for some more action from his mouth, tongue, and throat.

He gives my boys a little squeeze while sucking on my seven inches of firm knob. My meat plows his face numerous times. I gag him, holding the back of his head.

In truth, I'm going to shoot cream into his mouth before he wants me to. My last one-night stand against a bathroom wall was five weeks ago in some professor's apartment. Goo is going to fly and splatter in no time flat, this is how badly I need to come.

Tongue, teeth, lips, and tight throat all work together as a team on my Johnny. Cade's action is similar to that on the rugby field: hot, speedy, energetic, and efficient. He bangs his rugged-cute face against my skin, pulls away, and bangs into it again.

I refuse to be shy about thrusting my sweaty thighs forward and slapping blond balls against his chin and corded neck. So help me God, I will not blow his cordial invitation to spray man-sap down the back of his needy throat, disproving the rumor that he likes to eat cock. A rugby player must do what a rugby player does, right? Play with the team. Never underestimate a play. Win the game at all costs.

"Hold onto my hips and chew on it, dude," I coach.

Cade listens. Heavy slurping, cum-like strings of saliva hang from his mouth, and minor groaning enhances his star-quality knee-performance. Cade knows he has to get me off fast. If he wants a Zack-snack of sticky goo, he'd better perform better, and faster, whatever it takes to blow me away.

Who am I kidding, right? He is not going to have to work hard to get my rocks off. I'm holding a porn-load of goo in my balls, which was ready to burst two weeks ago.

His fingers and mouth quickly work together. Nipples are tweaked. Hips are held and released. His face buries itself into my skin, pulls away, and buries itself again.

Jolts of guy-connected-to-guy electricity zoom throughout my body. I cannot hold my load in much longer and feel a burst surface. Goo is released from my balls and up through my shaft. Cream oozes out the corners of the hooker's mouth, decorating his chin and drips onto his Nikes.

Once my satisfaction is over, no longer on a five-week sabbatical of fag-fucking and ramming a Razor, I push Cade away and toss a white hand towel in his direction.

As he stands and cleans up, consuming most of my shoot in his rippled belly, he says, "I didn't know you had it in you."

I reach down between his legs and give his nine inches of firm toy a shake and reply with curt ambition, "I haven't had it in me yet, but I'm willing to try."

None of the jocks on the team know that Cade and I fuck around in the locker room; we want to keep it this way for fear of getting booted out on our asses. In truth, it's pretty hard to believe that the star player of our team likes cock. No one would believe me if I told them, of course.

Following our naked twosome, we shower across from each other. Cade's shaft is fully deflated between his soapy legs. Lever 2000 lathers his hairy chest, pumped neck, and broad shoulders. He winks at me, still under my spell.

I don't return a wink. Instead, I turn around, lather up my ass with soap, and show off my bulbous bottom for him to use in the near future, an early visual treat for his primal needs.

Cade has to turn around to prevent a woody and embarrassing scene. He pretty much ignores me during the rest of our shower time.

It's like I've sealed the deal with him: Flyhalf is getting exactly what he wants from the star player. What Cade doesn't know yet – this is just the beginning of our naughty game.

Two days later, Cade is doing laps around Yattamere Field, keeping in shape. I get a text message to join him and show up ten minutes later.

Legs in motion, drops of man-sweat on plated bare chests, Reebok shorts riding up on chiseled thighs with every stride, we run side by side. The track is empty except for us. We put everything into the run, eventually slow down on lap seven, and decide to talk. Cade says, "Nice performance in the shower on Saturday. I was afraid of sporting a brick in front of the other guys and had to turn around."

"I'm glad you liked it. You think it was too much?"

"Fuck no. Not when it comes to you. It was a pretty solid tease for me. In fact, I wanted to come over to your spray and bang your bottom. Tito and Braun would have kicked the living shit out of me, though," he says.

"Kevin Braun is a dick-licker," I reply, speaking of the black and bald forward on our team. "Don't let him fool you. Something tells me he wouldn't mind sucking your joint."

Cade laughs. It comes across as being masculine and brutish, which I find attractive. "Speaking of suck-jobs, dude, you owe me one. When are you going to pay up?"

I haven't forgotten. The thought with him alone causes my prick to harden up and my mouth to water. I tell Cade, "Listen, meet me in the locker room and I'll pay my dues." I quickly spank his ass, make a right, speed across the field and opposite side of the track, and yell over my shoulder, "It's now or never, buddy! You decide!"

The locker room and shower areas are empty. It's just the two of us, alone and able to carry out some man-inside-man action. Cade is on the bench, lying on his back with his muscular hands behind his head. His knees are bent and his legs are spread open for easy access. His heels are planted on the narrow plane of wood for balance. A nine-inch spike stares up at me, ready to be plunged into the back of my throat. With a twinkle in his eye, he instructs, "Start with my pecs and work your way down to my cock."

I don't listen, though. His left armpit is looking mighty tempting, and I go for it with my mouth, nose, and tongue. I lap up his runner's sweat and devour his rough smell. My lips stray to his shoulder, neck, a cheek, and finally his mouth. I give him a kiss that he won't forget.

Cade tongues my mouth back, into our locker room gig. He begins to moan with pleasure, hypnotized by my touch.

Slowly I pull off and away. I find a hairy nipple and dab my tongue at its fleshy mound, which drives him crazy.

He lets out a grunt of excitement and asks, "What would the guys on the team think if they saw this?"

There's no time for talk. My tongue turns into a licking machine, devouring his chest. It travels down the hairy plane of his rock-hard torso and greets his fuzzy navel. I lick and kiss the dent, turning myself on.

Cade says, "You haven't even touched my cock yet. Get busy down there."

I have a promise to keep, which he isn't going to let me forget about until his pleasure is over. My mouth falls to his jungle-patch of triangular-shaped pubes. Cordially, my right hand finds his balls and begins to caress their furry orbs.

Murmurs and groans escape the star Razor. He coaches, "Slip it in your mouth. Go ahead and do it. I can't fucking wait any longer."

No one tells me what to do. I've been an independent thinker all my life, particularly in the company of a naked rugby player. I don't even come close to his pole.

Cade inquires, "What are you doing, man?"

"Trust me," I say, falling to my knees between his legs and pressing my mouth against his tight hole. I lap, lick, dive, pull away, and just about drive him mad with my queer tongue-tour. My hands find his knees and pull his legs apart. This gives me better access to his hairy core. I further investigate his hole with some more tongue-action, and spiral him into a state of heavy breathing and uncertainty.

"Fuckin' A!" Cade exclaims and quivers, totally into our connection. "I'm going to shoot a load if you don't stop that."

Again, I choose not to listen to him. I lap his core, balls, core, balls, and shove my nose and mouth into his hairy opening. I pull away and take some air into my lungs.

"Stop," he whispers in a state of elation. "My cock is going to burst on its own if you don't stop."

One index finger and my tongue work together, pleasuring his bottom. Both move together: in and out, in and out, in and out.

As planned, there is no blowjob for Cade Lewis. Not that this is unfortunate or bad luck for him. Not that I leave him in a state of pent dissatisfaction, either. I always get what I want and have control of the moment. Cade becomes my pet on the bench, captive under my tongue and finger spell, a game for me that I intend to win.

My free hand finds his shaft, and I begin to stroke it up and down. My tongue, finger, and hand all work together, and drive Cade wild. Beneath my touch, he groans, "Dude, you're in the zone. I'm going to shoot. I'm going to ..."

Although my seven inches of cock is a solid mass between my legs, ready to be played with by his jock-palms, Cade becomes my number one priority. I want to get him off, and make his juice to explode over his jock-chest.

"Zone," he murmurs, enjoying my trio of movements and tools. "I'm blowing, guy .... I'm shooting."

My right hand tugs on his stick: up and down, quickly and with a steady rhythm. My finger and tongue continue to tease his bottom, working him into sexual overdrive.

He shivers under my touch, almost lethargic, and grits his teeth, whimpering. "Zack ... Zack ... It's ending," he informs. His voice is raspy. His hips rise and fall to my movement. His teeth grind and he starts to moan. "I can't hold it in. I can't .... I can't."

Two creamy strings of Cade-come fires out of his joint and sticks to his furry abs and pecs. He continues to moan and pump my fist as two more arcs of the white sap juts out of his post, decorating his torso. Heaving for breath, spent in a matter of seconds, becoming sexually sated, he lets out a laugh, and begins to relax. Cade sits up with goo all over his chest, and asks, "Who taught you to do that, Zack?"

"Kevin Braun," I respond, and stand.

"No fucking way. You're kidding me, right?"

"Whatever," I say, and head for the showers, knowing he'll follow me for clean-up and a personal handjob, which he now owes me.

Less than twenty-four hours later, Kevin Braun has me pinned to my locker. His black, Hummer-size chest is snug against my weakling one. His ten inches of steel dong touches my stiff one. His ruby-red lips are only inches away from my pale ones. He asks, "Rumor has it you're fucking Cade Lewis."

Damn, Braun is pure muscle from head to toe, a fucking skyscraper, chiseled to the core, handsome beyond comprehension, a chocolate god. I put up a fight, and respond, "Look, it's none of your business."

Braun is not pissed at me, although he should be with my last comment. Instead, he informs, "If anyone is going to fuck Cade, it should be me." He gently places a kiss to my lips in his Romeo-manner, oozes with sweetness, pulls away, and pleads, "get me in the zone, Zack. I gotta have Cade."

I gently push him away and confess, "I'll see what I can do."

Braun returns to my face and kisses me long, hard, and with tongue. He rocks my world for a few seconds, pulls off and away. The chocolate god falls to his knees and ...

"What are you doing down there, Kevin?"

"Sealing the deal."

And I melt, inside his mouth as his lips curl around my cock, getting the best blowjob of my rugby career from the hottest guy that works for *The Razor*.

The Friday evening before our Saturday play-off game I hook-up with Cade in the locker room after practice. All the other guys have gone out to Petey's Pub for some beer and pizza. Not two minutes after they all leave, Cade has me straddling the bench. My ass is in his face, and his tongue is inside its hairless and puckered hole. His playbook action is top-notch stuff for the next ten minutes: tongue, finger, nose, lips, tongue again. Eventually he pulls away, finds some lube and smears it against my crack. Next, he finds a condom from his gym bag and slips it over his tool, presses into me and ...

"Jesus, Cade!" I yell, overwhelmed with his size as it splits me into two queers. I moan with bliss, keeping my grip on the sides of the wooden bench.

His hips slam into me, pull away, and slam into me again. All nine inches of his meat punctures my ass. He spanks my bottom a few times and calls down to me, "Hang on, buddy, we're just getting started."

I become dizzy, windblown, and lust-driven in front of him. His riding becomes a constant to and fro motion that numbs my ass and thighs. Cade's balls slap against my balls with his forced beauty.

Together we become balanced, intoxicated with each other. Lust is found between us: palms on hips, man centered by man, cock banging into a tight bottom.

Again, he spanks me, hungrily nailing my guy-core, bolting into me and pulling out with the speed of a rocket. Fingers continue to dig into my hips.

We groan and moan together. We move like jocks on the field, ready to score. We glide wildly, hungrily, passionately, in secret – man-lust at its top form.

102

Cade becomes intense behind me. Sweat drips from his torso and stings my back. He informs in a guttural tone, "I'm going to make you blow, buddy," and reaches around my right side, tugging methodically on my stiff wanker. The prized athlete allows his strident movement to become a naughty performance of ass-ramming. He coaches me, "Come, Flyhalf. Shoot your load onto the bench."

Huffing and puffing, my entire body shivers with his play-by-play movement. A state of elation is fully found in my ass and dick. I announce, "I'm blowing. Here comes the rush."

A wanted buzz of orgasm flushes throughout my bent-over torso. Guy-jiz explodes from my cock and the Zack-snack pools on the bench, sticking to the wood. A constant vibration swivels through my torso, dick, and ass with my blowing and Cade's continuous movement.

Behind me, Cade cheers, "Don't be shy. Let it all out. I'm coming next." He takes his palms off my hips and his swollen throbber out of my bottom. The hooker removes the plastic from his dong and informs, "I'm aiming for your back, Zack. You hold tight."

I look over my right shoulder and witness both of his fists at work. Cade thrusts his hips to and fro, working his beef. He grits his teeth and begins to growl. Sweat beads on his forehead, temples, nipples, and navel. He closes his eyes, continues to man-handle his meat, and ...

The sound of Cade's orgasm floods the locker room. Dick-glue flies out of his joint and splashes against my back. Arc after arc decorates my skin. Splotches of the ooze stick to and warm my skin. He looks like a XXX star behind me, draining his tool and relishing his moment of focused man-bliss, becoming spent.

103

Over. Done. He leans across my sticky back and nails my mouth with his own mouth. He says, "That was fucking amazing. I want you again. Maybe against a wall."

The kiss is magic without any conditions, exactly what I'm looking for in a hot rugby player. I say, "We'll see what happens. No promises."

"Sounds good to me. As long as I can still fuck you."

"I don't see that as a problem," I confess, kissing him again.

During this inebriated moment with him, the locker room door bursts open and ...

We're caught. So much for keeping our fucking private.

Kevin Braun stands in the doorway, possibly returning for something he has forgotten. A look of satisfaction and glee surfaces on his handsome face.

"Fuck," Cade whispers, shocked at Braun's appearance.

"We're busted," I whisper, winking at Braun and sharing a semi-smile.

There is no time to bolt to the showers. It is what it is: naked rugby players in a post-sex connection.

This is what Braun sees: Cade rising from my back, standing behind me; puddles of hot hooker-cum on my back; two still-erect shafts after heated sex; Cade's right palm resting on my hip.

Braun handles the surprise like a pro. He steps into the locker room and lets the door close behind him. He strips out of his clothes and moves up to our twosome. He says, "Can you make room for me? I need to blow a load, too."

Cade is a little caught off guard at first, but he mellows when Braun snuggles up to his side and leashes a palm around his chest for a quick man-hug.

Braun says, "You're secret is good with me. What do you say all three of us get it on?"

I don't object.

Cade doesn't object.

Black-steel grows hard between Braun's legs as the welcomed intruder begins some naughty with us and says, "I'm in zone. Ready or not, here I come."

LIKE A GREEN OLIVE
ON A TOOTHPICK
By Derrick Della Giorgia

How cliché are those vignettes where the inexperienced young pupil fantasizes about his statuesque swimming instructor and actually manages to get in his underwear? Honestly, how high are the stakes? That was my opinion about swimming pool erotic stories. Well, until I had the hots for a swimming instructor myself, desiring him with all the strength my body could produce, in as many ways as my crotch suggested my brain. Every single class, before, during and after the class, surrendering to the pathologically powerful sexiness that a wet ripped body can exert.

I had developed a sort of ritual at the pool. I changed, warmed up, took a shower, got in the water for my 45-minute class, changed again and went back home. In the lane next to mine, he taught the beginner course – which involved a whole lot of bending right in front of me and exposing his perfect rear. During the class, he awarded me with his triumphant nakedness and his water splashing and pupils hugging, which, like clockwork, gave me 'crotch bites and stings.' That was the best description I had come up with for the flames he provoked in my groin. Twice a week, that was what I ardently looked forward to. Until one day, my routine was altered by a totally uncalculated event.

My heart thumped against my chest blocking my steps at the sight of the water hitting his face and dripping down his chest, through his abdomen and into and around his mouth-watering emerald green Speedo. I had never caught him there before. I quickly looked around for a free shower and spotted the one next to his. I squeezed myself in between his elbow and the guy in the next space and turned my back to the wall as he stared at the trimmed hairs on my pectorals, before even saying hi. I activated the water and closed my eyes, trying to get adjusted to the sharp impulses that crossed my mind and burst into fire all over my body. I was scared that if I had looked at his body so close to me, my hands would have moved onto his flesh, without letting me any other possibility. Inside my head, my blood pulsed in synch with the currents of pleasure streaming from my stomach to my balls and my skin intensified every feeling – temperature, touch and even sounds. Then, I hit him with my arm. It was wonderful, like a little orgasm. The wet smooth skin of his back – I believed it was his back, but it could have been his arm or his abdomen – awakened my appetite for licking, eating, tasting, rubbing and swallowing.

"I'm sorry," I emitted, nonchalantly.

He didn't even answer, notifying me his approval for occasional rubs while showering. His neck was extended and his head thrown back, permitting the water to descend directly on his face, splashing on his forehead, teasing his parted lips and his half smile, or jumping in a long dive on the part of his body that protruded the most in that position. His bulge. The rich sack that couldn't be cupped in one hand – I was sure, part of his balls or the tip of his cock would be left out – and that divinely dominated his swimmer thighs. It was the only area of him I couldn't see. My body again was victim to wild impulses that ordered every cell of my organism to turn and grab that cock, pull that Speedo down and take everything I could into my mouth, deliver my tongue on his head, suck his skin swallowing his flavor, smell the sex that hadn't yet been washed away. I forgot how to take a shower,

108

unable to perform any movements, paralyzed in my thoughts and dreams. Prey of my hunger.

He kept receiving the water in that position, only now and then making circles with his hands on his abs and his chest. And then he went down with both hands, seconds after followed by his head, and concentrated his attention on the piece of fabric wrapped around his crotch. My mind was too buzzed to comprehend the purpose of his movements, but didn't miss his attempts at stretching the elastic and fixing the bow that the white lace of his Speedo was forced into, pressed against the meat that had enslaved me. He undid it, allowing me, from my position, to peek into his pubes and beyond them, in the darkness that surrounded his cock and his balls. My eyes became desperate, trying to get by the mass of his hands working on the lace and mentally photographing the forbidden beauties of his pouch. What it felt like interminable minutes of rummaging, ended with him turning to me and saying, "I can't tie this shit!"

My tongue – furiously hitting my teeth and my cheeks, managed to give back: "I know, it's so annoying!" Wanting to say instead: 'Can I help you? Let me put my hands in there …'

When I thought there was no other sense of mine he could possibly stimulate, he slowly turned, offering his back and his ass, and I had to lower even more the temperature of the water to interrupt the unavoidable and painful hard-on. In that fabric, his ass was firm, lush and shiny on top of his legs, like a green olive on a toothpick. I wanted to bite it and feel it on my lips! Lick it until my tongue was stuck in it! The same ass that I watched as he swam, getting in and out of the water, working hard against gravity and the mass of water, that same ass I had dreamed about, longed, envisioned in the sexiest positions, imagined spread open on my bed, was right there, next to me. Wet. Hard. Close.

109

I couldn't take it anymore, so I stepped out of his reach and hurried to my lane, hoping my class would help me forget about his body.

"Late for your class, huh?" He sent to me from under the roar of water that flooded his teasing face.

"Yeah ..." I exhaled.

Swimming classes served for me more as psychotherapy than anything else. As it was, I already spent every other day in the gym, doing weights. I had started to get wet when I realized that being immersed in water for almost an hour made me forget about all the stress I accumulated every day in court defending my clients. Twice a week, I dropped my suit, my hands free from heavy law books, and swam at my instructor's orders, enjoying the naked crowd in the lanes next to mine. Until Stephen showed up disrupting my perfect equilibrium and made my insides turn upside down with desire. Probably twenty-one or twenty-two years old, at least ten years younger than I. Stupefying. Dark short hair, dark eyes, big jaw, masculine forehead, smooth perfect body, naked for most of the time I spent at the pool. While my instructor diligently wore his uniform at all times, Stephen didn't resist more than twenty minutes in it and would strip wherever he was to get in the water with his class. Out of the water, giving instructions and orders in his wet Speedo by the edge of the pool. And then diving in again: arms and legs in position, ass tense and under!

That day, he looked less active, as if thoughtful, with his legs in the water and his ass on his flip flops, yelling to Marcus that his dolphin should have been faster and to Gwen that her legs weren't moving at all! I couldn't get the image of his body under the shower out of my mind. Not one lap was completed without me dreaming of thrusting my hard stick inside him. He would love it. I would love it.

110

But, it all came to an end when the relief I usually got at the end of the class, invaded my limbs as I wished my instructor a nice week-end and smiled to a Stephen wrapped in his towel.

When I got in the locker room, I was the only one there. All the benches and the lockers were empty and only the smell of chlorine and overheated muscles suggested a lot of hot swimmers had been there just twenty minutes before. I sat on the bench exhausted and took off my Speedo. Then I spread my legs and let my balls and dick hang there. My clothes lay next me, ready to accompany me home – across the street – where I would take my fully deserved shower. Stephen was still in my thoughts, especially the white lace buried between his balls, but my senses had been tamed by the hard swimming and, seeing him in his towel, ready to leave, had brought me back to the real world, where the pupil didn't get to fuck the swimming instructor. I stood up and stared at my body in the mirror in front of me. I was wet and the very short hairs on my legs and chest made my muscles sexier, without giving my skin that shade of blackness that confused the lines of one's body. I was feeling myself when I heard the door.

"Hey there. Enjoying your results?" Stephen materialized ten feet away from me and stopped for a second, making the water that was still trapped on his exposed body, drip on the floor around his feet.

"Hey ..."

He walked to his locker, and I eyed the swell of his crotch.

"Your abs are coming out very nice there." He commented staring at my naked body as I started to dry my hair in the most embarrassing excitement.

"Thanks," I hurried to reply before the delay revealed my fantasies. He walked out of his Speedo and

111

came near me again. He checked his body in the mirror from every angle, ignoring the fleshy bobbing of his cock. His savage dark pubes a sexy imperfection over the flawless white skin. His balls more tanned than the pale muscular thighs that protected them.

"I guess I should trim, too." He paused, increasing the tension. "It feels better, doesn't it?" He passed his fingertips over my stomach and noticed my meat awakening. "What do you think?"

"Yeah, maybe ..." I mumbled as our eyes locked.

"See?" He slowly grabbed my hand and pressed it under his against his pubes. I felt the heat of his body and then the smooth flesh of his shaft hardening underneath my palm. "I see how you look at my body," he continued.

"Your flesh heats me up." I confessed.

"And?"

"And ... I wanna fuck you." I told him as I cupped his balls in my hand.

"Go down there and tell my ass." He ordered me, without any hesitation.

I thought I was daydreaming, until I plunged my hands into his flesh, grabbing his butt cheeks and separating the muscles to get to the hole. I buried my tongue in it and teased his entrance as he moaned. Then I made him bend a little more, so I could control his body the way I desired. I pushed my chin into him and scratched his smooth skin with my twelve-hour beard. The more I pushed into it, the more he hardened it, almost suffocating me with sex.

"Yeah. More of that, please! I love your beard."

I embraced his lean and ripped thighs and rubbed my chest all the way up from where his balls hung to his lower back, while with my hands I felt his cock – that after

112

that treatment wasn't bobbing anymore, but pierced the air with its humid head.

"I've always wanted to be fucked by you, lawyer! I thought you weren't into twinks."

"I'm into you, you don't know how much. Every time you dive in ..." My mouth was open on his right ear, biting it as I slid my cock in and out the tight tunnel formed by his thighs and his ass. He turned his head and searched for my tongue, inundating my mouth with his.

"Fuck me." He implored, grabbing my ass and pushing us against the wall. His left cheek was smashed against the mirror, and he asked for more. I smacked his butt to get it ready and delicately wedged my thumb where he wanted it.

"Relax instructor, that's only my finger." My thumb was all in, and as I massaged his inside I used my other fingers to stimulate the area surrounding the pit. "Can I get inside you?" I whispered into his ear, more to enjoy the way he would have begged me to than to warn him that my cock was about to split him in half.

"You must." He adjusted his hips and spread his legs, granting me free access into his body. My cock was in paradise already, stuffed under his balls and enjoying the humidity that reigned down there – a mix of his sweat and a handful of lube. I just stepped back a bit and guided my head close to his secret mouth. As I expected, the resistance was high and the years of swimming made the difference against my hip bones. I positioned my hands on his deltoids – now that he had lifted his arms – and I dropped my whole weight into him. The warmth inside, the walls that caressed my cock, the movement he immediately started, brought me to the point of orgasm in no time, but I pushed more and nailed him to the wall, informing him it was going to be my way.

"Don't ever get out of me ..." A completely surrendered Stephen commented. I smacked his flesh and rode him the way he deserved. Dolphin style, front crawl, every technique I had learned, turned into sexual dance. I swam inside him non-stop, until he supplicated me to come, and I told him to turn around.

"I wanna look into your eyes when I come, Stephen." I lifted his tight body and locked it onto my waist. Then I reentered his hole and finished my task. He felt the hairs all over my chest and then worked on his cock, trying to balance himself as my thrusts rhythmically shook him.

The young instructor's white cream equally distributed on his chest and my abdomen. "Please, come on my face, lawyer!" He got on his knees and licked my balls like a puppy. A second after, I made his wish come true and directed the cum that had accumulated during all those classes to his beautiful face.

QUARTERBACK SACK
By Jay Starre

Mack the quarterback was in a mood. Quietly toweling off his battered body and separated from the last lingering few of his teammates by a line of lockers, he reflected on the bruising loss his team just suffered.

It was a savage game; late November in the pouring rain, muddy grass, cheering and groaning fans in the thousands, slamming bodies, the glorious football in flight in the glare of the stadium lights, the soaring elation of touchdowns, followed by wracking humiliation when the other side scored. Victory or loss, it was all part of the game.

But for Mack, winning was all. He hated losing.

CJ and Bruno finally dared face him now that the rest of the team had fled. A tackle and a guard, they'd been at fault more than most in the defeat. It was primarily due to their poor play that Mack was sacked no less than half a dozen times during the game!

Fresh from the showers the pair huddled just on the other side of the lockers from their moody quarterback.

"He don't want us bothering him, CJ! You know what he's like. He won't fuckin' talk to nobody til we win another fuckin' game," Bruno whispered to his giant buddy.

"That's just it, Bruno. We gotta break the cycle. He's a sore loser, and you know why?"

Bruno's massive brown thigh pressed against CJ's naked black one. His wide mouth broke into a grin, one side curled up and one eyebrow following as he attempted to solve the riddle his pal just presented. Thinking was not his strong suit; bashing other football players on the field was.

"Uh, why, CJ?"

"Cuz he feels like a loser when he loses. Now let's make him feel like a winner!"

With that, the pair sidled around the corner side-by-side. Their massive bulk filled the space between banks of lockers. It was a prime dressing location, with a pair of benches running parallel down the middle offering a big seating area, perfect for big football butts. Now, only Mack occupied the area. His teammates were giving him a wide berth due to his infamous moods.

He faced them as they approached, his hazel eyes glaring under pale brows, his generous mouth set in an unsmiling line. The buzzed blond said nothing, casting aside his towel and straddling the bench as he folded his muscular arms across his chest and awaited their expected apology.

For all the good it would do. He wouldn't forgive or forget until they won again!

CJ was first to spring wood. His black snake jutted outward and upward to rear in front of him as he approached the glaring quarterback. His full red lips curled into a sheepish grin, white buck teeth gleaming. The most easy-going of the three, he threw an arm over Bruno and spoke into the menacing quiet.

"Bruno and me, we're sorry we fucked up, Mack. We wanna make up for it, don't we?"

His gruff apology was followed by a wink at his buddy, who nodded enthusiastically and tried on a smile,

116

too. Bruno also tried on a hard-on, one hand dropping to cup his fat balls as his brown cock swelled up into a jerking tower thrusting out from between his massive thighs.

Regardless of the pair of stiff cocks approaching, backed by nearly 600 pounds of muscle, the tall quarterback stood his ground and maintained his stony silence.

Those big hazel orbs glared. His square face was set, the dimpled chin rigid, the long straight nose flared. His creamy pale complexion flushed pink. He looked about to explode. Definitely, he was in a real mood!

It was CJ who led the charge, dragging his less brave partner forward. They collided with the blond, lifting him off his feet and slamming him against the tiled wall behind. Their gargantuan arms wrapped around the leaner quarterback, cradling and pinning him with his thighs up and spread. His naked crotch was totally exposed.

Their intent was obvious as the ebony-skinned tackle once again initiated the play. With a toothy grin, he lowered his face into the quarterback's lap and swiped his broad tongue over the thick pipe flopping there.

"What the fuck?" Mack managed to gasp out as tongue played over the length of his dick with raspy heat.

"We're fuckin' 'pologizing, dude," Bruno blurted out in his face just before he clamped his mouth over the quarterback's. Both men had wide mouths, with plenty of room for the guard's fat tongue to swab deep. Drool immediately began to leak out to coat lips and chins.

Two mouths assaulting him, the blond quarterback snorted in air and grunted. His cock, a real grower, swelled inside the big tackle's hot face-hole, stabbing toward tonsils as its length increased dramatically.

117

CJ gurgled happily. He opened up his throat and allowed the probing knob to fill it. He was beginning to feel a little better about letting down his teammate on the field. Truth was, he hated losing, too, but most of all he hated letting down the handsome blond quarterback, who took it so hard. He hoped to change all that with this new tactic.

The black tackle took the lengthy pipe to the balls, feeling it swell as it insinuated farther into his throat and stretched his lips. Now that was a good sign!

Bruno wanted some of that cock-sucking action, too. The incredible length of their quarterback's tool was legendary. He pulled his lips off Mack's with a nasty slurp and lowered his head to butt against his buddy's.

"Gimme some dick, CJ! Don't hog all that fuckin' meat!"

The ebony-skinned tackle pulled off, snorting for air. "Don't choke on it! The thing's a monster!"

With a whoop, Bruno sucked up the bright pink boner. His buddy couldn't resist one of the inviting nipples in front of him, clamping his mouth over it and sucking. The quarterback's broad chest was smooth and firm and each nipple a prominent, totally suck-able, pinkish-brown nub.

The pair held up the 220 pound quarterback effortlessly as they took turns diving into his lap, vying for a taste of the drooling knob and competing to see who could deep-throat the most expertly. Black buzzed scalp bobbed enthusiastically, then was replaced by auburn-haired head. Non-stop slurps filled the air.

Drool pooled around the base of that huge pink shank and coated the hairless nuts dangling below. The quarterback bit his lip and moaned, thrusting up into either hot mouth, not caring which was which. His hands on their shoulders, knees up and legs in the air, he leaned back against the tiled wall and reveled in the gurgling spit-bath.

He wasn't about to admit it yet, but a good suck-job was just what he needed to take his mind off the night's defeat. If there was anything that could remotely compare to a game of football, it might, just might, be getting his big bone sucked! Still, he wasn't about to let his two teammates off the hook. Maybe if they offered up more than their sweet mouths ...

Meanwhile, in cock heaven, the pair of dick-sucking jocks were too competitive to merely look on and wait their turn. Both mouths attacked the pink pole simultaneously. Fat tongues ran up and down the thick shank on either side, gulped at the broad knob, spit it out and then licked back down toward the smooth balls. Chins, noses, and lips all massaged cock, a juicy lather of spit coating crotch and faces.

Jockeying for the juicy knob, their lips met, CJ's thick red ones and Bruno's wide pink ones. They kissed, cock-head between them, tongues swabbing together, spit dribbling down to coat the pulsing boner. They slurped up the knob, smacking their lips together, tongues stroking each other's wide open mouths until one of them grew too heated and had to swallow that cock to the root again.

CJ, with his blunt, dark features and buzzed bullet head, presented a real contrast to Bruno, whose light-brown complexion was almost always softened by that wide crooked smile. The guard had dreamy amber eyes and a long straight nose he now snorted in the smell of quarterback crotch with. His thick mop of auburn hair was always in disarray. Together, they bumped heads, sucked cock, licked balls, and tongued each other's mouths as eagerly as they slammed bodies on the playing field.

Breathless and grunting, the lathered-up quarterback finally asserted a measure of control. Slightly mollified, he was feeling a little better than ten minutes earlier. "You pair of fuck-ups have a lot to make up for. I'm gonna need more than a good suck-job ... get on your backs and show me your big cans!"

The blond's voice, even though it was husky and huffing from the fantastic blow job, was still commanding. The pair obeyed instantly, sharing a grin and wink as they lowered Mack with a speed belying their bulk. He was on his feet, gigantic boner pulsing in front of him as he watched the tackle and guard obey his orders.

In an instant the big jocks were sprawled out on their backs on the double-wide bench between the banks of lockers. Side-by-side, one gleaming black and the other sepia-brown, one smooth and the other coated in a light down of sandy fur, they locked one knee around each other's as they raised their feet in the air and spread them.

Two massive butts on display! They took up most of the space between the banks of lockers as they each placed their giant naked feet on the lockers in front of them, and leaned back to rest their massive shoulders on the lockers behind. Mack had to lift to their legs and squirm around in front of them to kneel and get a closer look at the butt-cracks offered up to him.

"Nice holes. You dudes are gonna get them stretched tonight, and I don't want to hear any bitching about it!"

"Don't worry Mack! Our holes are yours, bro! Stuff us full of dick! We're real sorry 'bout today on the field! We fucked up bad and we know it ... oh yeah! Eat my fucking ass," CJ babbled on until a rasping tongue suddenly swiped across his pouting asshole and began tickling it.

Bruno's bleat echoed his buddy's. "Oh hell yeah! We're real fuckin' sorry! Fuck yeah! Tease my hungry hole!"

With both powerful butts at his disposal, the quarterback wasted no time in deciding which to use. He buried his flushed face in the black butt and ate out that smooth slot, while he crammed his hand in the brown ass and began to tickle that quivering hole with his fingertips.

Hole pouted open to his tongue, sleek inner flesh quivering and sphincter spreading. A second hole clamped and convulsed against a pair of his stroking fingers. Both big cans squirmed under his attack. He didn't hold back, sucking noisily on black ass while tickling and stroking open the tightly puckered lips of brown hole. The guard and tackle grunted and begged.

"Fuck yeah! Ohhhhh ... unnnnhhhh ... eat me out, bro!"

"Finger my ass ... uhhhhhhhh ... hell yeah!"

The quarterback switched butts, stroking the hole he'd just swabbed with spit and eating out the hole he'd just rubbed open with a pair of fingers. The giant black tackle rode those rubbing fingers enthusiastically, his wet hole gaping into a maw that rubbed and strained against the quarterback's stroking digits madly. The amber-skinned guard's hole was deliciously snug, pulsing against his tongue as he licked it all over and tickled the tight entrance.

He knew which jock he'd plow first. It had to be CJ, whose black hole pouted outwards in hungry anticipation, practically crying out to be stuffed. The blond rose to his feet, fingers still tickling the tackle's black butt-hole, his drool dripping from the guard's amber pucker.

The jocks were kissing!

He liked that, and he liked the looks of their stiff cocks bobbing between gargantuan thighs. CJ's was a fat rammer with a huge knob while Bruno's was long and curved with a tapered bullet-crown. Both dribbled nut-juice in a steady stream.

121

Bruno's tangled mop of auburn hair fell over his pal's buzzed black scalp, his wide mouth covering CJ's and half his nose and chin, too! Both jocks were handsome in their own way, CJ brutish and dark, Bruno soft and sexy. They were quite a pair, and for the first time, Mack realized they shared more than the game of football.

He was a little bit jealous. All he cared about was winning, while these two had found something to get them through the tough times. It was a heady realization, but for now his dick was doing more thinking than his head, and a pair of steamy, eager holes were all but screaming for a good drilling.

"Here comes quarterback dick! Are you fucking ready for it?"

His growled threat succeeded in breaking up their slurping kiss. They turned to look up at him, eyes half-glazed, mouths wet and gaping. CJ was the one who'd made up the game plan, and so he was the one to bleat out the fact there was a bottle of massage oil up on top of the lockers behind Mack.

"Fuck, CJ. You had this all worked out, dude! In the future, I want to see some of that planning go into your play on the fucking field!"

CJ put on his humble face, blunt nose quivering, big red lips pouting and beady black eyes remorseful. The chastised look was spoiled somewhat by the lathering of Bruno's spit glistening all over his lips, chin and nose.

Mack's long arm whipped up behind him to the top of the locker where his hand groped and found the bottle of oil as predicted. He almost smiled, grudgingly admiring CJ's well-planned attack.

He flicked open the lid and squirted. A stream of glistening oil hit black asshole, pooled in the pouting entrance, then ran down the spread crack. He rubbed it in with his fingertips, staring at the distended lips pushing outwards in hungry need, the huge black butt heaving upwards. He aimed for the fat black dick and smooth dangling nads, hitting them with another full stream.

He quickly moved to Bruno and coated his wide-spread brown crotch with more oil. For good measure, he gave them both another generous coating so that they glistened from navel on down.

CJ realized it was his ass being targeted first when the fingers that stroked his hole moved aside to allow a bulging cock-crown to slam right in.

"Fuck! You're fuckin' guttin' me, bro!"

Mack, still plenty pissed-off, did his best to do just that. He slammed his knob past oil-primed sphincter and into the fuck tunnel beyond. Thrusting with his hips, he rammed home half his monster pole in one shove. Of course, he could tell the tackle was prepared for it, his asshole a hungry maw already opened up by a good tongue-drilling.

His right hand returned to Bruno's spread ass-crack. As he fed CJ cock, he crammed a finger into the brown-skinned guard's tight hole and twisted. The ass-lips went into snapping convulsions, but he gave them no time to get used to the invasion, shoving another finger inside, and then a third.

"Oh man … oh hell … oh fuck … my poor fuckin' hole," Bruno babbled, his right leg twisted around CJ's and his right arm under the giant tackle's shoulder. His wide mouth gaped, his big tongue out licking at his lower lip, his long nose quivering. His soft eyes stared up at Mack, full of an emotion the quarterback wasn't quite prepared to accept.

For good measure, he stabbed deeper with his fingers, amazed at the way the giant guard squirmed happily around the fingers stretching his asshole. To

123

Mack's surprise, that dreamy look on Bruno's face only got softer as his hefty brown can rose and met the twisting invasion.

Bruno was pleasantly imagining how the quarterback's thick pipe was going to feel when he had his turn!

That turn was coming right up. Merely testing out CJ's hole, Mack pumped his pink rod in and out only half-way, teasing the sensitive sphincter with his flared bulb and massaging those tender lips with his thick shank. He pulled out with a slurp and stepped sideways.

"Your hole is about to get dicked!"

The quarterback's warning was preceded by a savage twist of his fingers before he yanked them out and replaced them with his blunt cock-head. The flushed crown pressed against the brown ring of muscle, which had immediately tightened up. He pushed, feeling the muscle resist, then suddenly give way. The pink knob disappeared between the throbbing brown butt-lips.

"Hell yeah! I fuckin' love it!" Bruno shouted out to Mack's continued astonishment.

The hole seemed so tight, he could hardly believe the big guard was enjoying it so much, but the crooked grin on his face and that dreamy look told the truth. He thrust deeper.

And deeper.

Bruno's hole gulped and swallowed it all. In fact, he was able to bury that giant meat nearly three-quarters home.

He didn't neglect CJ's black butt. His left hand returned to probe the distended hole he'd just fucked. The tackle groaned loudly as he scooted forward to hump a trio of digits thrusting into his guts. The look on his face said it all. He was ripe for more cock.

124

A glint in the jet-black eyes and a half-smile on the plump lips revealed more than that. Mack could tell it was all going CJ's way, which should have angered him more than ever, but with the tight clamping of Bruno's fuck tunnel massaging his pumping pole, and the convulsions of the tackle's black sump pit around his twisting digits, he was beginning to lose his battle with his own emotions.

He was beginning, just beginning, to think of something other than football.

The blond pumped deeper and harder in and out of Bruno's deliciously snug hole a dozen more times while he cork-screwed his fingers in the tackle's hole before he switched again. This time he left his fingers in that gaping black maw as he crammed his flared cock-head back in.

"Fuck! Aggghhhh ... what the hell are you fuckin' doin' to me, bro? I ... fucking ... love ... it!"

Now the quarterback was actually grinning. His mood was definitely on the upswing. With three fingers, and his huge knob stuffed up the black tackle's hungry hole, he was in ass-heaven. He probed at Bruno's tight pit with a pair of fingers at the same time, feeling the snug orifice quiver as the giant guard strained to take them.

"Jerk each other off. I want a load out of both of you," he ordered.

He punctuated his demand with a deep thrust up CJ's hole. His giant pipe drove almost all the way in, pulsing against his fingers beside it. He bit his lip and shoved deeper, grunting with satisfaction as his pink balls finally slapped against smooth black butt.

The two jocks on their backs writhed around the quarterback's assault. They grabbed at each other's oiled dicks and began pumping furiously. Mack felt their holes respond, tightening and seizing his cock and fingers.

125

He drilled CJ's gaping slot with balls-deep punches, his solid hips slamming and squishing against oil-soaked round black ass, his pink cock disappearing and reappearing as the massive tackle took it effortlessly while fisting his buddy's stiff dick and panting like a bull in the ring.

Mack switched holes. Pulling out with a squishy slurp, oil splattering from both hole and pink dick, he side-stepped to bury that glistening pole between the brown ass-lips his fingers had just stretched then abandoned. Bruno's hips rose to meet the jabbing pole in his guts and then slammed down to gobble it up to the root with more squishy slurps.

"Fuck ... that is one tight ... sweet ... asshole," the blond huffed.

The steamy slot clinging to his cock had him tingling from head to toe. He fucked it savagely, driving in so hard he lifted the humongous brown ass off the bench with each powerful shove. His lengthy pipe slammed home, yanked out, then punched home again.

His fingers still probed CJ's slick hole, twisting and thrusting just as thoroughly as his cock reamed Bruno's snug slot. The pair of football players locked lips again while they jerked each other off and squirmed around the blond's anal assault.

He drove them both to orgasm, pounding home and digging deep. Black butt and brown butt heaved together, tongues buried in each other's mouths, hands pumping each other's oiled dicks.

They spewed.

CJ's black cock erupted first, a flying spray that hit the pair's lip-locked faces. Bruno was right behind, gobs of spunk splattering his brown belly and torso. They moaned around tongues and humped wildly over fingers and cock as their nuts drained.

Mack felt their holes clamp and quiver, his cock deep in Bruno's tight innards, his fingers way up CJ's sloppier slot. The fresh reek of cum assaulted his snorting nostrils. He fucked harder and faster, with dick and digits, supremely satisfied at his conquest of the squirming pair.

Their mouths parted as they gasped for air. Gazing up at the blond quarterback, they offered him apologetic grins. "Did that make up for our fuck-up?" CJ asked.

Mack, sweat dripping from his forehead, his pits and down his ass-crack, quickly decided not to relent, not just yet. He pulled out of the pair's well-fucked holes with a groan. He glared at the jocks with his hazel eyes just long enough to intimidate them before he turned around in the tight space and leaned up against the lockers behind him.

His lean thighs rose up to meet a solid, ivory-white can. He spread his feet wide apart and arched his back, opening up the deep crack and showing his pink pucker – smooth, sweaty, and snug.

"You boys got a lot to make amends for. Maybe after you eat some quarterback ass, you can fuck it, too. Then we'll talk about fucking forgiveness!"

He couldn't hold back a chuckle as he felt big jock hands grab at his butt and spread it even wider apart, just before a pair of faces crammed into his crack and tongues swiped out to lick up his sweat and search out his hole.

"That's it. Eat some quarterback hole. Eat it good. Real good!"

They were too busy doing just that to answer.

With tongues slobbering over his tender ass-lips, the blond jock sighed, knowing what would come next. Two big dicks, black and brown. Up his ass.

Now that would be a proper quarterback sack!

The gobbling football players fought as eagerly over the blond's hole as they had over his giant pink poker. Brown and black hands seized the pale butt-cheeks and spread them wide apart. Buzzed black scalp rooted in the open crack, butting against auburn-haired head. They tongued up and down the hairless valley, slobbering over the pink hole, flickering their plump tongues over the quaking lips, meeting there to kiss each other briefly then attack that sweet maw again. CJ's black fingers stretched the lips wide apart while his buddy gored the snapping slit with his tongue.

They took turns diving deep, stroking the grunting quarterback's innards, heating him up for the inevitable. Both football jocks sported resurrected cocks down between their massive thighs by the time that hole was gobbed good and pouting outwards.

CJ took the lead again. "You want Bruno to fuck you up the ass first, bro? Nothing against my buddy, except my dick is fatter and bigger. He could open you up so's it don't hurt as fuckin' much when I shove it in."

Mack, shaking all over from the awesome tongue-drilling, had something else in mind. Something a little more extreme, and ultimately more satisfying.

"You two fuck-up's still got some making up to do. Get your asses back up on the bench. Face away from each other and push those big lazy butts together!"

CJ, much brighter than his placid buddy, understood what Mack had in mind right away. He grinned with excitement and jumped up to drag his teammate back onto the bench and position him on his back with his legs in the air and knees pulled back against his chest. Things were definitely going as he'd planned!

He sprawled out himself, all 280 pounds, and scooted forward to press his massive black butt up against

128

Bruno's hefty brown can. Both their cocks reared up between them. He grabbed his teammate's around the thick base and pulled it toward his. The pair of boners rose up together in a twitching double-column of black and brown.

Mack's hazel eyes shone. He even managed a brief grin as he tossed one long white leg over the paired benches and faced CJ. His pale butt hovered in the air directly over those twin poles.

"Squirt out some more of that oil and rub it all over your dicks, boys! I want a slick fucking ride!"

Now, with that white butt beginning to settle down over their cocks, Bruno finally understood. Mack was about to take both cocks up his butt all right ... at the same time!

The big guard had the perfect view as that ivory ass began to squirm around over the two knobs, the smooth cheeks wide open and the pink hole all gooey with their spit. He followed his orders with a groan, seizing the massage oil bottle up from the floor beside them and squirting a wild geyser over both their stiff dicks. He reached out, meeting CJ's fingers already there. They pumped up and down the gigantic mass of paired cock, coating the brown/black column with glistening oil.

It was incredible to watch, and felt amazing, as that white butt wriggled around over the two cock-heads, the pouting hole gaping wider as the blond quarterback grunted and strained to feed himself that enormous bulk.

Both CJ and Bruno stared open-mouthed as Mack settled down over the paired crowns. His pink ass-lips strained, gooey spit dribbling out and over their oil-coated cock-heads, snug ass-lips slowly engulfing them, then as Mack let out a loud grunt, swallowing them entirely.

"Fuck, bro! I can't fuckin' believe it! You're taking two fuckin' cocks up the ass at once," CJ cried out. He hadn't planned anything as wild as this!

Bruno was just as impressed. "Hell yeah! Way to go, dude! You're the man!"

Mack's face glowed beet-red. His perfect features twisted up in a growling rictus of divine pleasure. His dimpled chin quivered. His blond brows arched over those piercing hazel orbs. The stretch on his sphincter was unreal. And he loved it! The idea of taking both the big football jocks' boners up his butt at the same time was a real nasty thrill. He had them where he wanted them, on their backs, their dicks trapped in his butt-hole, and from the looks on their faces, enjoying it as much as he was!

"Fuck yeah," he said with a gasp. "Now I'm going to fuck those dicks of yours like they've never been fucked before! You're both going to be the sore losers tonight, and I'm going to be the fucking victor!"

It was the simple-minded Bruno who blurted out the bald truth. "Fuck, Mack. There ain't no fuckin' winners or losers in this game. Everybody fuckin' wins!"

At that moment, as two cocks forced their way inside his straining gut, he was hit by the simplicity of that statement. For once in his life, he had to forget about winning! He just had to enjoy the game!

With deep groans, he managed to will his asshole to open up. He sat down on the pair of glistening cocks with steady insistence. His teammates stared wide-eyed as that pink hole engulfed more and more of the twin columns, straining, drooling and growing pinker.

The smooth white butt shook violently and so did the quarterback's muscular thighs as he straddled the pair of benches, crack wide open in that stretched position. He slowly and deliberately sat down over the two big poles. With a loud grunt he settled completely over

130

them, capturing them with his stretched ass-lips in a snug embrace.

All three jocks shouted out.

"Fuck!"

"Hell yeah!"

"Way to go, dude!"

The gored quarterback began to writhe and hump in a nasty dance over the sprawled jocks. They could do nothing but lie back and moan as asshole savaged their dicks and ass mashed their balls. The quarterback held nothing back, gritting his teeth as he humped up and down, writhing at the bottom viciously and then pulling back up just enough to slam back down. With their legs in the air, they rested their ankles on Mack's shoulders from in front and behind. Their big asses pressed tight together, their recently fucked holes rubbing together, still coated with oil and pulsing wildly. Their hefty butt-cheeks, coated in oil, too, slid against each other. Their dicks were locked in a squeeze inside the quarterback's pulsing gut. Bruno was treated to the sight of white butt spread wide and impaled to the balls by black and brown bone. CJ stared at Mack's pink cock rearing out from his crotch while enjoying the sight of their two cocks swallowed whole inside the quarterback's vice-like asshole.

They could feel each other's dicks pulse against each other inside that warm cauldron. It was amazing.

"Fuck, bro! It's like me and Bruno got one dick between us," he gasped out.

"Just like you got ... uggh ... one brain between you," Mack jeered between groans. "Next time on the field you better use that one brain to play a hell of a lot better! Uhhhhnn ... yeah!"

Regardless of the jeer, it was CJ who could see the change in Mack. His mouth hung open, the pink lips

131

curled up in a half-grin. His eyes no longer glared. Instead, they were now partially closed in a dreamy expression that rivaled Bruno's normal look of complacent innocence. The dimple in his chin quivered. He actually looked happy!

The tight butt-furnace massaging and stroking their cocks suddenly began to squeeze. The look on the blond quarterback's face told them what was coming. The half-grin was now a full-blown smile!

"Fuck! I'm gonna shoot!"

Mack's tongue lolled out, his face bright pink, his eyes squinting closed as he rose and fell in a savage drive to get himself off. Just as he dropped down to slam against his teammates' balls, his own nuts released their spew.

His cock erupted. The slit opened up to spray out an arc of creamy jizz that hit CJ's plump red lips and shiny black chin. The tackle guffawed, then groaned, as Mack's convulsing asshole squeezed and clutched at his buried black bone.

"Hell yeah! I'm blowin,' too! Up ... your ... hot ... white ... ass!"

That was Bruno. His giant body flopped on the bench against CJ's as he shot his load up the quarterback's asshole. CJ inhaled the stink of cum on his lips while lapping it up and still grinning. All that cum, and all that coming, set off his own trigger.

"I'm feedin' you a juicy blow, too, Mack! Fuck yeah!"

The quarterback squirmed his white butt around over the spewing cocks, gasping for breath as his own blow kept on squirting out to splatter CJ's heaving black torso. He seemed to have about a quart of the sticky goo in those big pink balls of his.

Supremely satisfied, but not quite done with disciplining his teammates, or at all ready to admit to caring about something other than football, he rose up off their cocks. Asshole gaping and drooling oil, the quarterback leaned forward to thrust his still oozing pink pole deep into CJ's black hole, pinning the giant tackle to the bench and staring deep into his sparkling brown eyes.

After a few thrusts to plant his load deep, he pulled back out, twisted around and did the same to the surprised guard. Shoving back his massive thighs and exposing his puckered brown oiled hole, the blond rammed his pole home. Bruno squealed like a girl, his own giant rod squirting out another gob of cum.

CJ was offered the awesome sight of the quarterback's beautiful white ass, clenching and pumping as he rammed Bruno deep. The pink hole between those smooth cheeks was stretched and pulsing. Cum and massage oil dripped from it. He couldn't help himself. He rose up and crammed his face in that inviting crack, gobbling and sucking on the quarterback's sloppy asshole.

A few minutes later in the showers, all three satiated and grinning, Mack allowed his teammates to take turns soaping him up before he made them do the same to each other while he watched. The two huge jocks laughed and joked as they ran their hands all over each other's naked bodies, and Mack felt a stab of jealousy for the second time.

He had to admit to himself he'd been consumed with the need to win every game he ever played. He'd neglected his teammates. As they turned to him with big grins and attacked him with bars of soap, he found himself giggling.

And not ashamed of it.

The very next game, the trio faced each other in a huddle on the field. The quarterback, tackle and guard all shared one thought. Victory tonight!

But of course that was not all they thought of. Pads bulging their powerful bodies, and regardless of uniforms hiding the vibrant flesh beneath, each recalled the other in the heat of nasty sex play. Big bare asses, pulsing holes taking fat dripping dicks. Grinning mouths gurgling over stiff cock. Cum rocketing out of straining knobs. Legs wide open, big jocks begging to get fucked good.

Mack stared deep in their eyes, believing he knew exactly what they were thinking. "If you two fuck-ups want more, you know what to do. Let's win!"

With more at stake than simply a game, the tackle and guard raised their hands and slapped them together with whooping glee. CJ was revved up more than ever to win. The thought of another chance to sack Mack's hot hard cock and sweet white butt had him growling for the other team's blood.

Bruno sized up his two teammates mood and, as always, went along. But he couldn't help thinking, although not his strong suit by far. His wide mouth curled up in that distinctive crooked grin. He wasn't smart, but he could add two and two.

Supposing they won. Sure, Mack would be in a great mood and they'd enjoy a hot round of steamy cock, ass, and hole play afterwards. But if they lost ... wouldn't Mack need a little cheering up, just like last time?

It seemed to him, victory or loss, they'd come out winners!

HOCKEY CAPTAIN TRIES NASTY PLAY
By Jay Starre

Goalies are a strange breed. Temperamental. Independent. Brave, too, with all those pucks flying at them. Although that last one, bravery, seemed to be a problem for our goalie lately.

Francois confronted me about it. "Hey Matty, what the fuck's up with Brock? He played like shit out there tonight. He ducked the fucking puck more than he stopped it."

As the Captain of our ragtag recreational hockey team, it was my responsibility to keep up morale. Usually if a teammate played poorly, his buddies would chew him out, no problem. But with goalies, no one wanted to irritate them with the wrong kind of comment.

I sighed. What to say to Brock? Just about everyone had dressed and left, but as was often the case, our goalie hadn't chosen to change with the rest of us. He was likely to be found in one of the quieter change rooms in the vast recreational complex where we played.

I wrapped a towel around my waist and padded down the long cement corridor toward the farthest change room. We'd played at midnight that night, not uncommon in a busy rink, so I wasn't surprised to meet no one except the last of the opposing team on their way out.

I offered a friendly goodnight to those two, as most of us in the league were on good terms – at least after the game. Afraid of finding our goalie in a funk and wondering how to approach the problem gently, I opened the door to that last change room quietly.

The locker room was arranged with one main change area and an additional two smaller change areas just beyond a doorway that led to the showers. The first room was empty, but I heard sounds coming from one of the rooms at the far end. Strange sounds. Kind of like grunts.

I didn't call out, still worried about what to say to our goalie, but also intrigued by those odd grunts. What the fuck was that all about? Quietly, I came to the doorway and peered around the corner.

I didn't find Brock in a funk. I found him bare-ass squirming over a bench with a big dildo crammed up his butt!

I froze in place, mouth agape and hand instantly dropping to my crotch to clutch a rapidly stiffening boner through my towel.

What a sight! Brock sprawled over a change bench face-down. He'd stripped off his pads, skates, pants and heavy-duty goalie jock. His creamy-white butt was totally bare. But above, he still wore his shoulder pads and chest protector, his team jersey, and even his goalie helmet.

He had quite the butt. Goalies are in a crouch most of the time, a permanent squat that clenches the butt-cheeks and creates buns of solid power. Brock, fair-haired and smooth, had a creamy pale can without a single blemish. Full and solid.

At the moment, that butt was spread wide open. Muscular thighs flopped, while pink asshole dripped shiny lube and a big flesh-colored dildo furiously rode in and out of it.

"Take that big fake dick up your butt-hole, pig! Take it like you love it! Next time you're on the ice, and I come at you with the puck, you're gonna remember this, and you're gonna fuckin' get out of the way, so I can score. Understand? Understand?"

Troy practically spit out those final two words, ramming the lengthy dildo balls-deep.

The brown-haired hockey player attacking our goalie with a greased dildo was a real prick. Troy played for the Burnaby Blades, one of our main rivals. We'd lost tonight against them, mostly because Brock had allowed two goals by this same prick.

Brock grunted deep as that toy rammed home, but also heaved backward to swallow it and hold it inside. His round butt squirmed as he fucked himself over it. There was no question in my mind that he was loving it.

It was obvious Troy liked it, too. Tall and gangly, he hunched naked over his prey. He'd discarded his own hockey gear, it was scattered on the floor around them, and had one long arm wrapped around Brock's belly, the other planted on the end of that greased dildo. His own high tight butt clenched dramatically as his dangling nads swayed between spread thighs.

Troy really was a prick. Hockey is all too often a game beleaguered by fights on the ice. Troy was one of those with a short fuse and scrappy personality who usually instigated the battles. He was a great forward, though, and a formidable opponent. Those long legs of his drove him across the ice at a good clip, and his equally long arms powered a mighty slap shot.

If Brock was afraid of those rocketing shots, he'd duck instead of block, and that meant disaster for our team. A true dilemma!

In the meantime, there was the exciting game happening right here and now in front of me. Our goalie's butt was truly awesome. The squishing dildo dug around inside him, slid out while pulling his pink ass-lips with it, then crammed back deep to his loud grunts. It was too damn hot.

I decided not to give away my presence. I hovered just beyond the corner wall and observed in silence. My hand pumped my cock under my towel as furtively as possible while the heated action continued. Troy berated Brock with nasty abuse while our blond goalie took it like a beaten cur.

The tall hockey player rammed that dildo in and out, full force. His back dripped sweat, a rivulet running down between his tight butt-cheeks. He was all lean muscle. Those muscles clenched powerfully as he pummeled with that fake dick as deep and hard as he could.

It was amazing how Brock took it. The dildo was huge and really long, too. His asshole just sucked it up as if it was nothing. His big butt heaved up and back to meet every shove and probe. The white flesh had grown bright pink, and the hole itself was a fiery slash of swollen ass-lips and pouting sphincter.

"I'm gonna blow a load! All ... over ... your fucking butt!"

The dildo was yanked out just as Troy hissed out those words. I gawked at the sight of the battered butt-hole gaping wide open between those hefty ass-cheeks. I bit back a groan as I saw Troy turn slightly sideways and reveal his lengthy prick for the first time.

Without even touching it, one hand gripping the base of the dildo and the other arm around Brock's waist, he blew his nut. His prick reared up dark purple, a wicked curve in the stiff shank and a swollen crown gushing goo.

The cum arced out to splatter Brock's heaving, just-dildoed ass. Gobs landed white and creamy all over his sweat-soaked butt-cheek to run down toward his pink ball-sack. That long prick kept on spurting, more cum than I'd seen a dude produce probably ever.

I shot, too. Inside my towel my fisted cock spewed. With my heart pounding and trying to stifle my groans, I quickly slipped away on shaky feet. I was still spurting as I stumbled back down the hall toward my own change room.

What to do? I didn't really dislike Troy. Sure he was a prick on the ice, but mostly it was due to a combination of his love of the game, his keen competitive spirit, and his short fuse. I really did like Brock, a quiet loner most of the time, but easy-going and never one to complain when his teammates let him down.

I had to do something. As Captain, I was responsible for my teammates.

I'd have to recruit Francois. We played on the same line and could practically read each other's minds. He'd follow my lead. "I'm going to set a trap for that bad-tempered hockey prick. I'm betting he'll bottom pretty fucking quick if we put it to him right."

Francois nodded his head vigorously, his shaggy mop of black hair bobbing. A Quebecois, his French-Canadian background lent him a dramatic flare. He'd perform exactly as needed.

Bright blue eyes contrasted sharply with his raven hair and gazed back at me with utter trust. He wasn't exactly stupid, but he was not a deep thinker either. He really had no idea whether my plot would work or not, he just figured I knew what I was doing.

Brock was not nearly so confident in my scheme. His flush of embarrassment when I confronted him with what I'd seen was followed by an apologetic plea for understanding. "He just gets to me. I can't help it. He's got some kind of kinky power over me I can't seem to shake."

"Just tell him you'll meet him again like usual after the game on Saturday night. Francois and I'll do the rest."

I admit it was a long shot, but I felt as if I understood Troy better than Brock or anyone else. Peel back that feisty bravado and you'd find a less confident and far more needy dude.

"This is gonna be fucking fun!"

Francois grinned from ear to ear as we prepared to set our trap. His wide mouth split a broad face with his trademark toothy smile. He could be counted on to always have fun.

I had to agree with him though. My plan wasn't just about curing our goalie's problems, or putting our enemy Troy in his place. All the elements fit in nicely with my own secret desires.

I was good buddies with the Iceman on duty, mostly because I kept my teammates in line and never left a mess in the locker rooms or let them argue when our ice time was over. He did us the favor of locking the spectator doors to one of the smaller rinks. When Francois and I skated out onto the empty ice, the stands were empty as well.

"Fuck yeah! Fuck it's cold though!"

Francois whooped gleefully as he took off in a spin around the rink. I followed with a whoop of my own. Both of us wore skates and helmets – and nothing else.

I snorted in frigid air, my bare skin flushed and dotted with goose bumps as I chased Francois's naked butt around the rink. The French-Canadian was short and stocky with a wide shoulders and a plump can that pumped seductively as his big thighs carried him effortlessly around the oval surface. A little on the fat side, he was not the least bit self-conscious of the fact and sexy as hell because of it.

140

A few vigorous rounds and we were both heated up. The one door that remained open to the rink led to the change rooms. I spotted a tall figure lurking just inside it, crouching behind the spectator's stand and peering out at us with big brown eyes.

Troy! Brock had done his part. He'd told the hockey prick to meet him here, and instead he'd found us, skating madly in circles in the nude!

It was time to up the ante. A few powerful strides, and I caught up with Francois. Without a word spoken, he knew what to do. Spinning expertly, he was now skating backward. I came into his arms, and we spun together, skates cutting deep scars in the clean ice.

Our bodies became one. Our cold flesh collided. Our flopping dicks mashed together. We kissed. A tongue dueling, lips mashing, drooling suck.

We spun right past the lurking Troy who tried to melt back in the shadows, his own mouth open and a hand down at his crotch clutching what was probably a big boner through his hockey pants. Even from a furtive glance, I could see how he was dressed. He'd taken off his skates and helmet, but hadn't shed the rest of his gear from our game, which had ended twenty minutes earlier. He was prepared to meet Brock in the hopes of pounding his hot goalie butt with a big dildo again.

Instead, dumbfounded, he watched two hockey jocks in a lip-lock as they skated in spinning circles around the ice, butt naked.

Regardless of the fact it was all a scheme to trap the punk, it was still a thrill. I'd always wanted to skate naked, and Francois had admitted he did, too, when I outlined our plot earlier. He kissed me with sloppy glee, his blue eyes peering into mine, his big body meshed perfectly with mine as we spun and darted and flew across the ice. Where his skin touched mine, it heated us both,

141

and where our hands clasped each other's icy-cold butts, blessed warmth radiated.

For Troy's benefit, and our own pleasure, we dug our fingers into each other's clenched ass-cracks while humping against each other's crotches. It was a nasty parade around the rink, and Troy was getting the show of his life.

As a pair our bodies contrasted sharply. Ginger-haired and spattered with myriad freckles, thick muscles from lots of weight-training, and taller than my buddy by several inches, my muscular arms wrapped around Francois's shorter, huskier frame. My naked ass was solid pumping freckled marble while his was full, fleshy and softly amber.

Our swirling dance was so much fun I could have gone on much longer but knew we had to move on or risk losing our prey. I broke the kiss and proclaimed loudly, my words echoing in the abandoned rink, "Let's take it into the locker room! Time to fuck each other up the butt!"

Troy heard. He disappeared out the door just as we approached the gate. Now, it depended on whether the hockey prick would wait for us or not. We skated off the ice, my longer arm draped over Francois's broad shoulders.

By this time, we both had full-blown hard-ons, regardless of the goose bumps dotting our naked flesh. The warmer air beyond the swinging doorway was a welcome relief, although now we were both aware of the sweat that frothed our pits, crotches and butt-cracks. Francois, with a goofy grin, couldn't help probing around in my ass-crack with his nimble fingers as we sought out the nearest change room. It was exactly the one where I'd discovered our goalie with a big dildo crammed up his sweet white ass.

We'd left our gear and clothes there, and we both tossed our helmets onto the piled equipment before continuing with our scheme. I was fairly sure Troy lurked beyond the door that led to the other smaller change areas and the showers. That's where he always met Brock, according to the blond goalie. He would have seen our gear and either went on his way, or stayed, hiding right where we wanted him.

My drama queen buddy got down to business. "Get on your back on the bench, Matty. I'm gonna sit on your face while I chew out your butt. Let's get our holes heated up before we do a flip fuck!"

Of course, Francois relished this part of the plot. He was a real butt-licking fiend, and loved to park his hefty can over a willing face. He did just that as I positioned myself with a view of the door to the other change areas.

Big ass settled over my face, pinning me to the bench. I grabbed two hands full and squeezed the enormous hockey ass as I buried my nose and mouth deep between the lush mounds. Hole, pink and pouting, opened to my tongue.

Francois lifted my legs, my skates still on, and dove into my crack like there was no tomorrow. His wide mouth opened up, moist lips slobbering all over, and fat tongue coming out to swab and suck. He let out histrionic groans and moans while making sure to slurp and smack his lips as loudly as possible.

I would have laughed myself silly if I wasn't surrounded by sexy, plump butt-cheek and busily chomping on sweet hockey jock hole. Satin lips swiped up and down my own crack while darting tongue teased my tender jock hole.

My Quebecois pal munched away contentedly, nearly forgetting his next part in our play. I had to nip at one of his plump cheeks to remind him. His husky body jerked slightly over me, but he took the hint.

His face came up out of my crack just enough for him to nearly shout out, "Fuck, Matty, wouldn't it be cool if some hockey stud came in now and fucked both our asses?"

It was Troy's cue, if he was bold enough, and stupid enough, and horny enough to go for it. Of course he'd probably be horny as hell, what with expecting to get his hands on our goalie's sweet can, and with his eyes full of me and Francois busy sucking out each other's buttholes.

I pushed up slightly on my bud's big ass and peered around it. Yeah! Success! There he was, totally naked and pumping his lengthy boner as he strolled toward us from out of the other room.

I took a moment to size up that wicked hard-on. It was truly prodigious in length and had a real curve to it. The head, flushed dark purple now, had a flare to it that would treat a sphincter to a real stretching.

"You pansy-ass jerks need a cock to fill those hungry holes? I'm your man."

Pushing Francois's hefty can farther out of the way, I stared right into Troy's big brown eyes and offered up our well-plotted dare.

"So punk, you want some hockey boys' ass? Well then first you gotta give up yours. After that, we'll give you a crack at ours. Get it? We fuck you up the ass, then you get to fuck us up the ass."

Francois's raven mop bobbed up and down as he nodded enthusiastically, staring up at Troy to gauge his reaction. His big butt was in the air, spread over my prone body, his crack wide open and his spit-wet hole nicely pouting in and out in a nasty display.

He was quite the actor.

Troy had approached boldly and was now hovering right beside my face and Francois's hot can. His large brown eyes grew wider as he darted a hungry glance at the sweet spit-wet slot between those lush ass-cheeks, then back to me. For all that obvious give-away, the rest of his expression remained the same. His lip curled up on the right in a snarl. That snarl looked almost exactly like his smile, which curled up in the same way. He snarled most of the time, only smiling when he scored. Triumph looked about the same as anger on him.

He knew me well enough. He knew I meant business. And he knew Francois. Once, when the scrappy forward had lost it and attacked my French-Canadian pal during a game, Francois had merely wrapped his husky arms around the tall jock and slammed him to the ice, burying him under all that bulk and winding him. The fight had lasted 30 seconds.

We faced off, all three sporting stiff, eager dicks. It was really only a matter of who was going to fuck whom, and in what order. Troy figured that out, and much as I suspected was deep down a bottom at heart.

"OK. My ass is yours first. Then, I'm gonna drill you both so hard you won't walk for a fucking week!"

Yeah, right, I thought. He just couldn't let go of all that feisty bravado.

Well we'd see how loud he squealed when Francois's very fat bone rammed up his tight hole! I couldn't wait to see that, even more than I wanted to pound my own dick up there.

Francois got to his feet with that toothy grin splitting his face and a lusty sparkle in his blue eyes while I merely sat up on the bench and spread my legs. "Suck on this while Francois lubes up your butt for his dick."

145

I said it in a matter-of-fact tone, careful not to rile our prey now that we had him where we wanted him. He was real unpredictable at times. But his hard-on led the way, and controlled his brain enough, so that he followed my lead just like Francois.

He came forward with his curved cock still in hand, his long limbs tensed as if he was about to start scrapping. I smiled at him in a sort of encouraging way, but was thinking inside how much sex must be just like another fight to him.

He dropped to his knees right between my spread thighs. He offered up a defiant glance before he settled down to business. He kept one hand on his own cock, pumping the curved length slowly. His other hand slid around the base of my cock and aimed it at his descending mouth.

Amazingly, that snarl remained in place even as he wrapped his lips around the head of my dick. I grabbed the top of his head, feeling the buzzed brown nap tickle my palm as I forced him down over my boner.

Instead of resisting as he might have, he swallowed like a champ. In fact, he gobbled savagely, nearly choking as he deep-throated me right to the balls.

"Fuck! Yeah! Drill his ass, Francois! Fuck him good while he sucks me off!"

I yelled it out, our signal to Brock, who was supposed to be waiting outside the locker room for just this moment. Francois, blue eyes bright under that mop of raven hair, had the bottle of lube in his hand we'd brought along. He stared at Troy's tight white butt with a hunger I immediately understood.

He tore his eyes from that ass and looked at me with a pleading look I couldn't gainsay. "OK. Eat his butt first before you fuck it."

146

My husky buddy dropped to his knees right behind Troy and burrowed in between his perky ass-cheeks. Both hands clutched at the tight cheeks and spread them wide. Troy mewled around the cock in his throat, arched his back, and wriggled back onto the lips and tongue attached to his tight little hole.

That's when Brock appeared.

The look on his face was worth all that scheming. Blond and green-eyed, he had regular features that would have been bland except for his full red lips and the intensity of his focus when he played hockey. That intensity transformed his face now as he stared at his nemesis, Troy, with a cock in the mouth and a tongue up the ass!

He'd changed out of his gear and wore sweat pants and t-shirt. A hard-on rose up to tent those sweats as he watched breathlessly. I nodded, and he came closer to stand right behind the broad back of Francois where he couldn't quite be seen by Troy. He shoved down on his sweat pants to reveal that thick cock all flushed and stiff.

Meanwhile, I was getting the suck-job of my life. The brown-haired brown-eyed prick between my knees sucked and licked and bit my shank like a terrier worrying a juicy bone. His tight ass wriggled back against Francois's tonguing while his head bobbed up and down in my lap at a furious pace.

He deep-throated my pipe almost effortlessly. Although he did gag and choke a bit that didn't seem to deter him in the least. He yanked on my balls with one hand while he stroked his own cock with the other. His tongue twirled maddeningly all over my cock-head and shaft.

I was hard-pressed to keep my head. But for our purposes, there had to be more. My heart pounding, I

147

yelled at Francois between ragged pants. "Get your tongue ... out of the prick's ass ... and shove your cock in there!"

That was the whole point of the operation. Brock needed to see Troy get fucked up the butt, and that way hopefully he'd break free of the spell the tall hockey prick had over him.

Francois's mouth unattached itself with a slurp. His head came up, an apologetic grin on his face as he licked his lips and winked at me. I rolled my eyes and bit my own lip as the suction-pump in my crotch only grew more intense. I didn't know how long I could hold out against that vicious suck-job!

Brock took the bottle of lube from Francois with shaking hands and squirted the clear goo all over that squirming white butt. With his boner in hand, the eager goalie reached over the kneeling Francois and thrust a finger between Troy's perky ass-cheeks – and jabbed.

Troy's lean body jerked and his lips clamped over my cock. The look in our goalie's green eyes was just as intense as when he faced the worst attack on the ice. Francois knelt on the floor in front of him, his own hard-on in hand as he lunged upwards.

"Here's some cock for you, Troy! I bet you're gonna like it. I bet your gonna like it so much you're gonna want more of it when I'm done. I bet you're gonna want Matty's cock, and I bet your gonna want ..."

I cut him off. We'd decided before that Troy shouldn't know Brock was watching, but in the heat of the moment Francois had forgotten. "Yep! You're gonna want our entire team's dicks up your ass!" I filled in for him.

Whatever his thoughts about that prospect, the brown-haired jock didn't argue one way or the other. He did make a lot of noise, just like he did when he was on the ice. He was known for his jeers, catcalls, dares, swearing, laughing at his opponent's mistakes and braying at his own triumphs.

And when I'd watched him cram a dildo up our goalie's ass, he sure had made a hell of a lot of noise. He didn't disappoint now. He grunted around the cock in his mouth. He arched his back and heaved his compact can against the fat dick being jammed up it. He spit out my cock for just long enough to let out a curse and a squeal.

"Fuck! Unnnhhhhhhhhhh! Pound my butt with that fat bone you goddamn fucker!"

He let out another high-pitched squeal as Francois thrust into him full-force, then just like a true fuck-pig he buried his face in my crotch to slurp and mewl over my cock.

"Fucked from both ends ... cocks in both holes ... just what you need!" I managed to blurt out. I said it for Brock's benefit, of course. He had to see his nemesis for what he was. Not the blustering, posing boss of the ice, but a true bottom who gave up his ass and mouth for his opponents ... and loved it!

Brock watched from just behind Francois' shoulder. His eyes remained intent on the steady pumping of the French-Canadian's thick cock in and out of Troy's stretched and battered anal slot. The heaving ass had grown bright pink and dripped sweat. Even now, Troy didn't just take cock up the butt, he fought for it with his twisting waist and writhing butt.

Francois grinned at me, thoroughly enjoying himself. He held onto Troy's lean waist with both hands in an effort to control the prick's wild gyrations, with only some effect. He jabbed mercilessly in and out, wincing now and then as Troy clamped viciously with his tight ass-lips.

I waged a losing battle myself. The brown-haired jock swallowed my cock to the root then spit it out to curse us both, then dove down over it again. That snarl remained, lips coated in drool and big brown eyes wild as hell.

"Let's fuck him on the bench," I managed to order.

I had to change it up or I'd blow my load in another minute or two. I also wanted to tame the crazed jock, if at all possible. This was also a cue to Brock to make himself scarce. He tore his eyes from the fascinating view of Troy's puckered hole getting pumped full of fat dick and scurried into the next change room to hide beyond the doorway.

We lifted the squirming jock together, perfectly in tune with each other just like on the ice. Francois's fat tongue came out and wagged at me, the twinkle in his blue eyes almost making me laugh. We turned the cursing Troy over onto his back and plopped him down on the bench between us. I straddled his face and Francois lifted his legs and scooted in to sit between them on the bench.

"Gimme some more cock, assholes! Give it to me hard ... then your turn's next ... uhhhnnnggg!"

I cut him off by pushing down on my dick and cramming the head between his snarling lips. He slurped and mewled as I fed it to him, my freckled thighs tensing as I rose and fell over his head and fucked his mouth.

Francois aimed for his lube-coated, flushed asshole. The hairless crack was bright pink from the pounding he'd already received and from his own violent exertions. Sweat coated his perky butt. I leaned over and watched as Francois planted the broad cap of his thick meat on target and shoved.

Troy let out a satisfying squeal as half that monster drove into him. His lean thighs flopped around in the air. I glanced up to see Brock hovering in the doorway, craning his neck to see the action. I nodded and he shuffled forward, his sweats around his ankles and his boner rearing in front of him. He moved in behind Francois again to watch the impalement of his enemy up close.

We had the brown-haired hockey prick right where we wanted him, cocks buried in both his holes. Or at least I believed so. But he wasn't about to give up without a fight. One of his hands moved down to his own ass and rooted around in the lube-dripping crack. Fingers came up coated in the copious goo ... .and whipped back up to cram into my own butt-crack.

Straddling the bench and his face, my ass was wide open for his surprise attack. He drove those fingers up into me, a pair of them stabbing right into my puckered butt-hole!

My own blue eyes went wide as I grunted like a stuck pig. Francois, seeing my startled look, let out a hyena laugh just before I stifled it with a sloppy kiss. I held the back of his head with my hand and tongued his wide mouth. I had to do something to offset the wracking sensations in my crotch and ass.

Those fingers rooted and probed forcefully, lube squishing as it eased the way. It felt totally awesome, especially with wet lips slurping all over my cock as I drove down into that gaping mouth.

The ache in my asshole as I squatted over those digging fingers only served to intensify the heated pleasure in my sucked dick. I knew what Troy was up to! He was going to force me to cum, and he was doing a damn good job of it.

We had to head him off! Nothing would be better than to have him shoot with cocks in his holes and Brock watching.

My eyes stared into Francois'. I nodded as I tongued his mouth. He understood, as always. One of his hands reached out to grip Troy's curved hard-on and started jerking it savagely. He drove deep into the hockey prick's

151

squishy asshole, faster and faster. So fast, in fact, he lifted the compact butt up off the bench with each powerful thrust.

It was a close thing. Troy attacked my butt-hole with renewed effort. His two fingers twisted and jabbed. His lips suctioned like hot silk. His throat clamped over my buried cock-head. I shuddered from head to toe, wondering if I could hold out another instant.

Francois came to my rescue. He knew how to draw a load out of a willing dick, and it seemed even out of an unwilling one. My raven-haired teammate fucked Troy's hole in a perfectly matching rhythm with his savage dick-jerking.

It was close, but Troy lost it first. His lean body, trapped on the bench between his rivals, suddenly rose upwards in a flopping convulsion. I broke the kiss with Francois and looked down just in time to witness it. His curved cock spewed.

It was so fucking hot I had to shoot, too. I pulled my dick out of Troy's gulping mouth and sat down on his face, his fingers still buried up my ass. As his dick-head erupted and jizz spattered his lean belly in big gobs, I added my own load.

My spit-soaked knob sprayed. Cum landed on his tensed abs to join the copious blow he was continuing to spew. He didn't disappoint. Gob after gob shot out of his dick.

Brock moved in to shoot. With sweats still around his ankles, he added his own load to the mess. His flushed face was totally intent. He was seeing exactly what he needed to see, I believed.

Francois kept on fucking. His thrusts up Troy's battered ass forced a steady spew from his curved cock. My grinning teammate also continued to pump on Troy's cock in an effort to drain his balls.

The dude could really come! I was emptied, and so was Brock, and still more goo came out of the fucked jock's dick. In fact, it was still coming when Francois lost it, too. He yanked his cock out of the clamping hole seizing it and blew his wad all over Troy's compact butt-cheeks.

Through a haze of satiated orgasm, I nodded to Brock. It was time for him to disappear. We'd agreed Troy wasn't going to realize he'd seen him get fucked.

With obvious reluctance, he pulled up his sweats and slipped out of the locker room. I knew why he wanted to linger. We'd promised Troy he could fuck our butts after we did him, and Brock wanted to see that, for sure.

But unless Troy could get it up after a blow like that one, we were safe for the night.

I hadn't counted on the dildo Troy brought to use on Brock!

"Fair is fair. You dudes gotta give up your asses for me now." Troy was as feisty as ever once I got up off his face.

I couldn't argue. And I really didn't want to. My asshole had a pleasant ache in there from the reaming Troy's pair of fingers had given it. And, I had a feeling I'd enjoy watching my buddy bend over and offer up his plump amber butt for Troy's use.

With lube squirted over his big round butt and straddling the same bench we'd just fucked Troy on, my grinning teammate took the flesh-colored dildo with a grunt, then a wriggle and a deep sigh as the lean jock shoved half the thing inside.

I knew what was coming. The dildo Troy had brought was a double-headed one. His snarled grin was followed by a nasty demand. "Get that butt of yours over here. Let's see the two of you kiss asses!"

I straddled the bench with my butt facing Francois's. Lubed dildo settled on my hole and began to slither in. Thanks to the rough fingering a few minutes previously, I was wide-open for it. With a sigh of pleasure, I sat back to swallow the slippery rubber.

Our asses met. Francois's hefty can was warm and sweaty against my solid one. Troy stood over us and laughed. And cursed. "Take that dildo up your greedy asses, punks! Take it and love it! You're both a pair of pansy fuckers who love to get fucked! You love it! You fucking love it!"

He never shut up the entire time we fucked ourselves over that dildo, our butts banging together, our dangling dicks finally growing stiff as Troy reached between our spread legs and pumped them with his characteristic viciousness.

It seemed that regardless of the drilling we'd given him earlier, and his own willing descent into total bottoming, he hadn't changed at all. He was still the foul-mouthed, feisty bad sport he always had been.

He laughed like a maniac when we shot our loads, dildo deep in our asses. He shot again himself, too. He aimed his curved cock at the junction of our impaled butts and unloaded another staggering wad over our sweaty butts.

We showered together with surprising geniality. Of course, Francois was unfazed by it all. He had enjoyed the wild romp and wasn't worried about who had come out on top. He figured Brock had seen what we wanted him to see, so that would be that.

I thought so, too. And, Troy actually did seem a little changed. His snarl was more grin than not, and he said nothing at all that could be construed as abusive or rude. That in itself was a minor miracle.

Our next game was all it should be. Furious and fast-paced, our rivals put up a good fight as usual. But, we triumphed as Brock performed with his usual intensity. Troy came at him like a steam-roller, but the blond goalie blocked every one of his shots, plucking them out of the air with a flying glove, batting them aside with a steady stick, or blocking them with his padded body.

I searched him out after the game to congratulate him. Flushed with victory and smugly self-congratulatory at the success of my elaborate plot against Troy, I barged into the last locker room and called out to Brock.

"Hey! You shut out those fuckers tonight! Congrats, pal!"

In the echoing silence, what did I hear? Grunts coming from the far change rooms.

I hesitated. What would I find there? Maybe a vanquished Troy with Brock's triumphant cock up his tight white butt?

But somehow I knew. I forged ahead anyway. Beyond the doorway I found them.

Bent over a bench, Brock's awesome big butt was wide open, shiny with grease, and stuffed with a dildo. And Troy, his head turned to face me, grinned around his perpetual snarl as he pumped that dildo home.

"Look whose butt is getting stuffed now? Not mine, fucker!"

I looked at Brock. His flushed face was turned toward me, too, as he lay over the bench with lower body naked and upper body still encased in his gear – and our team jersey. He smiled, and winked.

I turned and left them to it.

155

All my convoluted schemes had gone awry, it might have seemed. But not really. I was pretty sure Brock would play his best in the future. And Troy? Who cared?

I found Francois and sat on his face before I fucked his sweet, plump butt good. He loved it.

THE SWIMMER
By RJ Bradshaw

His butterfly strokes
Set my heart aflutter
His swift scissor kicks
Cut through me like butter

Cheesy poetry; result of being the Life Guard on Thursdays. Public Lane Swimming: 11:45 am–1:30 pm. Old men and him. He always shows up before noon and stays until the aqua yogis get here. Always alone. This time no different.

HIM: Mid-twenties. Fair skin. Lean. Confident walk as he searches for a free lane. Muscle definition in his feet and legs. Long toes. Body not shaved like a competitive swimmer. Tight grey swim briefs. I can see the outline of his shaft. Hairs trailing up to a broad furry chest. Freckles on his arms and back and face. Lengthy brown hair that looks black when it's wet, when it's flat against his head and tucked behind his ears; ears I want to nibble and lick. Dark eyes. A beard, bushy; it looks soft.

ME: Twenty nine; still get ID'd. Sitting in a chair beside the pool, keeping watch. Trying to look bored; pretend I'm not horny. A stranger to him, unnoticed. Skinny and pale. Awkward. Red swim trunks, tightened with drawstrings. Hairless stomach and chest, except a few hairs that pop out around my nipples; look like pubes. Fit, but not muscular. Light brown hair, curly, tight. Hazel eyes with hints of green. Three days facial growth, amounting to little. Big jaw. Wide nose. Nice smile, I think.

His dive gets me wet
With pre-cum and sweat

HIM: Swimming. Goggles. Strokes are imperfect, passionate; I'm guessing self-taught. Working on his backstroke. Left arm, right

157

arm, left arm, in and out of water. More thrust in his right. Right hand gripping his thick cock, pumping; foreskin sliding over the tip. Grin on his bearded face. Naked body dripping. Lets me watch him. Invites me closer. In my dreams.

ME: Stiff. Knees pulled up to chest, hiding my lust. Knees on the locker room floor. Lips wrapped around his dick. Tracing with my tongue. His fingers twisted in my hair. Smell and taste of chlorine. Back to reality. Obvious bulge. Sitting is safe. Please, please don't let anyone start drowning. Thoughts of lawsuits. Keeping watch, especially on him. Smirking at my rigid secret.

His backstroke has the knack
To make me stroke back

HIM: Front crawl.

ME: In the locker room. On my hands and knees.

His front crawl I salute
In the front of my suit

HIM: Behind me. Erection plunging in. Hands stroking me like water. Finding his rhythm inside me. Gasping air, so he doesn't drown.

ME: Sitting in a chair beside the pool. Cock ready to burst. Watching the aqua yogis walk in. Fuck. What time is it? 1:22 pm.

His paddle makes me smile
When he does it doggy style

HIM: Rising out of the pool. Peeling back goggles. Water streams over freckles. Heavy breaths. Exhaustion. Hair on his shoulders. Drops in his beard. Swim briefs cling, outlining. Confident walk as he heads to the locker room. Talks with old men. Laughs with them. Sexy smile. Voice rich. Screaming my name as he fucks me. Coming. Coming. Going.

ME: Knees pulled up to my chest. Throbbing and hard; need to do something about that. Waving hello to an aqua yogi. Not smiling. Craving to be in the showers, to really witness him strip off his shorts; old men don't know how lucky they are.

Cheesy poetry. Waiting for Thursday.

TOSSING THE CABER
By Michael Bracken

A real man knows how to handle a big pole, and the caber toss at the annual Highland Games involves the biggest pole of any sport. The men who toss the caber are all big, burly men who make my knees weak and my pulse race when I see them lined up in their kilts and kilt hose, but they aren't the only competitors at the games.

In addition to the caber toss, the other Heavy Events – the stone put, the Scottish hammer throw, the weight throw, the weight over the bar, and the sheaf toss – all attract former high school and college track and field athletes who may not have been good enough to go pro but who remain eager to continue competing against other men. And, they attract former athletes like me who no longer have any desire to compete, but who enjoy the companionship of athletes.

Scottish clans come from all over the region to compete in the Highland Games, and keeping everything organized requires dozens of volunteers. I work the competitors' tent, where Heavy Event competitors gather before and after events to adjust their kilts, tape their wrists, ankles, and knees, and guzzle Gatorade. I'm not there to play Peeping Tom, but I always enjoy seeing what Scotsmen – even pretend Scotsmen – wear under their kilts, and I have my chance in the competitors' tent, where I see everything from tighty whities to loose-fitting boxers to boxer-briefs to banana slings, all replaced or covered over by the chaste undergarment required of Highland athletes prior to each competition.

I try to keep my attention on the competitors' needs and not the rather explicit fantasies that run through my mind when I see big, burly men lift their kilts, but this past year one of my fantasies came true. I was cleaning up the competitors' tent late Saturday evening, long after the day's Heavy Events competitions had ended and most attendees had either returned to their campsites or were listening to the pipe and drum competition on the far side of the Highland Games site, when Derek Mackenzie, a caber tosser who favors tartan plaid boxers, pushed back the tent flap and stepped inside.

"I'm glad you're still here," he said as he crossed the tent to where I was working and held out his muscular left arm. He wore a black 'Made in Scotland' T-shirt tight over his barrel chest, a Mackenzie muted green tartan kilt fastened around his thick waist and hanging to mid-knee, a black leather and silver sporran hanging at his groin, black kilt hose turned down at the knee over tree-trunk legs, and well-worn black ghillie brogues. His sandy hair flowed in wild curls to his shoulders, and a full beard covered much of his face. "I need my wrist retaped."

"Been stroking the caber too vigorously?"

He smiled. "A caber as big as mine needs a lot of stroking."

I had him sit on the table while I used a small pair of scissors to cut the old tape away. His wrist was thick, his hands big and powerful, and I imagined them holding me.

To the back of my head, Derek asked, "What does a Scotsman wear under his kilt?"

It was an old joke, but I played along as I began re-taping his wrist. "I don't know, what?"

"Your boyfriend's Chap Stick."

He'd given it a new spin, and I looked up, into his pale blue eyes. "I don't have a boyfriend ..." I started.

"Oh? Have I misjudged you?"

"... at the moment." I winked. Then I finished taping his wrist and patted the back of his hand. "There. Good as new. You'll be stroking the caber again in no time."

"I'd rather not do it alone," he said. "I prefer team sports."

His sporran had shifted to the side, and I could see his kilt beginning to tent at his groin.

"I'm a True Scotsman tonight," Derek said, informing me that he had removed the undergarment required of Highland athletes.

"And you're prepared to undergo a kilt inspection to verify that statement?"

"I am, indeed."

Derek was still sitting on the table, and I was standing between his widespread legs. I placed my hand on his knee and slid my fingers under the hem of his kilt. When he failed to stop me, I slid my hand along his muscular thigh all the way to his crotch, where I found his caber ready for competition. It might never win biggest in clan, but was of substantial length and ample girth, and I wrapped my hand around it. I slowly pumped my fist up and down, the heel of my hand against his pelvic bone and then upward until my thumb and forefinger reached the spongy soft mushroom cap of his cockhead.

I wasn't satisfied just stroking his caber. I wanted more. I'd spent all day watching men in kilts, and I was so turned on that I thought I might erupt in my jeans. As I dropped to my knees, Derek slid off the table and stood before me. I lifted his kilt and ducked my head under it as if I was about to take a picture with an old-fashioned camera.

161

His caber was as I had imagined it – long, thick, and rigid, with heavy stones hanging from the bag beneath, all surrounded by an unruly nest of sandy hair. I took it in my mouth, covered the cap with my saliva, and then slowly took his entire length into my oral cavity. I drew back and then did it again.

Derek pushed his sporran to the side so that it did not bang against the back of my head as I face-fucked him. Soon he held the back of head through the thick material of his kilt and began thrusting his hips forward to meet each downward motion of my face. His heavy stones slapped against my chin.

Harder. Faster.

And then he came, erupting against the back of my throat, and I could barely swallow fast enough to keep his cum from spilling from my mouth.

I remained under Derek's kilt until his caber stopped spasming in my mouth. Then I released my oral grip on it and slipped from under his kilt.

He took my hand and helped me to my feet.

"Did I pass inspection?" he asked.

I licked my lips. "You, sir, are a True Scotsman."

The tent flap opened and one of the Highland Games organizers poked his head in. "You should have closed by now."

"Derek needed his wrist rewrapped," I said.

Derek held up his hand to show off the fresh wrapping.

"We were just finishing up."

The organizer nodded and disappeared.

"We should continue this someplace more private," Derek said. "I have a bottle of Glenlivet in my cabin."

Single malt whisky and a cabin was enough to entice me, so I disposed of Derek's soiled wrist wrapping, cleaned the scissors with alcohol, and then switched off the light.

"How did you manage to reserve a cabin?" I asked as we crossed the grounds past the pipe and drum competition. There were only two-dozen cabins available, and most people opted to camp in tents, bring their motor homes, or stay in one of the motels scattered around the area.

"I put my name on the waiting list two years ago," Derek explained.

Before long, we arrived at Derek's cabin. He reached into his sporran for the key, unlocked the door, and led me inside. The cabin was little more than a single room containing a queen-size bed, a dresser, and a nightstand. A window unit provided air conditioning in the summer, an electric heater provided warmth in the winter. A building thirty yards or so back the way we had come provided communal showers and restroom facilities.

After switching on the room's only light, Derek dug through his duffel bag and retrieved an unopened bottle of Glenlivet and two tumblers that had been wrapped in crew socks to prevent them from breaking. He didn't display any of the stereotypical stinginess of a Scotsman when he poured the Glenlivet, splashing a good three fingers of whisky into my tumbler and an equal amount into his.

He knocked his back and refilled his tumbler.

I sipped at the Glenlivet, not nearly the drinker my host appeared to be, using the whisky as much to rinse away the taste of Derek's cum as to provide me with a slight buzz.

Half the bottle disappeared before Derek suggested I shed my jeans. I wore black hiking boots, and I removed them first, dropping them with a pair of thumps to the

163

wooden floor. Then I peeled off my socks, T-shirt, jeans, and boxers, and stood naked before Derek. I'd been a runner when I was younger, and I still had a runner's lean body, though the years since school had seen the addition of a few extra pounds and a loss of the muscle tone I'd once had.

Derek removed his sporran and set it on the nightstand. Then he pulled me close, covered my lips with his, and thrust his tongue into my mouth. He tasted of Glenlivet and something smoky, and his moustache tickled my upper lip as we kissed. He reached between us and cupped my rapidly rising cock in his hand, toyed with it for a moment, and then spun me around and bent me over his bed.

A half-used tube of lube appeared from out of Derek's duffel, and he squeezed a thick glob onto the two middle fingers of his right hand. He teased my sphincter for a moment, and then slid one slick finger into me. A moment later, he slid a second finger into me, stretching me and preparing me for the caber that was about to come.

He flipped the front of his kilt over my back and pressed the spongy soft head of his caber against my sphincter. I was ready for him, and I pushed backward as he pressed forward, his entire length disappearing into me in one smooth motion.

Then Derek grabbed my waist and held me as he pumped into my ass, drawing back and thrusting forward harder and faster. By then my cock was swollen with desire, bobbing in front of me as Derek continued pounding into me from behind.

I wrapped my fist around my cock, realizing as I did that I wasn't nearly as long or as thick as Derek, but I certainly had no reason for shame. I began stroking myself and was surprised when Derek reached around and knocked my hand aside, replacing my fist with his own.

He jerked me hard and fast, faster than he was slamming into my ass, and I came first, spraying myself in the chest because I was still bent over the bed.

And then Derek came with one last, powerful thrust that would have knocked me off my feet if my legs hadn't been trapped between Derek and the foot of the bed. He held me upright for a minute, maybe two, and then we both collapsed onto his bed.

We didn't talk much after that, but we did finish the Glenlivet, and we did fuck twice more before Derek fell asleep – or passed out – and I slipped out of his cabin. I showered in the communal facility before returning to my tent, and I slept soundly until one of the pipe and drum corps woke the entire camp with a rousing, screaming-cat rendition of "Reveille."

I stopped for hot coffee and scones at the volunteer tent, and then prepared the competitors' tent for the day.

I didn't see Derek until it was time for the caber tossing finals, and neither of us mentioned our night together. I re-taped his wrist and wished him luck, just as I wished luck to every one of the Heavy Event competitors I assisted in the tent.

One of the other volunteers manned the competitors' tent, so I could watch the caber tossing finals, and I licked my lips with appreciation when I saw all the burly men in kilts waiting their turns. It took three men to carry the caber – a large wooden pole similar to a telephone pole – to each competitor, and then that competitor had to toss the caber into the air so that the top end landed closest to the thrower and the bottom end – the end that the thrower had been holding – landed pointing away from him. Scoring is based on how the caber lands as if viewed as the face of a clock. In a perfect throw, the caber lands at straight-up 12:00.

165

Despite my best wishes, Derek came in second, with a toss landing only a few degrees shy of perfection. After the competition ended, Derek returned to the competitors' tent with me and had me remove the tape on his wrist.

"Are you going to be here next year?" he asked.

"I plan to," I told him.

"I've already reserved my cabin," he said. "I'll bring another bottle of Glenlivet and ..." He glanced around to ensure that no one was listening to our conversation. "... and I'll let you toss my caber again."

My cock twitched in my jeans and I smiled. "I'm looking forward to it."

A real man knows how to handle a big pole.

And I know

MY HIGH SCHOOL GYM COACH HAD THE CUTEST ASS
By Shane Allison

I was running out of breath. I could hear my heart beating. Sweat was trickling down my face in buckets. I licked pearls of it from the corners of my lips. My eyeglasses were slipping off my face, from around the bends of my ears. I pushed them back up on the bridge of my nose, on my fat, rotund face. I was tired of being fat. I made up my mind after Thanksgiving break that I would do something about the love handles, the stretch marks and man-titties that sagged from my chest, so I signed up for intramural track and field. I had lost ten pounds my freshman year, but gained it all back by the time I reached my senior year.

Every muscle in my body was hollering, but that's the price I'm paying if I want to see my dick without bending over.

"Let's go, Allison, one more lap!" Coach Teter yelled. "Getcha legs up, let's go!" I could hear my classmates laughing under their winded breath.

"Let's go, Fat Albert," Brian Miller said. It was easy for him. His body was perfection. Like something out of a fucking fitness magazine. His mama didn't feed him fried foods and sugar when he was old enough to have teeth to eat it. Thanks to mine, I'm a social outcast. Brian Miller, the All-American boy next door baseball hero, the teacher's pet, who didn't need to study for SATs, 'cause he had a nice, fat athletic scholarship to Nova University. Brian Miller with his brand new 2001 Dodge Ram that all the big-haired blond girls wanted to be taken for a ride in,

Brian fucking Miller who all the guys worshipped and wanted to be like. And to think I'm busting my nuts to look like him. Our laps were drawing to a close. My whole body was on fire. Track and Field was the last class of the day for me. I told my guidance counselor I wanted it that way. I didn't want to go to a class after sweating and smelling funky. I couldn't run anymore but walked the rest of the way to the set of bleachers where Coach Teter was sitting. As we passed him, he blew his whistle and yelled, "Hit the showers." My glasses were fogged from sweat from the workout Teter had given us. Damn, my legs hurt, I thought. But it was what I deserved for being a fat ass. Brian Miller and his fellow asshole friend, Andy Salley, taunted me, as we all made our way to the field house.

"Get your legs up, fat boy!" Coach Teter wasn't the only one who made me pay for my glutinous ways. I was a real disappointment to my daddy 'cause I didn't come out like him: a hetero pussy-hound. I'm a walking embarrassment, but I don't give a shit 'cause as soon as I save up enough money from my job at the movie theatre, I'm gonna pack my clothes and Janet Jackson posters and haul ass to New York. I have an aunt who lives in Queens, and she says I can stay with her as long as I want. She's like forty-seven, but acts seventeen. She's totally awesome with my being gay. I came out to her in an email. I guess that wasn't the way to go, but oh well, whatever. Coming out is over fucking rated anyway.

Sometimes I think I deserve the abuse, to be picked on for being a fat loser.

I had a crush the size of Disney World on Coach Teter. He had the build and the looks of a seventies gay porn star with his dark hair and thick black 'stache around a set of candy-red lips. He wore a different color pair of shorts for everyday of the week that showed off a nice bulge, a pert ass. The white T-shirts he wore were like tissue paper-thin that showed off his nipples, little hairs around them netted under a sheath of cotton. His body looked like something from a Greek statue. 'Cause of him I wore an extra pair of shorts under my sweats so no one would notice that I had wood.

I never showered with the guys. I couldn't stomach looking at myself naked, so the thought of strangers gawking at this pudgy temple disgusted me. I would sneak off to a room opposite the showers to change, and towel dry the sweat from my face and armpits. I would spray on cologne to cover any scent of musk. One day, I was getting dressed when I noticed this hole in the wall. I peeked through. It was Brian and Andy. They had huge dicks for their age. Andy's was curved slightly off to the side. His soaped up balls hung low while Brian's stuck straight out. His dick was like I had always imagined it during many after school jack off sessions in my room. They had lots of pubic hair. More than me even. Andy had skin that came over the head of his dick, but not Brian. I pushed my hand down into my shorts and started to tug at my dick as I watched the lather trickle down their narrow chests into a thick patch of crotch hair. I fantasized of blowing them both under the hot shower water, the three of us cloaked in steam. To watch them soap up their dicks, moving fingers along chests, stomachs and nipples, made me crazy. What I saw next, you could have knocked me over with a fucking feather. Brian and Andy started to wash each other, soaping up each other's backs and asses. Holy fuck, I thought. Andy was standing behind Brian, his arm wrapped around his neck, while his fingers ran along the crack of Brian's ass.

"Oh my fucking god," I whispered. I wasn't where they could hear me. I thought I was by myself 'til I felt a hand on my shoulder. It scared the shit out of me. I quickly jerked my hand out of my shorts, and turned around. "Like what you see?"

It was Coach.

"Sorry, Coach. I um ... I was jus' ... um ..." Coach Teter looked through the gutted hole at Brian and Andy.

"Looks like they're at it again."

"You know about them?"

"I've seen things that would curl your ball hairs. These two have been at it off and on for 'bout three weeks now. Here every day like clockwork. I always wondered why they were the last ones to shower. So what are you doing here?"

"I was dressing back in and noticed this hole in the wall. At first I didn't think anything of it."

"Got a pretty nice group this year." Coach Teter started to pull at his crotch.

"What are they doing now?" I asked. Pipes ran along the wall above his head. I could hear water from the toilets rushing through them.

"Mr. Salley is blowing Mr. Miller." I asked if I could see like I was some kept slave. Coach Teter moved over to make room. Andy was sucking off Brian. They were both sloppy with soap as shower water pelted their bodies. Brian slid himself in and out of Andy's mouth. As I watched, I felt Teter's hands on me again, fingers coasting along my skin and shit. I acted like I had not felt his fingers hook over the waistband of my shorts. He tugged at them gently, moving them down past my ass to my bent knees. My dick was bone-hard watching Brian getting his worshiped by Salley. Teter and I were just getting warmed up. He felt heavy behind me, his breath warm on my ear and neck. He ran a single hand under my shirt. I was nervous as fuck. My throat tasted salty. Teter's touch was enough to tear me away from the steamy shower scene between my bullies who were really fuck buddies in secret. When I felt his hand gliding up toward my nipples, I stopped his actions. I wanted him more than anyone, but I couldn't bear the thought of him discovering the love

170

handles, the man-titties that were the reason I never wore shirts that accentuated my short comings, or muscle T-shirts that were made to show off muscles I didn't yet have.

"What's wrong?" He asked.

"I'm not in the best of shape."

"You're already on the right path to getting your body where you want it." He continued touching me as he laid the ground work on building my self-esteem. "I've seen a big improvement since you first came to me."

"You really think so?" I asked.

"Absolutely. You'll start to see the difference."

"But when? I look at myself every morning and there's no change."

"You won't see it overnight. Give it time."

I believed the sincerity in his words. I wanted to tell him of my crush on him, but said nothing. He lifted my shirt up over my belly, chest and off my arms. I used them to cover the flabs of fat. So disgusted with my faults, I couldn't look at him looking at me. I thought of how grossed out he must have been. All I could give him were quick little glances. He peeled off his shirt. His body was perfect of course, the one I laid off cheesy beef burritos to get. Strong shoulders, firm pecs, taut abs. All the muscles I had yet to see on myself.

He moved in closer. Teter's lips were wet and stuff. He pressed them against mine. Thought if I touched him, his hot body would burn my fingers. His skin felt like Egyptian silk. A trail of hair ran down his stomach. I undid his shorts. His dick tented the thin blanket of cotton. When I pulled everything down, his dick plopped out. It was uncut with a single vein trailing down the middle of the shaft. I was scared of getting caught.

171

"Does anyone else know about this?"

"No one will notice. You said it yourself. You didn't think anything of it."

I pulled back the skin, and started to lick the head of his dick. It was hot-pink. I dropped to my knees. The field house reeked from musky gym clothes. I took the rest of Coach's dick. He was rough, fucking my face hard. My eyes watered. I gagged a little. I pulled away if I couldn't take it.

"Come on, suck it," he whispered. His dick would slip from my mouth, but I would put it back in.

"That's it. Take it slow." Teter held my head down on his dick. My throat was stuffed with what I lusted after for months. I kneaded his ass in my mitts. I looked up at him as drool dribbled from the corners of my mouth. I held his dick at its base. "Move your hand away," he said. I could taste precum, his dick tensing. He was close.

We were well into it, until we heard a commotion of pleas on the other side of the cindered wall. "Fuck is this," I heard someone say. It sounded like Brian.

"Fucking faggots!" We heard someone shout, and then a shot rang out. I detached myself from Coach's dick.

"What the fuck?" Teter said. He looked cautiously through the peep hole.

"Oh my god!"

"What is it? What's happening?"

"They shot 'em! They fuckin' shot 'em!"

I watched him fuss with his clothes, putting on the shorts I had peeled off his ass. I looked through. Andy and Brian were lying on the floor of the showers. They weren't moving. A trail of blood ran from their heads and naked bodies.

"I'm gonna go see what's going on," Teter said.

I grabbed his arm, pulling him. "Are you fuckin' crazy? There's somebody with guns out there!"

"I just wanna check it out. Stay here."

I reached for Teter again with protest, but he was off before I could grab him. He turned to me and said, "No matter what happens, just stay put." More shots rang out throughout the campus; each one was like a bullet through my own heart. I didn't know how much time had passed before I got up the nerve to rear my head, fearful it would get blown off. When I entered the halls, they were strewn with bodies, puddles of blood. I stepped past the dead, and ran out of the royal-blue double doors in the opposite direction of the shooters. I ran into the woods facing the east side of town. I thought of Coach Teter, hoping that what was happening had not fallen upon him. I felt my pockets for my cell phone. Nothing. I figured it must have dropped out back at the gym. I ran until I could make out a street of bustling cars. I ended up behind a church on Paul Russell Road. I tried to wave someone down for help, damn near getting plastered by a Suburban. A guy driving a black and white Mustang stopped.

"Please, do you have a phone I could use?" He was hesitant.

"There's been a shooting."

"Who's shooting?" he asked.

"At the school. I heard gunshots." He finally let down his window and handed me his phone to call for help.

"Thank you. God bless you, thank you." I called 911 and told them what was going on, and then I called my parents. Daddy answered. I was breathing heavy, hollering on the guy's cell.

"Boy, what's wrong wit'choo?"

"They're shooting. At the school, they're shooting."

"Who shootin?" he asked.

"I don't know."

"Where you at now?"

"At the corner of Paul Russell and Blairstone."

"Ok, jus' stay there, and I'll come getcha." I handed the guy his phone back.

"Are you gonna be ok?" He asked.

"I'm fine." The guy sped off. I made my way across the street to a gas station, and waited for Daddy. I was in a daze of shock and disbelief, all those bodies, the blood, Andy and Brian dead. I wondered if Coach Teter was okay, if he survived. Even after going through the worse time of my life, I thought of his dick in my mouth, his firm ass in my hands.

Ma and Daddy arrived thirty minutes after the stranger left. I wiped my tears. I didn't want them to see me crying.

"You all right? What happened?" I said nothing, but just hugged him. He hesitated, yet was able to put his machismo aside to return the sentiment. I told them what happened.

"Boy, I'm so glad you all right," Ma said. I wanted to go to the cops, but they wanted to take me home.

"You hungry? You want some t' eat?"

"I'm just going to go lie down," but I couldn't sleep. Not after that. The reverberation from the TV in the living room caught my interest. I heard 'shooting at high school,' and switched on the TV in my room. The anchor woman talked of body counts, and the shooters that were responsible. I knew them: Richard Kelly and Sammie

Azoum, two boys a part of the Dungeons and Dragons clique at school. She said they then turned the guns on themselves. I cried for the students and some of the staff that were killed. I knew some, while others were just familiar faces in the crowd. Coach Teter's wasn't shown.

It doesn't mean he's alive, though, I thought. They called parents to find out who was ok, who had survived, and when it was appropriate for them to return to school. Ma and Daddy wanted to pull me out of Rickards, but I wanted to show the shooters that they had not won. The campus reopened on a Tuesday morning. It was quiet. You could cut the fear with a plastic butter knife. There were flowers, candles and blown up yearbook pictures of the slain set out in the main courtyard of campus. Students, teachers and faculty gathered to pay their respects. I saw the pictures of Andy and Brian. The memory of them getting it on would be filed away in the chest of my mind. We all wept. I felt a hand on my shoulder. It was Coach. He was alive. We hugged happy to know that we had both survived. The shooting changed everyone and everything in Florida. There was more beefed up security at our school with weapon detectors set up throughout the campus. I wanted to mess around, but Coach Teter didn't think it was a good idea because of the position it would put him in. Honestly, I think us having sex would remind him too much of the shooting.

I graduated that year. The Civic Center was standing room only. There was a tribute led by the governor, to those that had lost their lives. I tried to keep in touch with Coach, but he never returned my calls or emails. I guess it was for the best. We both had some healing to do. I still think about him today, wonder where he is, if he's married with kids or in a relationship with a man. I wish I could thank him. Thank him for believing in me.

WELCOME TO THE CLUB
By Lew Bull

All my life I had told myself to be happy in whatever occupation I decided to take up, and everywhere I went people would say you should have job satisfaction; well I took very little notice of this advice until I was thirty and then I decided that perhaps all these people must have had some insight, so I should start thinking about my happiness where I worked.

I won't say I was a drifter, but I had spent much of my younger life flitting from job to job, mainly because I really didn't know what to make of myself. However, when the big 3-0 arrived, I decided to settle down.

I had always played sport in my youth and had been to college where I earned a sports degree, so I decided to get into sport perhaps as a physiotherapist or a coach. I went back to my college to ask my professor if he knew of any upcoming jobs and was very surprised when he informed me that the Sharks, the local football team was looking for a physio. He gave me the number to call, which I did immediately, and an interview was set up. The interview went without a hitch, and I was duly offered the position of physiotherapist, which I gladly accepted.

My accepting the offer was two-fold: on the one hand I thought I would be happy doing something connected to sport, and secondly, I realized that I could be near all those hunky jocks. Let's be honest, what better sight is there than seeing a group of men wearing shiny, tight pants with equally tight muscle-padded tops and then knowing that under those seductively enticing outfits lurked packages waiting to be unwrapped from their jockstraps! I couldn't think of a better incentive to want to become a physio.

I also realized that the down side of all this was that I would have to be wary about how I treated the guys when they came for physio – self-control would be needed, but what the hell, I'd cross that bridge when I neared it.

I joined the team and was duly introduced to everyone on my first day. I surveyed the faces and bodies with interest. There were short, tall, muscular, stocky, African American, White, Latino guys and all looked enticing in their own individual way. At the first practice, I watched as they sprinted, tackled and generally tried to get their match-fitness up. It goes without saying that there was the inevitable niggles such as sprains and tired muscles, but nothing major happened on the first day.

As the practices continued, I began to notice guys whom I found attractive, but remained celibate. At the weekend, we had our first game and for the first time I saw all the guys decked out in their match gear. What an awesome sight! The guys were in their tight, shiny silver shorts of butt and dick enhancing Lycra, with pale blue tops. I had been in the locker room when they all arrived and watched with extreme interest as they changed from their ordinary day clothes into their ball-hugging jockstraps and pulled on their tight shorts. I could feel myself becoming aroused as I watched these peacocks of the game strut their naked and semi-naked bodies around the locker room. I've always been a tight shorts man and particularly if the shorts are semi-see-through, as these were. To see their jockstraps outlined through their shorts was an immediate turn-on for me. I could see the straps outlined at the rear and how they hefted many an ass, creating some superb bubble-butts. The sight was even more pleasing when I noticed how the white jockstraps were enhanced against the dark skins of the Latinos and African Americans. It was at times like these that I realized that I was definitely happy in my job.

178

As the team left the locker room to go to the field, I also left with the coach and his assistants to watch the game. It was exciting to watch our guys run with the ball and tackle; some of these tackles made me wonder how they didn't do more damage to themselves than what I had to deal with. During the first quarter, Juan Fernandez, the captain, took a heavy crunching tackle, which laid him out flat. I gasped when I saw the ferocity of the tackle and watched as Juan had to be stretchered off the field and down the tunnel to the locker room. I followed hastily and once he was placed on my table, the stretcher-bearers left to go back to the field.

"Where's it hurt, Juan?" I asked looking at this macho man, lying whimpering on the table.

He groaned as he looked up at me.

"It's my thigh and groin," he sobbed.

I thought it strange that such a macho man should be sobbing the way he was, but perhaps he'd torn something, which was producing excruciating pain for him. Gently I place my hands on his lower left thigh and asked if it was painful in that area.

"Higher," came the sob.

I moved my hands a little higher and prodded gently. Juan cried out and I said, "There?"

"Yes and a little higher. Both legs."

I felt in the same area of his right thigh and Juan once again let out a cry. Gently, I massaged the area on his right thigh.

"Is it here?" I asked.

"Uh, that's it."

My hands moved smoothly over the soft-feeling Lycra silver shorts, rubbing his upper thigh in movements toward his groin.

"Aargh!" cried Juan.

I could see the bulge in his shorts and decided that apart from his pain, I wished I could see him naked. Juan had typically Latino looks: dark hair, tanned, with Hispanic features.

"Can you take off your shorts?" I enquired, but Juan merely shook his head.

"In that case I might have to cut you out of them," I retorted.

I grabbed a pair of scissors, inserted the point at the leg and began slicing up toward the groin area. Juan raised his head, and I could see the desperate look on his face as I neared his crotch.

"Don't worry, Juan, I'm not gonna cut your dick off, if that's what's worrying you."

He smiled a pained smile and lowered his head again. I snipped all the way up to the waistband, making sure that I didn't cut his jockstrap. I did, however, notice that as I neared his crotch area, it seemed to have grown in size. Slowly I peeled off the shredded shorts, leaving Juan in his white jockstrap. This was indeed a beautiful sight: the sheer whiteness of the coarse material against the muscular, tanned skin.

I rubbed some oil onto my hands and began a slow, systematic massage of his upper thighs. My hands slid over his muscular legs toward his crotch, and each time I could feel his muscles tense.

"Relax, Juan. Did you say the groin area was also painful?" I casually asked.

Juan grunted, which I took to be a 'yes.'

I let my fingers slip effortlessly over his thigh and gently rub up against his hefty package, nudging his balls each time. Juan lay with his eyes closed while I ventured across his heavenly body. I could see that his cock was growing inside his jockstrap, and soon I noticed the tip peeping out over the waistband. I moved my attention to his other thigh and began the same tactics. A little dribble of pre-cum oozed from his piss slit as it peered over the top of the waistband. Casually, I wiped his tip, taking his juice onto my finger and then placing it in my mouth to savor his taste. Juan never reacted. I continued to nudge his balls and on one or two occasions, I let my hand graze casually across his coarsely covered cock. I noticed how it throbbed as I did this and soon whenever I did it, Juan would give a slight upward thrust with his hips. During all this, neither of us spoke. I wasn't sure how far I could go with Juan, so I stopped massaging his legs. He opened his eyes and looked at me.

"Why have you stopped?"

"I'm sure that you feel better now, don't you?"

"Actually it's deeper in my groin that hurts most."

I oiled my hands once more and, with a slightly harder pressure being used, pushed my fingertips in his groin. Juan once again closed his eyes. I also let my hands slip between his legs, aiming for the direction of his hot, Latino asshole. Juan raised himself slightly as if to allow me greater access. My fingers were now massaging his lower buttocks, but at the same time, my fingers were surreptitiously sliding into his waiting hole. His breathing became heavier and his cock was drooling more rapidly now. As I slid my slender fingers into his tight opening, I noticed how he had brought a hand up to his crotch and pulled the waistband of his jockstrap down, to reveal his long, dark rod. It was a glorious sight to me. His hood had slid back to reveal a glistening cock-head, waiting to be sucked, while his slim, long shaft was hard and stiff. Keeping my fingers attacking his opening, I maneuvered myself to the side of the table and lowered my mouth to encompass this macho piece of Hispanic meat.

181

I let my mouth work its way along his shaft, lubricating it with my tongue and then dragging my tongue along the underneath area. Juan groaned softly as my mouth traveled along the smooth dark flesh.

I released my fingers from his ass and pulled his jockstrap down further to reveal two large balls, their sac pulled tight over them. I licked both and them plopped each into my mouth, one at a time and rolled my tongue around their firmness. The dark pubic hair surrounding his fine balls, tickled my chin, as I licked my way back up his shaft. I took hold of his stiff shaft with my oil-slicked hand and began sliding my hand along his length. The tighter I held his hard cock and the more my hand slid along its length, the more Juan groaned in ecstasy. I watched as his foreskin slid effortlessly over the head and then slide back and each time I revealed his head, I would lick and kiss it.

"You're getting me close, Greg," he moaned.

"Good," I replied, increasing my hand speed and my licking.

"Aargh! I'm coming," groaned Juan.

"Shoot!" I exclaimed placing my mouth tightly over the top of his cock but continuing to jack him off. I felt the first of his warm, tasty Hispanic cum hit the back of my throat, then my mouth filled with his seed. I swallowed as fast as he shot, sinking my mouth to the root of his shaft.

As I felt his eruption subside, I continued to suck on his rod, trying to keep him hard. His body shuddered with each throb from his cock, but still I held on to him. Eventually, I opened my mouth and allowed his slick cock to escape, but even then I didn't stop making love to it. I caressed it with my lips and mouth, kissing it and sucking on it. When I felt that Juan's breathing was back to normal, I raised my head and smiled at him. His eyes were now open and twinkling.

"I think your groin and thighs are fine now, but if you feel that they still need some treatment, let me know," I said, casually wiping my hands on a nearby towel, while Juan slipped from the table, pulling up his jockstrap, tucking in his slowly subsiding manhood and tossing his shredded shorts into a nearby bin.

"Thanks Greg, that was great. I think you're going to fit in well here."

"Thanks, Juan, but what do you mean?"

"A couple of us have been watching you and noticing how you eye us guys out, especially when we're in our jockstraps or in our shorts. Do you dig what you see?"

I blushed profusely because I knew that Juan was right.

Juan laughed when he saw my reaction and said, "See you," and headed to the showers.

I smiled inwardly to myself knowing that this was going to be a job worthwhile.

# # # # #

In the following two weeks, Juan visited me three times with pseudo injuries, which I helped to 'heal,' but something special happened after practice one late afternoon.

I had sat watching the practice, along with the coaches and reserves and then wandered back to the locker room to tidy up. Often when I had very little to do, I took it upon myself to help tidy up the locker room. When I entered, there was the usually manly smell that permeated the locker room and there was the inevitable jumble of discarded clothing lying on the floor. I started to collect the clothing that was lying around and fold it into piles. As I picked up a pair of jeans, a packet of condoms and a tube of lube fell from one of its pockets. I picked up the objects and wondered whose jeans these were, but there was no name or other indication on them, so I replaced the objects and folded the jeans.

Also on some of the benches were the silver shorts of the guys. I picked up some and folded them, but there was one pair which felt damp to the touch. I felt the dampness and realized that it was in the crotch area. I held them up and turned them inside out and there on the inside I saw the telltale remnants of some cum. My heart almost skipped a beat as I realized that someone on the team must have jacked off or something happened for him to come in his shorts. I looked on the inside and saw the initials M.G. I smiled broadly to myself, realizing that M.G was Mike Green, the quarter back; he of the broad shoulders, trim waist and well-hung appendage – the man with the soft blue eyes, the bulging biceps and the thighs like tree trunks. Now my heart really skipped a beat.

As I busied myself, the team came into the locker room and began showering and changing. Nobody needed any treatment, so I sat in my office and watched through the doorway as the guys fooled around with each other. As I sat there, waiting for them all to leave so that I could lock up, Juan came into my office.

"Hi Greg, sorry to trouble you, but could I speak to you when the others have gone?"

Immediately I became excited thinking that Juan needed 'treatment' again.

"Sure thing, Juan, I'll be waiting for you here."

The singing, back-slapping and general horseplay continued for some time and then silence fell over the locker room. When I heard nothing, I left my office to check the showers and locker room in readiness to close up and wait for Juan.

As I returned to my office, I saw Juan sitting on my massage table, dangling his legs over the sides. Before I

184

had a chance to say anything, I also noticed two other people in the office. I entered.

"Hi guys, this is a surprise. What can I do for you all?"

In the office were Juan, looking ravishing in his Sharks kit with the tight silver shorts. Then I noticed that Mike Green was also there, dressed like Juan and the third person was Horse Harrington, who was built like a brick shithouse. He was tall, broad-shouldered and his ebony skin glistened in the light. Although I had never seen either Mike or Horse naked, I had heard why Horse was so named.

Horse was the first to speak.

"I hear you give good head," he said sauntering closer to me. "I put it to you straight, I like a guy who gives good head and I need that," he continued towering over me.

"I see," was all I could say.

Suddenly Horse grabbed my crotch and squeezed. I yelped from the instant pain and crumbled to my knees, holding onto my balls. Mike and Juan surrounded me. All three stood around me dressed identically, rubbing their ever-growing erections. Because of the tightness of their shorts, it was easy to see that they had chosen not to wear jockstraps under their kit, so I could see the outlines of their engorged cocks. Both Mike and Horse clearly had large mushroom-shaped cock-heads and long shafts. From the view I had, I could see that Horse was by far the guy with the biggest and thickest cock, although Mike was not to be outdone. They advanced a little closer until their swollen cocks were at eye and mouth level, and the pain in my balls had subsided.

Instinctively, my hands traced the outlines of their shafts, and my mouth traveled over each one's manhood. Inside of my shorts, I knew that I was leaking pre-cum,

185

having these huge men wanting me to service them. I took hold of Horse's shorts and pulled them down, allowing his gigantic ebony cock to flop free. His cock was so heavy it had difficulty standing erect, and although he was hard, it appeared as if he was only semi-hard. I kissed the tip and licked off a droplet of clear juice, then let my tongue encircle his head. I spread my mouth wide and attempted to push his girth into my waiting mouth. It was difficult, but I was determined to take this man down my throat. I could feel my jaw stretching, but eventually, Horse slipped into the warmth of my mouth. I sucked and began to slide down his shaft as far as my throat would allow. I nearly gagged, but controlled my descent. Although I couldn't reach the base of his cock, it felt good to have been able to take him. Mike and Juan, in the meantime were stroking their cocks, having pulled down their own shorts.

I slid to the top of Horse's cock and popped it from my mouth and proceeded to take Mike. By now my jaw was aching but it had been exercised enough to take Mike's cock all the way down until I bumped my chin against his balls. I noticed that Horse and Juan were jacking each other, their mouths locked to each other, while at the same time, Juan had gripped onto Mike's nipples and was pinching them. With each tweak from Juan, Mike gave a deep thrust of his cock down my throat.

Soon it was Juan's turn to be 'treated' while Horse and Mike got into each other. Mike knelt next to me and took Horse into his mouth. Out of the corner of my eye, I watched as Mike sank down to the root of Horse's cock and held his position. Horse gasped as Mike held him tightly in his mouth, sucking as he began to rise to the tip again. I was surprised how easy it had been for Mike to take Horse, but then I wondered if they hadn't done this before.

I felt a pair of sturdy hands go under my armpits and lift me to my feet.

186

"Come, Greg, we're gonna give you a royal treat," said Juan, leading to my massage table.

The men stripped me and laid me on my back on the table. Horse bent my legs so that my feet were placed apart on the edge of the table, then he positioned himself between my legs and began to massage my pulsating hole with his tongue. Oh boy! My hole and body quivered with his touch. His tongue felt like a sharp blade entering me, and the further he sank his tongue into me, the more I groaned with pleasure.

Juan positioned himself above my crotch and took my cock into his mouth, while I took Mike's as he was standing above my head. My body was wracked with pleasure as each man created a sense of heightened erotic fulfillment. To have three men pleasuring me was what made my job all the more enjoyable.

"Please fuck me," I groaned, in between sucking Mike's cock deeper down my throat.

My ass was wet from Horse's tongue washing and was ready to be attacked. Juan left my cock and wandered off, but when he returned I noticed that he had the packet of condoms and the lube that I had seen earlier. He ripped open the foil and unrolled the condom onto Horse's long, thick cock, then returned to taking my cock down his throat.

Horse hoisted my legs above my head, and I felt the cold lube and then his circumcised cock head nudge my pucker and waited as Horse slowly pushed forward. I tensed in anticipation of the pain, which would arrive as soon as he broke through, but it never happened. This giant of a man was so gentle.

"I'll take it easy," said Horse, reassuring me.

He sank slowly into me, my ass muscles trying to prevent his entry, but my brain saying, Yes!, Yes! Fuck me!

Mike and Juan watched eagerly as Horse's ebony bargepole began to disappear into my warm entry. Every now and again, Horse stopped to allow me to become accustomed to his girth and length, but I think I was ready for the onslaught. I lay still, waiting to feel his balls slap gently against my ass. I felt the warmth of his body as his finely-haired balls caressed my ass, and I knew that he was well embedded in me. I breathed a sigh of relief and then he started a slow and methodical fuck routine. As Horse slid in and out of me, I gobbled on Mike's swelling cock, while Juan sucked and licked my balls.

Horse sure knew how to work his thick rod, pushing deep inside of me and slowly withdrawing as my tight ass muscles clamped firmly onto his shaft, not allowing him to exit completely. Each time he sank into my depths, I could feel my chute stretch to accommodate his thick shaft, and then I would feel his mushroom-shaped cock head nudge my prostate, gently massaging it and driving me crazy with excitement.

After Horse had enjoyed his time in my tight warm ass, he slipped out and allowed Mike to enter. Horse had really loosened up my ass, so taking Mike was not a problem. I could feel Mike's cock-head, which I think was more bulbous than Horse's, rubbing along the sides of my chute and also hitting my prostate. This constant rubbing and nudging was driving me wild with ecstasy and causing me to shudder and gasp with pleasure.

"Oh fuck, Mike. Be careful, you're getting me close!"

Mike instinctively pulled his cock closer to my opening and proceeded to deliver short, sharp jabs into my ass, which didn't do much to alleviate the pressure that was building within me. Instead he was driving me closer to the edge. Again I warned him of my situation. This time he stopped all together and left his cock throbbing inside of me. I loved its feel as it throbbed. This man sure knew how to please a guy and was skilled at using his weapon.

188

To save me from shooting my load, Mike pulled out and let Juan take over. I had always only given Juan a blowjob, so this was a first for both of us. As he entered me, he smiled and pulled my body closer to him so that I sank deeper onto his cock. Mike had taken to deep-throating me while Horse plunged his stupendous weapon into my waiting mouth and down my throat.

Juan's actions on me were very different from the other two. He used quick, short stabs that seemed to just break through my opening. There was none of the long, deep plowing of Mike and Horse, but it made no difference to me because I was enjoying all three men's approaches.

"Oh, fuck! I'm coming!" exclaimed Juan as he fired into me, his cock throbbing with each burst of cum.

No sooner had he shot his load, then Horse replaced him and re-entered my waiting hole. Horse pounded hastily, bringing himself to climax within four or five deep thrusts. All the while, Mike had stood watching each man fire into me and pinching each man's nipples to encourage their climax. Now it was his turn.

I lay expecting to explode any minute with my own orgasm when Mike slid into me like a stealthy hunter coming upon his prey. His bulbous cock head once more did the damage and my body again trembled with excitement.

"Mike, you're getting me going!" I shouted, as Horse and Juan stood on either side of the massage table, tweaking my nipples and playing with my balls and cock.

I could feel Mike's enormous cock head rubbing my prostate.

"Aargh! Fuuck!" I yelled and the first of a number of shots fired from the tip of my cock. Mike held onto my legs, hoisting them even higher and ploughed into my pucker, which clamped tightly shut on his shaft. The two of us rocked and shook as our bodies collided into each

189

other. My chest was becoming covered in a milky stickiness, through which Horse ran his hand, smearing my chest with my warm cum. I heard Mike gasp and felt a deep solid drive of his cock into my warm ass and then felt his cock throb as he fired his load into me.

As Mike and I descended from our high, all three men bent over my cum-soaked body and gently kissed me.

"Welcome to the club," said Juan. "Now you're officially one of the team, and we hope that you'll stay happy working with us."

I gave them an exhausted smile.

"If my stay is anything like what I've just gone through, I'll definitely be staying forever."

THE RIVAL
By Stephen Osborne

As a baseball team, the Laugh Line Players were a bit of a joke. With a name like that, how could we not be? We were improvisational comedians, not athletes. The fact that we usually only played one game a year (against a rival improv troupe, the Circle City Follies) didn't give us much of a chance to practice and improve either. Still, our five year record was an abysmal 0 wins and 6 losses.

Not that we cared, of course. Our little troupe was more popular than Circle City Follies, having a more prominent downtown venue for our shows. Follies had their theater on the far north side of the city, an area notorious for snarled traffic and delays caused by endless road construction. It didn't hurt that we'd been around a few years longer either.

Our annual charity game against Follies was quickly approaching, and I was, in absentia, made Team Captain. That'll teach me to miss a board meeting. My protests that I knew nothing about baseball fell on deaf ears.

"None of us knows squat about baseball," Barry, one of our directors, told me. "Honestly, Alex, don't get yourself worked up about this. No one expects us to win. It's all for fun, anyway."

And so I gathered our players at the field on Saturday afternoon for a practice session before the big game. I had planned on boning up on the game of baseball and had even bought the book, *Baseball for the Complete Moron*, at the local Barnes and Noble. I got so bored that by page three I was ready to gnaw my own arm off rather than read further. I tossed the book in the trash and decided to wing it.

Luckily my team, consisting of six guys and three girls, knew as much about the game as I did. We gathered at the pitcher's mound to assign positions. Then we took a few minutes to figure out just what those positions were. Finally, we began our practice.

Well, the word practice implies that we were attempting to get better. I suppose in the broadest sense we were, but only because we couldn't get any worse. In the outfield Ryan and Tom continually collided in their attempts to catch the ball. Our shortstop Evan screamed every time the ball came anywhere close to him. And the bat, with our batting skills as they were, was in no danger of cracking.

We worked for several hours, during which Abner Doubleday undoubtedly spun in his grave. I was so intent on watching Sally try to catch a pop fly that I didn't even notice the small group of people that had gathered at the visitor's dugout until they burst out laughing. Sally missed the ball and somehow fell flat on her ass.

I glanced over to see the Follies team. They were wearing matching uniforms of purple and black and all had a cap with the Follies logo on it. Standing slightly in front of the group was a guy I recognized – Kyle Turner.

I hadn't known that Kyle had joined the Follies troupe. I hadn't even seen him since high school, when we had both been up for the lead in the Drama Club's production of *Charley's Aunt*. Kyle, with his matinée-idol good looks, got the role.

"My goodness," he said with a nasty chuckle, "if it isn't Alex Martin. They told me when I agreed to Captain this team that we wouldn't have any competition. I can see they weren't exaggerating."

I felt my cheeks flush. I could take making a fool of myself playing baseball. I could take losing yet again to the Follies team. I couldn't, however, take losing a game of any sort to Kyle Turner. Not after the great *Charley's Aunt* affair of 1999. He had been insufferable in his victory, and I had never forgiven him.

As our time of use of the field was over, the Laugh Line players gathered their gear and headed over to the clubhouse to shower and change. I stayed behind, hoping for a word with good ole Kyle.

The same thing must have been on his mind because he immediately instructed his team to head for the center of the field to warm up. Then he strode over to me.

Kyle had been a fox in high school and had only improved with age. He could have passed for a younger, taller, and more butch Tom Cruise. He certainly had the grin down pat. I'd always wondered what he'd be like in the sack, but our theatrical rivalry, not to mention his insufferable conceit and my stubborn pride, made that impossible. Still, I wouldn't mind getting his cock down my throat.

He slapped me playfully on the shoulder. "Bet you're surprised to see me here, eh, Martin?"

I had to remind myself that I didn't like this grinning baboon. Now if only someone would tell my cock that we didn't like him. I could feel the damn thing growing in my jock.

"I didn't even know you were still in town," I said, trying to sound nonchalant.

"I was out in Los Angeles for a few years," he replied, "but everyone out there is so phony, you know? Besides, I missed the change of seasons."

Translation: I went out to Hollywood but couldn't make it as an actor, ran out of money, and had to come back home.

"Nice seeing you again," I said, lying through my teeth. Okay, my dick was glad to see him, but it has never been a great judge of character.

"So you ready to lose a ball game next week?" he asked, still smiling.

I bridled. Even after all this time he could still get under my skin. "We won't be losing."

Kyle laughed. "From what I've heard, you guys have lost every game you've ever played!"

"Not this time."

"You sound pretty confident." Kyle jiggled his eyebrows. "Care to make a little side wager?"

I shrugged. "Fine by me. Twenty bucks?"

His grin turned sly. "I had something a little more interesting in mind." Glancing around to see that we couldn't be overheard, he said, "How about something like the loser becomes the winner's locker room bitch after the game? Anything goes."

Surely I hadn't heard right. I gaped at him in astonishment. "Excuse me?"

Kyle chuckled. "You heard me. I always thought you were kind of hot in high school, but you seemed to have had some kind of grudge against me, so I never pursued it. Now I'll see what I missed out on." He eyed me carefully. "I think I'll like having you as my bitch."

The conceit of the man! He just assumed I'd agree! I emitted a hollow laugh. "You're on, but we'll see who is going to be whose bitch." And I turned to walk away, which would have looked more impressive if I hadn't tripped over a baseball glove someone had left and landed sprawled out, face down in the dirt.

Laugh Lines didn't have enough in the budget to allow me to buy uniforms for the team. I did buy us each a red T-shirt with our logo. We all agreed to wear black shorts and long black athletic socks so that at least we almost looked as if we were wearing uniforms.

Because I didn't want to lose, especially now, we had a few extra practice sessions before Saturday's game. That didn't help.

Finally, game day arrived. We had a fairly good crowd in the stands, even if most of them were friends or relatives. I hadn't had any further contact with Kyle since that day at practice, and when I saw him again, I swear my heart skipped a beat. God, he looked good, even in that purple uniform. Too bad he was such an ass.

The game began and our team was first at bat. Kyle pitched for the Follies. I have to admit he was pretty good. Good enough to strike out Mike, Sally, and Carl in rapid succession anyway.

We hit the infield, and I took my position in right field. Sammy, being the most athletically inclined of us, was our pitcher. It soon became obvious that the Follies team, with the exception of Kyle, was just as bad as we were. During Kyle's turn at bat he hit the ball fairly far into left field. He got to third base, but then no one on his team managed to get a hit. Their last out was a pop fly caught, more by accident than design, by Sally.

The innings went by, scoreless, with only Kyle and Sammy showing any talent. On our part, every time anyone on the Follies hit the ball, Ryan and Tom ran and collided with each other, even when the ball came nowhere near them. On their part, the Follies players seemed unable to hit the ball nine times out of ten.

195

In the seventh inning we actually scored when Sammy hit a home run. Our team cheered as he crossed home plate, and I looked over at the Follies dugout and stuck my tongue out at Kyle – a childish gesture to be sure but strangely satisfying.

"We still have two innings to go," Kyle shouted at me.

The eighth inning went scoreless. We failed to get another run during the ninth, but as long as we could keep them from scoring, the game was ours.

Their first batter actually managed to get a base hit. Kyle was next up at bat. I can't swear to it, but I think he turned to right field and winked at me as he stepped up to the plate. Sammy threw one right down the center and Kyle whacked the ball with force. It flew out to my area. I got right under it. I had to catch the damn thing. I had to take Kyle down a peg or two. It meant everything to me. And while I normally can't catch to save me, this one looked easy. I had my glove ready.

It would have been easy if Ryan and Tom hadn't also gone for the ball and the two of them bowled into me just as the ball came down. When I disentangled myself and got to my feet, Kyle was skipping lightly across home plate. We had lost again.

I'm sure the mighty Casey, of poetry fame, felt pretty bad that day in Mudville, but had he agreed to be someone's locker room bitch after the game? I think not, or Ernest Thayer would surely have mentioned it.

To be honest, no one on our team seemed to be that upset over the loss. After all, we'd actually scored, which was a victory of its own. Both teams headed for the clubhouse and quickly showered and changed. Everyone was laughing and joking. No one had taken the game seriously. Except me, I guess.

Not knowing what Kyle had in mind, I held off on joining the other guys in the men's shower. Kyle himself was nowhere to be seen. The last I'd seen of him had been on the field when he'd been gathering up his team's bats.

Minutes went by, and everyone was leaving. As he was heading out, Mike came up to me, all smiles. "Some of us were going to get some grub at Arni's Pizza Parlor. Want to come?"

I pulled at my T-shirt. "Haven't showered yet," I said. "I might catch up with you guys later."

He waved a cheery goodbye and went out the locker room door. The sudden silence made me realize I was the last one there. Had Kyle forgotten the bet? Had he been kidding? Was I off the hook?

Just then Kyle entered, still in his purple and black uniform, with bat in hand. The smile covering his face was infuriating. "Well, well, well," he said, "I guess this means you're now my bitch."

I sighed, but more for effect than anything. After all, it wasn't like Kyle was an ogre. If I was to be someone's bitch I could think of worse. And my dick liked him. It was already excited just looking at him. "Let's get this over with," I said.

Kyle came over and sat down on one of the wooden benches. He took off his left sneaker and then peeled off his sock, which he tossed to me. "To get started," he said, his eyes mischievously flashing, "I want you to sniff that."

Ugh. Surely he wasn't serious.

He was. "Sniff it," he said, a harsh edge creeping into his tone.

I put the sock up to my nose and gave it a quick sniff.

197

"Oh, no," he exclaimed. "Remember you're my bitch! A long sniff. Really hold it there!"

I did. My nostrils were suddenly filled with the acrid tang of sweaty cotton. He might be good looking, but Kyle Turner had smelly feet.

"That's enough," he told me. I immediately threw the vile sock aside. I'm into some mild kink, but smelly feet aren't among my turn-ons. "Now," Kyle said as he stood up, "kiss my bat."

I looked at the wooden bat he'd set down by the bench. Kyle laughed. "Not that bat! This one." he gestured to his crotch.

Now we were talking. Unless his dick smelled as rank as his sock, this could be enjoyable. I got down on my knees in front of him as he pulled down his shorts. His nicely filled jock was staring me in the face. Jocks were among my list of kinks. Nothing sexier than a guy in a jock strap. I nuzzled the fabric with my nose and then began sucking and licking, enjoying the taste of the cotton.

Kyle moaned and threw his head back. I pulled his dick out of one side of the jock strap and began to suck. God, he tasted good. Maybe I hadn't lost after all! I rapidly swallowed his shaft and was rewarded by Kyle's entire body shivering with pleasure.

"Why didn't we do this," he muttered breathlessly, "in high school?"

Why not indeed? Now that I had his gorgeous dick in my mouth our petty rivalry over the lead in some stupid play seemed trivial. I deep throated his cock and Kyle let out a long hiss.

"Boy, you're good at that."

After a few more minutes of sucking on Kyle's pole he gently pulled my head away. "You're going to make me come," he said.

"Isn't that the point?" I asked, looking up into his cute face.

Kyle smiled. Now the grin didn't bother me. It was sweet, not cocky. What had I been thinking? "Yeah, but I'm not ready to shoot yet." He helped me to my feet and tugged at my T-shirt. "Let's get naked."

I nodded in agreement. In less time than I took for me to strike out at bat we were standing in each other's embrace, totally sans clothing.

"What do you want to do?" he asked in a whisper.

I blinked. "I thought I was supposed to be your slave. Your bitch. What I want doesn't matter."

Kyle caressed my cock, making it twitch. "Who the fuck cares about the stupid bet at this point?" he asked. "I just want to have some fun."

We kissed passionately. We finally came up for air, I said softly, "I want you to fuck me."

I lay down on the wooden bench as Kyle rummaged through his gym bag. He came back with some lube and a condom. Unlike me, Kyle had been prepared. Maybe I'd known, deep in my heart that I'd be on the losing end of the bet.

Kyle placed my legs up on his broad shoulders and slowly entered me. He began fucking me slowly, but it was obvious that neither of us was in the mood for nice and slow. We wanted it rough and hard. Soon he was slamming into me so hard that we were scooting the bench slowly across the cement floor and both of us were screaming like banshees. We came virtually simultaneously, him throbbing within me and me spewing all over my own stomach. When I could actually form words again I chuckled and said, "Now I can't wait until next year's game. Same bet?"

Kyle's chest was still heaving and his words came out in gasps. "Surely you don't want to wait that long."

I smiled. "I guess not ... but when?"

"Give me a few minutes," he said, "and we can go another inning!"

UNDER DAWGS
By R. Talent

Two burly arms tightened around my chest, stapling my limbs to my sides. I was angry, pissed, standing there at the top of the ramp mean-mugging and shouting back. I was being restrained, denied from running back into the ring. Denied to pull out a keg of whup-ass on The Invaders, standing center stage, getting booed by forty thousand screaming fans that obviously saw what the dumb-ass referee didn't.

"C'mon, Kush, let it go man," Drake said holding me back.

"Naw, man, they cheated. Everybody knows it. Punks!"

No matter who you are, everyone seems to have an opinion whether or not professional wrestling is fake. The truth of the matter is that people on both sides of that argument are absolutely correct. Those superstars, those that have reached the top of that mountain, in licensing deals with their names and images on everything pretty much just have to show their faces, do some moves that look pretty spectacular for the camera before they are spit out into the abyss. Much like anybody else however – before any of them got to be known as the stars that they are they started out like us – scrappers. Gladly jockeying for position, cuts and all, in this dog eat dog world of wrestling fame and entertainment. Because the more the audience sees us, the more they love us or hate us, and the more they hunger for us, one way or another.

Drake and I were just there, right at the cusp of stardom when it was snatched away by The Invaders, a tag team crew that were on their way out of the limelight.

"Forget them! Let's get out of here," Drake said pulling me back.

I was so consumed with venom and rage that time just seemed to pass by in one big blur. One minute we were in the back changing clothes. The next we were out to dinner followed by a trip out to a local club with fans. By the time we made it back to the motel, I was dead tired, ready to hit the sheets. My tag team partner Drake, on the other hand, was in the shower ready to go back when I heard a pound at the door.

As I made my way over to it, catching a glimpse of my shirtless ripped body in the mirror, I had a good idea of who it could be. I tried not to give it too much attention knowing that it could very well have been an associate manager making sure everyone was in for the night.

"I know you're corny asses didn't just roll up over here," I said to the two men with broad shoulders and wife beaters barely covering their chiseled chests.

"Eh, a bet's a bet, Kush," MoneyMan, one half of The Invaders team, said, devilishly showing his pearly white teeth as he cupped the hefty hunk of meat stirring in his pants.

"Bet my ass. The two of you didn't play fair."

"Who said anything about playing fair, Lil' Man? I play to win … by all means necessary, pimp," His tag team partner, Pushaman said, stroking my clean-shaven face, making his way into the motel room.

I slapped his hand away.

I tried intimidating the two of them back onto the other side of the doorway, but they stopped short of getting back to the threshold.

Even though I was highly respected as a professional athlete and good at holding my own, I was still a bit sensitive about my short stature, which I well compensated for in my very manly muscles-out build.

"Whoady, Kush, I was just fucking with you! I didn't mean any harm. I just came over to claim my prize."

His prize, I thought. How did it get to here? Pretty much, it began with the four of us having one thing in common – we were the only four buff big black men in the white-dominated sport of wrestling entertainment. It wasn't like it was us against them, or that we had any sort of beef with the other wrestlers. For the most part, they were cool to the point that they were just a blast to hang out with. But as it usually goes, like attracts like, and we were very much 'in like' with each other, becoming very good friends. And it didn't hurt either that they had jumped many of the hurdles for us, so we could be even be considered to join the organization much less being put on the road to superstardom.

One night after we ended up getting into a match (being that we were the token blacks, which happened quite often), my man Drake decided that his career could sail to the moon if he didn't have a tag team partner. So, we have our little spat, getting ready to throw down when The Invaders stepped in and separated us for the night. Drake went off with MoneyMan, and I stayed behind with Pushaman.

Even though Drake and I continued to get along in the ring, winning most of our matches, we stopped being as tight outside of the ring as we once were, as we were still keeping our new sleeping arrangement as stated earlier. I didn't mind. Pushaman turned out to be a good hanging out buddy than I first thought. We had a fixation for pretty much the same things and cracking on each other about our weird and sometimes bizarre dislikes.

We were all happy-go-lucky one night when Drake and I won a match against the makeshift tag team duo of Cowboy and Big Samoa and The Invaders won a match between two wrestlers by the name of Ether and Granite. Because we knew that we were heading out super early to catch a flight to Glasgow, our routine to check out the local scene was put on hold for a stack of cards and a six-pack of vodka shooters.

Everything was going good until my middle lower back started giving me the blues. I had to lie down. It wasn't until after I done so that I thought about grabbing a bottle of ligament to rub to solve the problem. Being a good friend, I thought, Pushaman reached over and grabbed the bottle and started massaging my back with those wonder-touch hands of his. His gentle massage went from that to something a bit more sensual. Spine-tingling and dick-hardening. I tried not to let him know what was going on between me and the mattress beneath me. However, one simple smile of the eyes had him laughing and grinning as if he already had me. His hands started going lower and lower down my back, and then without notice his band just slapped my bare ass like it was nothing.

I always thought Pushaman was sexy as fuck with his shiny, shaven bald head and a sexy chin badges that made his big lips even more pronounced without the distractions of a moustache. I had a feeling that he messed around, but was too focused on my career to go there with him; one false move and it's over. He was looking good, though, and I was feeling it. The motherfucker could've gotten it to if he didn't start in on that 'Lil' Man' shit.

In the other motel room, Drake was starting trouble with MoneyMan, telling him that he didn't need any of this tag team shit. He decided to prove it by brawling with him. The fight ended in a draw, but it was enough to drive a wedge into our friendship with them. When we fought in the ring, we fought. Many of which we won. We were doing such a good job of annihilating them in the ring that everybody was certain that they were on their way out. This meant that we were about to enjoy the good life, riding on our names product endorsements and more. For The Invaders, however, it was beginning to look like the end of their careers, at least as a tag team duo. As their popularity declined, they often reached across the table with truces that were short-lived, but showed that as the only blacks in the league weren't at each other's throats.

In our last attempt to squash our beef, we made a friendly wager. Since Pushaman was so fond of grabbing ass in and out of the ring, and MoneyMan the same with low blows, I thought surely Pushaman wouldn't mind breaking his own 'bread' for some sweet swinging dick of mine. Surely, with the track record Drake and I had, we thought we were invincible. We would've still been if it hadn't been for that lame MoneyMan taking a steel chair to my back so that Pushaman and his pecker could pin me down for the count.

"Your prize?" I barked. "You're lucky I don't grab a steel chair over there and come across you head like your boy came across my back."

"All is fair in war and ass, man," MoneyMan smirked.

MoneyMan wasn't bad looking either. He held his own quite well with his cornrows and razor-thin beard; and he had these beautifully slanted eyes, giving the appearances that at least one of his parents hailed from somewhere over there in China somewhere. The thing was, though he was fairly good-looking like his boy, it was his swagger that stood out above anything else.

"I don't know what y'all think is about to go down, but it ain't about to go down like that!"

Before I could finish my sentence, MoneyMan hoisted me up off the ground. I swore up and down with my crotch in his face that he was going to pile-drive my aching body onto the nearby bed, if not the hard floor. I was anxious, suspend in midair with my kneecaps over his broad muscled shoulders, somehow someway, waiting on his next move. There were other moves I could have made. But with everything having a sharp edge to them, I decided that my best course of action was just to react to any act he did. Damning the consequences of hard edges or not. What I was not expecting was for him to try and nuzzle my dick awake.

"What the hell?" Drake asked coming out of the shower.

"My boy, Moneyman, likes to play with his toys for awhile before he breaks them in," Pushaman said.

"He ain't breaking in shit," I yelled, balancing myself against the ceiling.

"By the time I get my tongue up your ass, not only will I be breaking it in, you'll be wanting it broken in!" MoneyMan said definitely looking up into my eyes.

He put his face back into my denim-covered crotch, kissing and nudging it hard, trying to get a stir out of me. We both sort of knew if he did tongue my ass half the battle would've already been won. But, even through my jeans, the worthless fuck was feeling good. So good in fact that by the time I came up for air, Pushaman and Drake were deadlock trying to wrestle the other into submission, grunting and groaning talking smack to one another. I was so caught up in them, the next thing I know I'm being body-slammed onto the cheap bouncy bed.

I tried rising up but my shoulder blades locked, frozen solid, and my arms were fanned out couldn't bend or do anything. There I was one of the best in the business, couldn't even get up off my back as this

206

motherfucker started rubbing his index fingers in between my sweat, hair-filled crack left exposed by my jockstrap.

His touch did nothing for me. But my dick betrayed me just the same with Pushaman on top of Drake looked very hot, forced yet intended.

"I knew your ass was easy," MoneyMan said, unbuttoning my jeans and moving my codpiece below my balls.

"Fuck you."

"I plan to."

This was sort of fucked up, if I thought about it too much. In the ring, Drake and I were the ones that whipped ass, and now we were about to have our asses served on a silver platter to us.

I tried not to put my focus on what I couldn't do, as I looked on at Drake figuring that if he could get out his hold, he could help get out of mine. I looked on, praying that though his tight scrunched-up face that he had some sort of trick up his sleeve.

"C'mon, fuck," I mumbled, thinking that he had to do something.

"Shit, I give," Drake said in cowardice.

"What?" Pushaman asked putting him to the screws.

"I give, folk."

Noooo!

"I give, folk! I give!" Drake cried.

"He gives, folk," MoneyMan mocked looking at me, and then turning his attention to his tag team partner. "Hey, Push, come over here. Don't you think Lil' Man got some pretty-ass lips."

Pushaman nodded, standing above me. "He got those pretty pink pipe-smoking lips."

"He probably got a sweet throat. Why don't you check it out for me?"

I shook my head, thinking that Drake might get at them while their backs were turned.

"Man, you better gon' with that shit."

Pushaman looked me dead in the eye and started stroking his mean meat in the same bravado his partner had earlier.

"I ain't playing," I said taking my last stand.

"It don't look to me like your pretty ass got much of a choice, Lil' Man. But don't worry we'll take good care of it for you," MoneyMan said, taking my jeans off far beyond my steel-toe boots.

Pushaman shucked off his pants exposing a buttery toasted-color dick while I tried to kick MoneyMan away. I thought I was successful at it. Then Pushaman with his soft, smelly dick straddled my face and obstructed my view, giving MoneyMan the advantage of grabbing my legs and making his way between them.

I was no punk, though. With Pushaman kneeing my arms, he rubbed the tip of his scummy dick across my lips, begging me to take it. I fought hard, turning my head every which way believing that Drake was going to come through.

"Oh, no," I groaned at the invasion of a warm wet tongue snaking up my crack to my hole.

My mouth betrayed just enough for Pushaman to work his dick in my mouth, as he warned me to watch my teeth. My legs sold out, spreading as far as they could give MoneyMan a full access to bury his face up in there.

He and his tongue were feeling so good that I wasn't even aware that he was fucking my mouth like it was some good pussy until I felt that I was about to choke on that thick meat pole. Adding to the claustrophobic factor of his hard eight-pack looking like a brick wall in front of my face. I seemed to go in and out of conscious into subconscious with every flick of his tongue in my hole, causing me licking around every salty inch of flesh in my mouth.

"Ah, man," Pushaman's voice vibrated through me. "That's what I'm talking about! Lil' Man can deep throat!"

Pushaman was jabbing it in and out of me, and MoneyMan ate me out like he was dining for his last supper. I didn't know what to do. I thought I was about to explode. I guess Pushaman beat me to the punch because I felt his dick swell in my mouth, followed by grunting and warm spurts hitting the back of my throat.

"Sorry about that, folk," Pushaman said.

He was looking me dead in my eyes, taking his half hard dick out of my mouth. "That shit was feeling too good to hold back. I tried though."

Fuck you! I thought.

My throat was clogged with his seeds to say anything. And even if I could, I don't think it would've been toward him. I had plenty of suppressed screams that need to be let out from the tongue-lashing I was getting across my butthole. Pushaman stayed on top of me, keeping his eyes on me, and slowly climbed off, looking for Drake to 'swab the deck,' which was code for him to use his mouth to clean up his slimy mess.

I looked on in disbelief. I knew that I had to do what I did because I was stuck. Drake had the freedom to bounce while the two of them were on me. Instead, he stuck around to be the cleanup boy. As this was going on, Moneyman had my knees pinned the sides of my chest, had cracked open my buns like he was breaking bread, trying to tongue fuck me. But the problem was that even though he could get me open like he wanted to, MoneyMan didn't have access to my hole like he wanted to. With both my arm and legs locked, MoneyMan flipped me and had me face down on the mattress, having at it.

I was trying to hold in this pleasure that was running through my body, up my spine, trying its best to escape through my lips. I kept quite as much as I could not letting on that he was doing an excellent job turning me out, rising, though, ever so often to tuck my pulsating dick under my body.

"You're just going to town with it, aintcha?" Pushaman said, out of the corner of my eye, still between the beds with Drake on his knees, eyeing the action.

My best to try to hold it all in came out in one big sob, a few minutes later, only stopping short of telling him to fuck me.

MoneyMan got off on this, somehow eating me out with some sort of renewed enthusiasm. It didn't stop there either, as I also noted that Pushaman was slowly getting harder and showing inches growing out of Drake's mouth. Wordless, he pulled out and disappeared behind MoneyMan.

A few moments later, MoneyMan pulled his mouth off my asshole, and raised me up on my knees. The next thing I know, I'm pretty much forced to get on my hands as somebody got between my legs and started sucking my dick. This wavy of euphoria was short-lived when I felt something thick and hard slide against my hole.

It was not a tongue, not this time.

I wanted to say something, bound to, but I was still riding that wave of ecstasy from earlier. It had me trembling along with whoever had my dick in his mouth. I quickly learned that it was Pushaman, after he pulled off

210

to tell Drake to get over there and get back to work on his dick.

My heart began beating through my chest as I remembered the thing bumping at my backdoor. I guess I was more scared than I thought with a whimper seeping through my lips.

"Don't worry partna, I got a rubber on it," MoneyMan assured me.

It was good to know, but it wasn't my immediate concern as he shoved this enormously long jellied thing into me, digging into the flesh around my waist along the way. He had me. He began mounting me like a wild hound to a tamed bitch, going up in me with unforgiving force. I should have been in all-out agony. My body was split between pure pleasure and pure pain, or rather it couldn't tell the difference between the two. He was stretching my hole with squeaky, impossibly wide strokes and knocking against my prostate with every passing lunge.

These feelings were complicated even more when the man beneath me started tweaking my tits. I wasn't sure if I was going to bust a nut out of my ass or my dick. I felt like I was going to lose it at any given moment, knowing that my only saving grace was to get MoneyMan to bust one first. I tried squeezing my ass muscles and grinding back against him, hoping that I was helping him along the way.

"Oh, fuck!" MoneyMan gasped.

I could feel it. He was close. Screaming and cussing and telling me how good it felt. I can't agree more, shuddering through this whole ordeal to the point I was burying my head into the pillow.

My bending over even further like that must have done the trick because he was soon bracing himself against me.

211

"Whoa, that's some good ass," MoneyMan panted getting his last couple of bucks in.

"Oh, no," I cried out.

My body took note that I was no longer getting fucked and just sputtered a hot nut into the awaiting mouth beneath me.

I collapsed from exhaustion, not caring one way or another how Pushaman was going to get out from underneath me. MoneyMan slowly pulled his dick out of my ass, snatched off the condom and poured his package onto my cheeks.

The room pretty much went silent after that, except for the constant slurping that Drake did that filled the room before Pushaman muffled his screams in my crotch while he came.

Truth is, while that was a memorable night. We never were the same after that. Anytime either of us stepped in the ring there was always a hard dick pressing against another for the count. Even when the four of us ventured into solo careers, it seemed that it went from bad to worse. Sometimes forgetting through our elaborate moves in the rings that we were among tens of thousands of people watching, a fact that was almost forgotten when were face to face, skin slapping against skin.

I had to give it all up, though. It became too much. After one match when I almost copped a feel of the bulging dick in front of me along with almost leaning in for a kiss in front of all those people – almost. But it turned out to be a nice pay off because in giving up my career to become a trainer to other up-and-coming wresters, Pushaman and I hooked up. MoneyMan became an exotic dancer and began an escorting service pimping out Drake on the side

POWER STRUGGLE
By Cliff Morten

Chapter 1: Power Struggle – Battle of Words

"Why do I always have to do the donkey work for you, no matter at which positions we play?"

The intonation is sharp, attacking, and by the look in Jason's provoking green eyes, Nico can tell the tension smoldering throughout the day is about to go up in flames.

After the coach finished the training and dismissed them until the game the next day, Jason and Nico sat on the grass in the little garden in front of Nico's terrace, drinking beer and discussing soccer politics like so many times before. Nico has invited his friend – who also became his teammate recently – in order to relax the atmosphere. But soon, an edgy undertone creeps into their conversation.

And, now this question.

"Why?" Nico shrugs, casting intrigued looks over Jason's face. "It's all just about tactics. You see any problem? Haven't you been the one who always stated that personal vanity has to stay back for the sake of the team's success? Or wasn't that totally honest and doesn't count as soon as you are involved?" Nico knows he's aiming at Jason's most sensitive point. Jason shifts in his seat, unconsciously licking his lips.

"I never lie." Pride and indignation add a metallic color to his voice. "But it's not fair. Additionally, the coach high-handedly made you the Captain of the team. He didn't even allow an open competition to find out which of

213

us might be better suited for the job. You got the leading position from the start, only to avoid the conflict."

"What?" Nico is astonished at the passion he hears in Jason's voice. He's usually not one of those who is constantly muttering about the coach's decisions. And, Nico always thought official titles like Captain wouldn't matter to him. "You used to say it's destructive to criticize the coach as long as we are winning. And we've been winning for weeks, haven't we?"

"Come on, man, what would you say in my place?" Jason growls, waving away whatever comments Nico had poised on his lips. "I didn't imagine it would be like that when the club bought you in. I thought it would be a chance to increase my capability and effort due to inspiring concurrence with you, but instead I'm pushed aside to a marginal position and might sit on the bench sooner or later, just because I get no chance to show what I can."

Nico never noticed before how dark the vocals were rolling in 'concurrence,' threatening like rumble of thunder.

And again the defiant look, forehead high.

"I did support your transfer to us," Jason continues. It's true. They had both been looking forward to playing in the same team, and secretly Nico even had hoped for more. "But we both knew that meant we had to carry out this rivalry in honor," Jason explains with grim determination. Nico chews at his lower lip and swallows down the remark that this hadn't been so clear to him. Ironically, it seems they had been less of opponents to each other as long they were still playing against each other. "But now the confrontation is cowardly avoided and I must bite the bullet." Jason snorts with contempt and cools his heated tongue with a large gulp of beer. "You know I strictly separate private life and career. It has nothing to do with personal envy. I only think the team should be led by the one who is best for the task, and with all friendship and respect, I think that's me. We have agreed to openly talk about such issues," he adds justifyingly, and Nico nods. Jason's honesty is one of the qualities he especially appreciates in his friend.

"If that's the way you see it, I'm not surprised you simply couldn't bring yourself to pass the ball over to me today ..." Nico grins, Jason frowns and grumbles. Every time Jason was expected to cooperate with Nico, the action went wrong. Jason is an extraordinarily talented soccer player, and his failure is clearly not the result of a lack of ability but of his inner resistance against his seemingly subordinate role.

"Or ..." Jason doesn't answer and Nico proceeds further on dangerous terrain, "... has there been another reason for your problems today ...?" A sneaky whisper enters Nico's voice. Jason swallows. Nico smiles, his tongue plays behind his teeth, wily crinkles curl around his eyes.

Nico knows he exactly can't expect an answer other than growling and grumbling. His remark hints at the hard bulge he felt between Jason's legs during the partner exercises, when he repeatedly, deliberately but discreetly rubbed against him. His own erection blossomed right from the start when the coach assigned Jason as his partner, who at this point lay on his back, panting fast and heavy, still exhausted from the hard jogging training. It was an integral part of the coach's innovative methods to encourage the teammates to help each other with the stretching exercises as well as to apply mutual massages for muscle relaxation. Besides the physical aspects, the coach expects it to facilitate the bonding of the team, and today he certainly had chosen Nico and Jason as partners for each other intentionally, after becoming aware of the aggressive undercurrents in their interaction.

215

"Ow!" Jason complained because Nico's hard knee hit his inner thigh as he knelt down between Jason's legs, getting in the starting position for some gymnastics to increase the general flexibility.

"Spread your legs wider," Nico admonished and in an instant he saw flying red spill all over Jason's cheeks, his eyes blinking with awkwardness.

Long before Nico's brain could grasp the meaning of this reaction, his cock had its own interpretation ready and stretched out, curious for more.

During each of the following exercises – and thankfully there was a whole long series of them – Nico took more and more advantage of his position. Having Jason's body before him and almost beneath him like this allowed him to lightly stroke Jason's thighs, press his abdomen close to Jason's. Jason's scowl deepened when this intrusive behavior got approval, the coach being quite content with Nico's enthusiasm for the partner gymnastics after all the quarrelling during the game.

There was no way that Jason could have missed the intent behind his teasing, and his increasingly bad temper had much to do with Nico's shameless delight while he touched and cuddled Jason. Before the change of positions was announced, Jason managed to get away under a transparent pretext, something along the lines of having to make an urgent call.

Nico almost didn't dare hope that Jason would accept his invitation after that. But he simply had to try. Since he had changed from his old club to Jason's, he had waited for more signs, that Jason's feelings for him exceeded mere friendship – signs that had been relatively frequent before – and a hard cock seemed to be a reasonable reliable hint.

When he asked Jason to join him for a beer, Jason just murmured, "Why?"

"We should talk it all out," Nico said awkwardly. Jason grunted acceptance. But obviously he had a different topic in mind than Nico.

Jason is clearly not in the mood to comment upon Nico's remark now.

Instead, he snaps, "Who wants you as Captain? People here know me. I've played for this club since B-league of the youth, in good times and bad, while you went from team to team abroad, only looking for whichever club was willing to pay you best! Do you believe the people here think it's okay that the coach chose a stranger as Captain and prefers you to me, who they know and respect?"

Silently, Nico partially agrees with him, but Jason's arrogance is beginning to rub him the wrong way. "You're forgetting that soccer games aren't decided by democratic elections, Jason," replies Nico matter-of-factly. "The wishes of the people don't matter, and if you ask me that's fine, especially if you look at the delusional psychotic they elected for president some years ago."

He hears the sharp intake of breath and knows Jason takes the last remark as a comparison. It wasn't meant that way, but that doesn't matter anymore now. His blood slowly starts to boil. "It's not your popularity with the masses that makes a good soccer player, but speed, technique, intelligence and strength."

"I'm faster than you and my dribbling is better."

"And I'm stronger than you."

"Ahhh ... is that so?"

"May I suggest we don't let people vote to decide that question, but settle this between ourselves ...?"

"And how, pray tell ...?"

"With a fair wrestling match."

217

He is ridden by the devil to suggest that. But his desire to feel Jason pressed up against him once more, to roll over the ground with him, and also the increasing want to try his strength and fighting skills with Jason tempt him to challenge the other man.

"So, you want to fight?" Jason stands up and begins to rid himself of his T-shirt.

"Okay!"

Chapter 2: Power Struggle – Wrestling Match

"Might as well take off the belts, too," Nico says, facing a half-naked Jason with complete nonchalance. "You could cut yourself with the buckles."

Jason shrugs as he removes his belt. He's eager to put the arrogant Captain in his place once and for all.

"Wrestling only," Nico reminds him. "No kick boxing. No knife fighting. No amok running ..." he adds slightly worried, a little intimidated by the murderous look on Jason's face. A memory flickers in his mind, standing alone against a schoolyard bully, 'Biting and kicking don't count!'

A blue-black glance slides over Jason's well-built body. Not that he hasn't seen him stripped to the waist before. But now, tensed in anticipation, his swelling pectorals rising and falling with the rhythm of his fast and deep breathing, skin flexing above the clearly defined six-pack, he is more beautiful than any sculpture Nico has ever seen.

Nico tears his eyes away from him, tries to lock up the secret admirer and to set free the warrior in him. Holy shit, this nonsense was his idea! Now there's no chickening out without serious damage to his honor.

Nico undoes his own belt, draws in a breath then sends a silent signal of readiness. At once, Jason flings himself onto him.

Shit, he thinks as the breath is knocked from his chest, the man has experience with punches and a store of dirty tricks. His grip hurts right from the start, as he bends Nico's arms to positions his joints refuse to accept, digging his fingernails into Nico's skin so painfully that a high-pitched grunt escapes his lips.

Jason's aggressive onslaught has taken Nico by surprise, but he defends himself as best he can, wiggling like a snake. Both end up clinging to each other in a fierce clutch stronger than steel, intertwined like an inextricable knot.

Jason's sweat mixes with Nico's, fusing them together; Nico clings to Jason like someone drowning, and they stumble across the grass in a zigzag pattern like drunken Siamese twins, until they fall. Nico knows seconds before it happens that Jason will bear down upon him far too hard, and then abstract paintings are shimmering in front of his eyes until a vibrating black screen blinds him.

Nico successfully remembers how to breathe but finds himself in a position less than preferred during a wrestling match, flat on his stomach with Jason hovering above him. His arm is wrenched painfully behind his back, and Jason's hand clasps around his throat. Jason's hand glides up to Nico's chin, then pulls the other man's head back roughly, shoving his arm higher in his back till he's arching like an Olympic gymnast.

Jason bends down, his lips slightly stirring Nico's hair.

"Now ... Captain," he says, sarcasm dripping from his voice. "What do you think I should do with you now ...?"

Jason's lips are tickling his earlobes.

Nico sighs and lets his shoulders sink in what Jason thinks is capitulation.

Enjoying the fruits of his victory, Jason feels too secure, pays little attention to his captive's now-relaxed posture. The second Jason lowers his defenses, Nico smiles to himself. He can always rely on Jason to react impulsively, never seeing through Nico's much more calculating mind.

Nico shoots up, bursting out of Jason's grip.

"No need to worry about that," he hisses, out of breath. "That's a waste of time, because you will lose ..."

He's above Jason now, wrapping his arm tightly around his neck, taking him into a clinch hold then a throw that without question would have sent Jason to the ground ... but one accurately placed blow hurls him back in circles.

Nico squirms and stares at Jason with shock-wide eyes. The next blow crashes against his ribs and Nico staggers back, finally caught against the fence like a fly in a spider's net.

That's unfair, but Jason doesn't look as if he's willing to negotiate the rules any longer at this point.

And suddenly, Nico understands the genesis of Jason's seemingly senseless violence toward him. If Jason was stronger than Nico, their fight would have been Jason's chance to deal with his frustration and get over it, to let out his rage and disappointment at being robbed of the leading position in the team. It's finally clear why Jason has resisted every attempt at flirtation since Nico joined his team, even though Jason's desire for Nico was visible to anyone familiar with the body language of intimacy. Of course Jason must fight his feelings of being drawn to Nico as long as he considers him a rival to his career.

Nico almost laughs, but it turns into a tortured cry after Jason's next attack.

220

Supposedly Nico is an ambitious bastard who chooses even his private contacts by measuring up their usefulness for his career, while Jason is known as the simple soul to whom friends mean more than success. But now it's Jason who is unable to differentiate between private life and career. That is all more than obvious, but he hadn't expected it from Jason of all people, and therefore had been blind to it up to this moment. Unfortunately, enlightenment arrives somewhat too late. And it's rather useless to contemplate complicated psychological complexities while well-aimed blows are hailing down on him.

He is stronger than Jason. And that's the problem, because if Jason can't win by regular means, there's no doubt he'll use whatever means he can, striking in the heat of the moment.

Nico reviews his options.

He can't defeat Jason by playing fair when Jason ignores the rules, but he's not prepared to let the fight get out of control, to strike back with the same violence and risk hurting Jason severely.

Nico dodges away from a punch aimed at his chin.

Is he willing to let Jason win?

That might be a good idea. There's a lot less risk in that – and again Nico ducks under a fist. His friend would calm down, would probably be satisfied and able to overcome his inner tensions and contradictions.

Nico locks eyes with Jason. He sees a green-eyed wolf, snarling, struggling for the first place in the order of ranks. An alpha male, demanding submission from his opponent –

– from Nico.

Let him win?

NO.

Not on your fucking life.

Nico's never been a violent man. But there's a primal instinct lurking within him that comes to the fore.

He can't – won't – give in to Jason.

Nico dances aside to avoid taking another hit, but realizes this tactic won't help him much longer. His patience is slowly fading, and he's quickly running out of ideas to peacefully diffuse the volatile situation.

Perhaps ...

Nico falls down. Jason's own momentum makes him stumble, and he lands on top of Nico. He grabs Nico's wrists and pulls them down to the ground. His face is inches away from Nico's, the eyes throwing green-gold sparks of triumph.

Nico's never seen his friend's face so furious and wild, his rugged features expressing hatred, power, and euphoria, and god, he is beautiful ...

"Now, surrender, Ge ... hmmmpf ..."

Nico's tongue in his mouth ruins his victory speech. Nico's head shoots up, driving his tongue between Jason's lips and he sucks, licks ... ahhh ... Jason tastes salty and sharp from the fight, you could poison yourself with an oral overdose of testosterone from that kiss, and Nico nearly forgets his plan, because he's finally kissing Jason ... he's kissing Jason ... Jason ... Jason ...

Thankfully, his brain enters the wicked stage again, like Judas thinking of betrayal while kissing. He fumbles for one of the belts – he has made sure his fall went in the right direction, just near the heap of clothes.

Jason will not beat any records with his reaction time. Frozen in shock by Nico's kiss for several seconds, now he jumps as if bitten by a snake, and Nico catches him unaware, hurling him down and catapulting himself over him.

While sliding forward he raises Jason's arms over his head and wraps the belt tightly around them, grateful that the *Little Book of Knots* came in handy.

Jason is ranting and raging now, but with his hands bound it's no real fight.

Nico finds the other belt – and okay, that a thin tree stands nearby is pure luck but you have to be lucky sometimes – Nico throws one end of the belt around the tree and binds Jason's hands to it.

Jason kicks and writhes into exhaustion until the slim leather cuts his wrists, until the veins on his biceps are swollen to bursting, and his hair clings in strands on his wet face.

Jason collapses tired, worn out, panting helplessly.

"Do that again," Nico purrs, very approvingly. "It's nice to watch."

"Untie me, you sick bastard! You asshole! Let me free! That's unfair! That's deprivation of personal liberty!"

"I would classify it as self-defense," Nico strokes his bruises accusingly and pats gingerly at his hurting ribs where Jason's fist hit like a comet.

"Fuck! Let me free!"

"I would consider the first option," Nico muses out loud, causing another fierce struggle from Jason. The blond man squirms and writhes. Once he sees the look of cool amusement on Nico's face, he forces himself not to move.

He'd be damned if he'd give that damn bastard something else to get hot and bothered over.

His eyes are haunted like the eyes of a wild animal caught in a trap, but he's desperately trying to control his temper. Nico is watching in fascination how Jason's eyes seem to change their color with the emotional roller coaster, turning from raging hatred to shame for the suffered defeat, from panic to resignation, from defiance to humiliation.

"Nico, please. Untie me," He pleads softly with a rough and breaking voice.

Nico looks at him like a predator sizing up potential prey.

Chapter 3: Power Struggle – Make Love Not War

Jason's body shivers from pent-up frustration, shaking from boiling rage like the lid of a pot clattering before the heated water spills over in founts.

He shuts his eyes, and Nico bets he's focusing on meditation techniques like before the penalty kick in the sudden-death play-off after overtime, to calm himself and slow down his heart rate.

Nico has never seen anything in his entire life that compares to the glorious sight of this strong, proud man bound.

A captured hero. The pathetic suffering of a noble chief at the stake.

He approaches him cautiously, watching out for signs of danger. He sees Jason tense up even more as if preparing for a last attack.

"Kick me and you'll pay for it," he warns, his voice low and cold. "I don't think you need me to explain that you're at my mercy now. One stupid move, and I'll whip you."

Jason growls, clinging to some last shreds of rebellion, but both know it's an empty threat. Nico crouches between his legs, like during the partner

224

gymnastics, now confident that Jason will not try anything. He leans over him.

It takes every ounce of willpower Jason has to hold himself down, trying to avoid Nico's searing gaze.

Nico reaches out, touching his cheek gently.

"Jason. You know that I know."

Jason tries to look as if he hasn't a clue what Nico is talking about so miraculously.

But Nico can see the truth in the lambent green orbs. He even knows that Jason knows he cannot deceive him.

"God, Jason, you were so hard I'd probably have felt it through plate armor." He bows down a little closer and continues in a low, seductive murmur, "And so was I. You know that, too. Isn't it foolish to deny that to each other?"

Jason doesn't answer. In fact, he doesn't react at all. He even seems to have forgotten his situation and his urge to escape, lying perfectly still and calm.

"I'm not a beginner, Jason," Nico goes on, stroking him lightly, tantalizing the other man's senses. "I've seen the heat in your eyes when you look at me and think no one else is watching. I know that look, Jason. I've been with enough men to know what it means."

Nico leans down for a kiss, but Jason flinches away, wrenching his head to the side. Nico takes hold of his face with both hands, cradling it with a gentle force that will not be denied.

"Look at me and tell me it's not true. I hope I don't have to remind you that you never lie ..."

Jason gives a desperate sigh – Nico never knew such a simple sound could contain so great a confession – and he smiles at Jason with fondness.

Nico slowly starts to kiss him again, tenderly and playfully exploring Jason's mouth. He doesn't do much in the way of returning the kiss, but there's little resistance. Only when Nico begins to kiss his way down Jason's throat, following the curved line of his collar bones to his shoulders, leaving a trace of wet kiss-steps and little sizzling spots where he sucked until Jason's blood rose to the surface, Jason finally interrupts him with a choked voice.

"Stop it ... Please."

Nico gazes at his friend's face, and is filled with compassion as he sees the battlefield of contradictory feelings that are in war with each other. It's more than indecision; Jason is literally torn apart inside. Minutes ago he was insane with rage, but it was a rage partly born of suppressed desire, and now the feelings bait and switch like a disoriented magician who can't make up his mind in which shape to appear.

He doesn't quite stop stroking Jason, massaging his sides with deft hands, already sure that Jason's body is joyfully joining the game, whether Jason's mind likes it or not.

"Nico ... perhaps it's usual for you to feel this way, but for me ..."

"Really," Nico asks quietly, struck by the sheer helplessness in Jason's eyes. "Never once?" His voice is full of affection and respect and wonder, and maybe it's the fact that Nico doesn't make light of his inexperience what finally convinces Jason to let him continue his kissing research mission once more.

Nico acquaints himself with the parts of Jason's skin he missed during his first descent, making sure not to ignore a single inch; Jason is trembling and sighing from the intensity, his former anger and rage melting quickly into lust like a glacier into a roaring waterfall.

226

Jason hisses quietly as Nico opens his jeans and pulls them down, freeing an achingly hard cock. Your cock certainly doesn't lie, Nico thinks to himself, soft eyes swallowing the length and breadth of Jason's erection. And Nico goes down, licking and sucking, tasting all of Jason's musky male flavors.

Jason groans in desperate need. "Please, Nico. Untie me," he begs, as if remembering his situation for the first time. "I want to touch you."

Nico's mouth slowly travels upwards celebrating a short reunion with Jason's navel and nipples.

The two men lock passion-filled eyes.

"Only if you really want me to, Jason," Nico whispers, lying stretched out on top of Jason, full of urgency and hunger. "But, please, Jason ... let me have you like this ..."

Pulsing desire nearly strangles him, lust glowing in his ocean-dark eyes as the image of a bound and naked Jason is forever seared into his mind.

His voice is ragged and husky. "Oh god, Jason, it turns me on to see you like this ... tied down and naked in front of me ..."

Jason lowers his lashes. Nico senses shame but no outrage. His body language reveals awkwardness - the virginal flush, the way he averts his eyes from Nico's – and the contrast between these gestures of shyness and innocence and the rough beauty of his manly face is thrilling.

Nico's desire is so powerful it's almost frightening. A part of Jason wants to deny his request, but the refusal hovers there, just on the threshold of his lips, unwilling to formulate the words under Nico's intense stare. Jason opens his mouth, shuts it, and tries again, takes another go, but after several failed attempts the battle within is over.

Jason returns Nico's demanding gaze with a mixture of fear and trust.

Surrender has never had such a beautiful face before.

Interestingly, Nico thinks to himself in the span of a few moments, how practical matters always reinsert themselves, ruthless toward romantic situations.

"Hang on a minute, love ..." Nico whispers, and disappears into the house, to rummage through drawers and return with a bottle of lube.

Very funny, Jason thinks with a certain wry irony, as if he had any other choice.

With Nico no longer covering him, that undeniable heat no longer clouding his senses, Jason's fears and doubts once again rise to the fore, though intrinsically, he knows the arguments against his feelings are weak.

Still ... what his body wants ... he doesn't quite understand.

He does desire Nico. He has for a very long time, it seems, but ...

... but the panicked look in his eyes will not melt away so easily and by the time Nico returns from his quest, he realizes what happened.

Nico's glad he left him tied up, otherwise the man would have vanished on him.

Isn't it possible to leave the boy alone for even a minute?

"Nico – untie me," Jason begins again, and can't he ask of anything else? "I'm just not ready for this. I can't ... I can't."

Shit, Nico curses silently, having managed to get so far only to watch it all unravel right before his eyes and having to begin again like some fucking game of dice.

"Jason," and Nico covers him again, hunting for the rest of his patience, which has disappeared the moment his libido took over practically every rational thinking process. "You have thought of it before ... you know you want to try ... why not now?"

He takes up his caresses again, first with gentle persuasion and then with tender demand. He prays he'll do it right and not blow it all with a mistake, do it well, not too fast or too slow. Never has he wanted anyone as much as he wants this rough, golden-haired man laid out before him like a feast. Somehow he has to make Jason want him just as much or else it will all be for nothing, and he will feel like a complete flop for the rest of his life. What use is it to have successfully picked up every single chance for a goal when you fail in the most important moment of your life?

Nico's hands are all over him and he's whispering soothing words in his ear, "I'll go slowly, Jason ... don't be afraid. I want you, Jason, please."

Ironically it's Nico who's pleading and begging with a tied up man, but he doesn't give a damn as long as it works.

After a while he can feel Jason relax.

Eyes meet again and Nico is relieved beyond imagination because he doubts he'd have the discipline to release Jason at this stage, even if he insisted, and he really doesn't want to think too long on that scenario ...

But he wants to hear Jason confess. "Say the words."

And Jason does, shaking from desire. "I want you, Nico." he groans, the green eyes heavily lidded with uncontrollable need.

The floodgates open and there's no turning the tide.

"Get on your hands and knees," Nico orders.

Jason maneuvers into the required position and both are thankful the restraints have enough give for this to work.

Jason's well-muscled buttocks are a temptation Nico cannot resist, stroking the smooth skin, while using a lubed finger to lightly probe the cleft.

A faint cry of Jason, muscles already clenching.

God, Jason's so damn tight, to prepare him means work. Nico uses his arm to wipe the sweat off his forehead

Ok, he's done that before, he knows what to do, shouldn't be an insurmountable handicap after all the trials and tribulations he has overcome in the last half an hour, and since Jason said he's a virgin what did he expect? If he only wasn't so nervous, like some candidate for exam who's forgotten all he's ever learned.

Nico goes slowly, opening Jason up to new sensations, stroking and soothing him, whispering words to inflame and incite. With each gasp from the man beneath him, he pauses, allowing Jason to adapt and adjust.

He stretches him expertly, carefully – one finger only, murmuring, "Relax, Jason ... feel me inside you ... like this ... yes ... come on ..."

Jason obviously has other ideas. Craning his head over his shoulder, he snarls at Nico, "I'm not one nag shying or running wild, mate! Can't you just shut up and do it?" If Jason was a horse, he could be ridden a hell of a lot easier, Nico thinks to himself, then ceases to think at all as the image of giving Jason what he's asking for nearly undoes him.

"Is that what you really want, Jason?"

"Yeah, Nico ... just do it."

There is no way to enter Jason without hurting him, at least at first, in spite of the preparation and the generous amount of lube he's used to slick himself up and to coat Jason's entrance.

He has to push hard to force him open and get in just a few inches. The sensation of tight heat is overwhelming. Though he doesn't want to hurt Jason, he can't help moaning a deep shuddering breath of pleasure even as he feels Jason twitching with pain beneath him, quietly whimpering.

Hands gripping Jason's waist tightly, he waits, allowing Jason to accustom himself to the fullness.

Jason moans, the outer ring muscle contracting, unsure about this invasion. He relaxes, taking in deep breaths as Nico slowly breaches him.

Slowly and evenly, as much for his own benefit as for Jason's, he begins a steady rhythm with strong but not brutal thrusts, his hand stroking Jason's cock as he trembles beneath him.

Nico can sense the moment of Jason's surrender.

A sudden softness and pliability washes through his body, as if Jason's muscles and nerves, every fiber of his being were connected to Nico's central nervous system, no longer obedient to Jason's will but Nico's. He feels totally in control of Jason and a rush of lust for power floods his veins, more intoxicating than any drug Nico has ever sampled.

Yes, he will possess Jason, in every way possible – heart, mind, spirit, just as he possesses his body now. He will have him, claim him.

He looks down again at Jason, bound to him, begging with his sighs and hot whispers, and lust flickers within him like tongues of flame.

But there is no thought of abusing his power. He needs to please Jason, to hold him, to love him, to make him want it, want it again, and want it forever and ever again.

He strikes Jason's sweet spot over and over, urged on by Jason's deep-throated moans of pleasure. At the same time, he strokes his cock with calculated pressure, making him last, longing, starving, until every single cell in Jason's body screams for orgasm and he's begging, not only with passion-ragged words, but with his whole body, offering himself to Nico completely, feverishly shaking with need.

Only then does Nico show mercy, finishing him with one last forceful surge, and Jason is gone, crying out and coming so hard he shoots hot onto Nico's hand and on the grass below him, whispering Nico's name again and again until the last splashes and drops are spent.

Now it's suddenly so easy to bend him even further, spread his legs wider, fuck him deeper.

"Down."

Nico's hard hand shoves his face down in the grass, holding him fast.

Nico has the perfect angle to fuck Jason practically into the ground, and there's nothing Jason can do about it.

Only one thought, one want left – to fuck Jason, fuck him, fuck him in his tight ass, fuck his hot clenching hole, take him, take him, take him.

The force of Nico's orgasm causes him to cry out from the sheer magnitude of sensation that tosses him about. He comes hard and deep in Jason's body, collapsing on him and bearing him down with his weight.

Spent and almost drained, Nico starts to rise from Jason's back.

"Stay," whispers Jason.

Nico hesitates, unbelieving.

"I like to feel you on me," Jason says simply, and as Nico covers him with his body again, he sighs, satisfied, like a child rocked into sleep.

# # # # #

The game is going on in full action, and so far, Jason is doing well, the couch admits it to himself. The relief changes to concern and tension again as he watches with baited breath how Jason tricks one opponent after the other, storming forward on the left wing, while Nico keeps pace in the center field, intelligently making use of the gaps in the other team's defense.

Jason passes by his attackers elegantly, dancing with acrobatic skill. The whole stadium is death-silent with awe, everybody's attention is utterly absorbed by Jason's incredible performance. He sends the ball. The cross shoot comes in, following an ideal line, the exact segment of a circle. The coach's lower jar simply drops. Is that the same Jason who couldn't get one single cross shoot right only yesterday? The ball and Nico meet at the perfect point. He barely does more than hold his foot out – and goal!

The two men fly toward each other' with a big jump Nico flings himself onto Jason, and they roll on the grass, tightly hugging each other until they stop with Nico lying on top of Jason, leaning down like for a kiss.

What the hell?

The coach raises an eyebrow. The last thing he sees are Jason's shining eyes looking up at Nico before other teammates throw themselves onto the pair and one of the joy-celebrations akin to mass copulations that drives morally strict soccer fans into indignation begins.

The coach shakes his head. Soccer stars. One never knows what's going on in their twisted little heads. He hadn't considered Jason a 'diva' but, well, soccer stars, you know?

Moody as hell.

THE TAKEDOWN
By Kale Naylor

The clock struck 6:00 p.m., and the freshmen doorman shut and locked the gymnasium. Most of St. John Preparatory Academy's wrestling team was present. It was Friday evening, and while typically the faculty was long gone for the weekend, the organizers weren't taking any chances on the biggest grudge match in the school's history being interrupted or canceled.

The chatter in the bleachers ceased when the two gladiators stepped onto the blue wrestling mats. Their uniforms did little to contain their massive chests and the rest of their chiseled builds. The two eighteen-year-old seniors epitomized the alpha male specimen. This was why today's match was inevitable. Both popular and star wrestlers, there could be only one alpha male at St. John's, and this showdown would settle the matter once and for all.

Jeremy scowled at his foe while Bryce wore a cocky smirk. A smirk Jeremy silently vowed to remove very shortly.

"All right gentlemen, this is what you've all been waiting for," announced Nathan Abrams. "The brawl to settle it all. In this corner, the challenger, Jeremiah 'The Jackhammer' Seiver!"

Jeremy remained poised, glaring at his foe, unfazed by the raucous cheers.

"And his opponent," Nathan continued. "The champion, your student body president, your wrestling captain, Bryce 'The Golden Boy' Mallory."

With raised fists to the roaring crowd, Bryce beamed.

"All right this is an unsanctioned match and winner takes all," Nathan continued. "If Seiver wins, he becomes the new wrestling captain. However, if Mallory wins, then Seiver becomes ... well ..." he snickered, "Mallory's personal manservant."

The spectators guffawed.

"No points, no technicalities," Nathan said. "This match will be won by pinfall or submission."

The two combatants stepped forward, locked in an intense glare down.

"You guys ready?" Nathan asked.

"Oh yeah," Bryce said. "This'll be quick."

"That what your girlfriend says?" Jeremy quipped.

"All right guys," Nathan said. "GO!"

The two gladiators circled each other like a pair of jaguars while their teammates roared. Without warning, they pounced. Arms interlocked, they struggled to press forward but neither could gain any ground. Jeremy gained the first takedown when he viciously hip-tossed his foe to the mat. Before he could capitalize, Jeremy was quickly leveled with a single-leg takedown. The two tangled again. Jeremy landed on top and secured a chinlock. Bryce attempted to power out, but Jeremy maintained a firm grip.

"Ready to tap out?" Jeremy asked.

"We're just getting started," Bryce grunted. He gripped Jeremy's crotch and gave it a firm massage. "Did we forget to wear our cup today? Gotta say Seiver, I'm impressed. I bet you kept your boyfriend at Dalton's a happy man."

236

Jeremy froze. His worse fear had become a reality. Not only had someone discovered his past, but also it was his worst foe of all people. The brief distraction was all Bryce needed. He slipped out of the chin lock and clamped Jeremy in a sleeper. His legs firmly coiled his opponent's waist, Bryce tugged back. The students yelled in excitement. Jeremy flailed his arms and attempted to pry Bryce's bicep, but his vision blurred and his strength dissipated.

"Don't fight it," Bryce chided. "Just go to sleep."

Jeremy's struggles became weaker.

"Don't worry, Seiver," Bryce whispered in his ear. "I promise you're going to love being my bitch."

Jeremy continued to faintly tug at Bryce's arm, even as everything faded to black.

The torrents of cold water jolted Jeremy from the familiar tile floors. It only took him moments to realize he had been unceremoniously dumped in the locker room showers. The snickering informed him that he wasn't alone. Terrance and Frankie, Bryce's enforcers, leaned against the doorway.

"Bryce is waiting for you," Frankie said.

Terrance tossed Jeremy a towel, "And lose the wet gear. You won't be needing it."

When he arrived in the locker room, Jeremy found his new master lounging idly on the bench with a Cheshire grin. Like Jeremy, Bryce only adorned a wrapped towel around his waist.

"Your posse gone?" Jeremy asked. "I didn't think you could function without them."

"I thought this first time should just be you and me."

"What do you want?"

237

"Eager. I like that. I thought we'd start with something simple, like a massage. Mopping the floor with you was a bit more of a workout than I expected."

The wrestling captain removed his towel and brandished his cock which was at half mast. As much as it pained Jeremy to admit it, it was impressive. Long and thick, it was little wonder his nemesis was a cocky son of a bitch.

"Massage huh?" Jeremy said. "You sure you can trust me?"

"Oh I know I can. I've already kicked your ass once. Anyway, you agreed to this. If word gets out you broke your word, you can count on the school making the rest of your year a living hell. Besides, we both know you're going to enjoy it."

He removed a bottle of massage oil from his duffel bag and tossed it to Jeremy and lay face down on the table, his smooth muscled ass proudly on display. Bryce grinned as he saw the torture Jeremy endured. Yet he continued to pretend he didn't notice his new manservant's tent in his towel.

"Ah yeah," Bryce moaned. "Those hands are nice. I bet you used to do this with that beau of yours all the time."

"How did you find out?"

Bryce chuckled, "You think I didn't do my homework? That tidbit of intel was the whole reason I challenged you to this match in the first place. Nathan's cousin goes to Dalton. Getting caught getting fucked in the janitor's office. I guess if you're gonna get expelled, you could do worse. My thighs could use more oil."

"So this was all a setup."

"Plan was simple. Get you on the mat, psych you out, beat you in front of everyone and establish myself as

238

the alpha dog." Jeremy gritted his teeth and scowled at his teammate. "Oh don't be like that," Bryce continued. "You got played. It happens. Well, not to me."

"You are a truly a pompous ass."

Bryce sighed and nodded, "This is true. And speaking of ass, mine could use some attention from those magic hands of yours."

Jeremy grimaced as he squirted oil on his new master's backside and rubbed it in.

"Fuck!" Bryce groaned. "Damn I'm going to get used to this. You know, for what it's worth, you put up one hell of a fight."

Jeremy scoffed.

"I'm serious. I may not have always liked you, but I've always respected you. Take the match. Several times you had me worried. I honestly thought my plan was going to backfire. You got skill and you're probably the best wrestler on the team. We've got a great shot at state this year, and you're going to be our trump card. You've only got one weakness."

"This oughta be good. Okay I'll bite. What would that be?"

"You're unsure of yourself because deep down you're ashamed of who you are."

"You are so full of shit."

"And yet you're the one serving the whims of another man. Think about it. You're literally hiding in the closet, a janitor's no less, cause you're ashamed of what you are. You think I could've gotten in your head otherwise?"

"What do you know?"

"You think you're the only at this school who's ever enjoyed cock?"

Jeremy gazed down incredulously at a smirking Bryce.

"That's right Seiver. The difference is that I'm not conflicted about who I am. I like me, all of me. And that's power. Yeah I keep it discreet for obvious reasons, but it's not out of shame, I can tell you that."

"Wait until the wrong person finds out."

"That's their problem, not mine."

"Why the fuck are you telling me this?"

Bryce lifted himself from the table and for the second time that day he cupped Jeremy's package. "I thought it'd be obvious at this point."

Jeremy started to leave, but Bryce pressed him against a locker.

"You're not going anywhere," Bryce said. "To the victor goes the spoils. I still own your ass, and I plan to put it to good use."

Jeremy gasped as his rod was stroked and a tongue snaked around his ear.

"How long has it been?" Bryce whispered. "When's the last time you had a big cock inside you? You been craving it, I can feel you trembling. That ass has been waiting to be filled. For someone to be inside you, take control, dominate. Stop thinking about it. Just let go."

Something snapped within Jeremy. He grabbed Bryce's face, and the two locked lips. Their tongues wrestled while Bryce gripped the ass of his newly won prize. He clenched a handful of Jeremy's hair and yanked his head back.

"On your knees boy," Bryce ordered.

240

Jeremy eagerly did as instructed and allowed his tongue to lap away at his master's taught abs. His hands kneaded Bryce's rock hard pecs and massaged his nipples.

"Fuck!" Bryce moaned.

The wrestling captain clenched two fistfuls of hair and slammed his cock into his slave's eager mouth. Jeremy was brazen with lust. An animal unleashed, he eagerly slurped away the massive meat in his mouth.

"Suck that dick boy," Bryce groaned.

He bent Jeremy over the bench and spread his ass cheeks apart. Jeremy cried as the hot tongue repeatedly plunged into his hole. Despite his bucking, thrashing and protests, Bryce kept him planted with two firm hands around his hips.

"If you like that, you're gonna love what's coming next," Bryce chided.

"Give it to me!" Jeremy cried.

Needing no more invitation, Bryce slid his pole into Jeremy's ass. Expecting much resistance and having to wait for Jeremy to adjust to the size like his former conquests, Bryce was thrown by how easily he took every inch of him.

"Come on big boy," Jeremy said. "Fuck me hard!"

Like a piston, Bryce repeatedly drilled into Jeremy who rutted like a wild beast and slammed back into each thrust. The mounted wrestler was a bitch in heat, unleashed and uninhibited. The friction increased the intensity; Jeremy's hole maintained its tightness, never loosening. His body tensed and drenched in perspiration, it took all of Bryce's willpower to keep the impending orgasm at bay.

"That all you got?" Jeremy asked.

241

In response, Bryce grabbed his hair and yanked his head back. Not missing a beat with his anal assault, Bryce plunged his tongue into Jeremy's mouth.

"God damn that ass is tight!" Bryce cried.

"And insatiable, too."

Jeremy pushed Bryce on his back and mounted him. His hands firmly planted on the wrestling captain's oiled, chiseled pecs, Jeremy bounded off his conqueror's rod like a man possessed. Bryce gasped and braced Jeremy's ass while he endured the onslaught.

"God I love this cock!" Jeremy cried.

His ring clenched the massive staff, which elicited a cry from Bryce. The senior jerked Jeremy's rigid dick.

"I'm cumming!" Bryce cried. "FUCK!"

Jeremy felt Bryce's pulsing cock erupt within him. Torrents of hot cream nailed his prostate. That's all it took. Like a chain reaction, Jeremy's cock spewed white hot cum over Bryce's oil and sweat-slicked chest. Drained, Jeremy slid off of the softening cock and collapsed on top of his teammate.

Bryce remained in a post-orgasmic haze while Jeremy continued to lap away at his spent cock.

"That had to be the most mind-blowing fuck ever," Bryce said. "Why are you laughing?"

"You were right. About letting go and not being ashamed. And I can't believe it took all of this to learn your weakness." Jeremy massaged his cock. "I'm gonna enjoy exploiting that weakness again and again."

"Wait, didn't I win the match?"

"And I won this one."

"The hell you did."

"The hell I didn't."

"What do you propose?"

"Best two out of three?"

"You're on. You're going down. Again."

A beaming Jeremy grabbed Bryce's face and their lips locked once more.

A GEEK'S DEFLOWERING
By Garland

My legs felt like an oversized bowl of Jell-O and the stitch in my side stabbed me like a dagger. My breathing was erratic. It felt like bags of cotton had been shoved in my throat. I was choking. My lips were parched and cracked. Sweat dripped off my face. The already skintight track suit clung with greater desperation to my body leaving nothing to the imagination. The finish line was close. Only another thirty meters to go. Digging deep inside myself, I forced my legs to pick up speed. Slowly, I began to pull ahead of the other runners. I could feel my heart assaulting my chest, trying to burst free of its claustrophobic confines. I could hear it pounding in my ears. Everything seemed to slow down as I crossed the finish line and collapsed. The crowd and my teammates went crazy. The cheerleaders let out massive war whoops, jumping up and down, pom-poms shaking enthusiastically. But, the only thing I could focus on was Tim leaning against the bleachers nodding approvingly.

I didn't think it was possible, but my heart actually beat faster. I figured it was just the post race excitement I often got. Smiling slyly, he clapped and joined the rest of the team as they congratulated me.

"You looked good out there, Berland," he said slapping me on the back. "Keep that up, and you'll lead us to state for sure. Maybe even win it for us."

His words made me blush. Tim, the captain of the track team, the most gorgeous and popular guy in school actually believed in me! Me! A skinny geeky guy who wore oversized glasses and spent all his free time studying.

"Nice job Berland," Coach said. "Pretty good birthday, huh? Happy eighteenth."

"Thanks Coach," I said still trying to catch my breath.

"It's your birthday?" Tim asked.

"Yeah," I answered.

"Happy birthday, bud!" He said before getting the team and fans to sing Happy Birthday to me. It was corny as hell, but Tim had the whole school wrapped around his little finger. The charismatic senior could have ordered the whole team to walk into a volcano, and we would have gladly obeyed.

I waited until all the other guys had left the locker room before I dared strip or shower. When you're surrounded by hot well-muscled horse-hung guys who look like they stepped out of an Abercrombie catalogue you'd be a little shy, too. When I was sure the coast was clear, I ripped off my tracksuit, set my glasses down in my gym bag and dashed into the showers, hands covering my penis.

Standing there under the hot stream, I closed my eyes and let the water wash the sweat from my body. The water, hot as I could stand it, felt great. My body began to relax a combination of fatigue from the race and the magical effect of the water.

Turning off the water, I leaned against the wet tiles, closed my eyes and breathed in deeply. The swirling mist surrounded me and seeped deep into my pores. It felt as if I was in one of those Indian sweat lodges I'd read about. I stayed there until the hot steam grew cold and goose bumps sprouted on my body like weeds.

As I made my way toward the locker room, I sensed that I wasn't alone. Squinting, I wished I hadn't left my

246

glasses in my gym bag. When it comes to me and my glasses I'm like Velma from *Scooby Doo*.

"Missing something?" A voice I knew all too well asked before slipping my glasses on my face.

Standing in front of me, nude and smiling, was Tim. And he was hard! It was like something out of a wet dream. He smiled like a fox and took a step toward me. Gulping, I involuntarily backed up until I bumped into the hard tiles, glistening with little droplets of water. Tim, the captain of the team, the most masculine guy I knew, the guy who was dating the head cheerleader, got within an inch of me. He was so close I could smell him. I could feel his hard penis lightly pulsating against my navel. Why was this man's man so friggin' hard?

"What are you doing?" I asked, my voice a whisper, eyes darting furiously back and forth wondering if this was some kind of trick. "Tim," I choked out trying to stay focused on his deep baby blues. "What are you doing?" I repeated more forceful.

"Happy Birthday," was his simple reply as he put his arms up on either side of my head trapping me. "You're eighteen. Barely legal," he raised his eyebrows and smirked as if we were in the middle of some bad clichéd porno.

Suddenly, striking like a cobra, my track mate's lips were on mine. His hands wrapped around my penis and squeezed making me rise orgasmically onto my toes. Pressing his body against mine, he took my hand and blindly lead it down to his penis. He wrapped my hand around his thickness and pumped into my fist. I could feel it throb and grow as his desire boiled over.

"What are you doing?" I questioned, out of breath and dizzy with lust when he finally came up for air. "Tim, I'm not gay." At least I didn't think I was.

247

"Neither am I, Berland. I'm just a straight horny nineteen-year-old dude, who likes gettin' off. I enjoy suckin' cock and gettin' my cock sucked. Nothin' gay about it."

I didn't say anything, but I thought that was the definition of gay.

Kneeling in front of my flaccid penis, he lightly stroked it with his fingers.

"Let's see if we can get this guy hard," he grinned up at me.

Tim's more experienced mouth easily deep throated my penis. Though with my size I'd hardly say that was an accomplishment. As he loudly licked and slurped my penis began to grow. My eyes grew wide, and my mouth opened in a silent euphoric scream. I clutched his hair and shuddered when he stuck his middle finger into my tight hole. A low throaty moan spilled over my lips. Tim sped up his finger fucking, sending me over the edge and causing me to come in his mouth. God I had never come so hard in my life!

"Yum," he said after he swallowed every last drop. "Now that wasn't so bad. Was it?" He asked lightly stroking my cheek.

"No," I answered. It was the greatest thing I had ever experienced. Even better than jacking off. But what now? Was it good manners to offer some form of reciprocation?

"Do you want me to ...?" I asked indicating his still hard penis.

"Only if you want to. You ever sucked a guy off before?"

"No," I confessed face flushing magenta. "I'm a ... virgin," I whispered the last word as if it were a plague.

"Like a guy virgin or a virgin virgin?"

"The latter," I confessed before add, "both." My eyes drooped to the wet floor like a wilted rose. I felt like the biggest loser in the world.

"Then you don't have to do anything you don't wanna, bud," Tim said. "I think we could have a lot of fun together. You're pretty cute."

Not exactly the words I expected to hear from a 'straight' guy, but Tim was so hot I wasn't complaining. I had no idea where that thought came from. It scared me. Was I gay? Bi? Questioning? Straight curious? As if senior year wasn't hard enough, now I had to deal with this shit?

"Tell you what," Tim said breaking me out of my thoughts. "I'll leave my number on your bag. Use it. Anytime you wanna train or ..." His voice trailed off as he disappeared into the locker room. I watched, hypnotized as his round, smooth ass jiggled with every step he took.

When I left the showers a few minutes later, I was alone. True to his word, Tim had left his phone number on my gym bag. Picking up the paper, I stared at the ten digit number. Shoving it into my pocket, I hastily got dressed and ran all the way home.

The next day, Saturday, I couldn't stop thinking about what had happened in the locker room. My first sexual experience. I never thought it would happen with a guy and a criminally gorgeous guy at that! Hell, I never thought it would happen period. Lying on my bed, I thought of Tim's soft lips, the color of fresh raspberries against my mouth. I imagined his hot mouth closed over my hard penis. The way he had looked up at me and smiled as he squeezed my balls. My penis grew as I remembered the way his finger had felt inside my virgin asshole as he lightly tickled every erogenous zone I hadn't even known I had. Pulling down my pants, I wrapped my fist around my penis and stuck my finger deep inside me.

Stretching my ass, I slowly moved my finger in and out as I masturbated, pretending it was Tim's penis. After I climaxed, I picked up my cell and dialed the number I had already committed to memory.

I dialed and hung up at least a dozen times. My heart was pounding, and I was sweating from places I didn't even know could sweat. The truth was I was terrified out of my mind. What if this was just some big joke? Tim and I weren't friends. We had never hung out except during track, and now he's sucking my penis and saying I'm cute and talking about how we could have a lot of fun? Of course, I was suspicious. On Monday, the word fag could be scrawled all over my locker. Or, I could agree to meet Tim for some 'straight boy' sucking and find myself surrounded by his jock friends ready to play a rousing game of smear the queer.

Despite my better judgment, I finally allowed the call to go through after I dialed. Nervously, I paced back and forth across my bedroom as I struggled with trying to remember how to breathe. I wondered if it was truly possible to wear a hole in the hard oak floor. Bet my mom would love that.

"Hello?" Tim's hunky baritone finally answered. He sounded out of breath, and I couldn't help but wonder why. Had he been running? Working out? Or ... My throat went dry as I imagined him jacking off or maybe Tammy was there and they had been fucking. I'd love to watch him fuck. Bet he's great. Tender? Gentle? Or maybe a total animal? God I wanted to find out. I was nervous, and turned on, I forgot how to speak.

"Hello?" Tim repeated again.

"Hey. It's Bryson," I squeaked out.

"Berland!" He sounded genuinely pleased. "I was hoping you'd call. 'Sup?"

About five inches I thought.

250

"Want to go on a run?" I asked.

"Sure. Meet me at the school in fifteen."

My body was convulsing uncontrollably as I ran to the school. When I got there, Tim was there wearing a pair of very short, very tight running shorts. His smooth, muscular chest gleamed in the sun. I was instantly hard.

"Glad you called," he said.

Good God he was beautiful! Like one of those ancient Greek statues. I was glad I called, too!

"So you want to do some laps?" I asked as I willed my ever growing hard-on to go down.

"Sure," he said.

It was a slow jog around the track. Tim and I talked about everything. School. Our hobbies. What colleges we were hoping to go to. What we wanted to do with our lives. It was the first time I had really ever hung out with a guy before. I liked it.

"I must say," I said after we had stopped and were leaning against the goal post sipping water, "I am a little surprised about all that's happened."

"You mean yesterday in the locker room? Why are you surprised? We're buds. Buds do that," Tim answered casually.

"I've never really had any friends," I answered, voice a whisper in the wind.

"What about me? We're friends. We've run track for the last four years."

"Yeah, but we've never really hung out. We run with too different crowds. We're different. The only time we're together is when it's track season."

"So who gives a shit?" Tim asked. "Look, we should have hung out more. It's probably my fault. Most of high

251

school, I've let other people control whom I'm seen with, and I'm tired of all the high school bullshit. You're a nice guy. So let's start now. We'll hang out like real friends do."

"I'd like that," I said smiling. "So you ready for some more laps?"

"Actually, I'm not really in the mood for a run," he said.

"So what do you want to do?" I asked though judging by the bulge in his shorts I had a pretty good idea what was up.

"I think you know," he said voice going low. "It's the reason you called. The reason why you're tentin'," he said smiling at my shorts.

Quickly, I covered them as I felt my face burn. Tim removed my hands and smiled at me as he brought my hands to his pants and rubbed them on his bulge. I could feel his penis quiver through the thin fabric.

"Don't cover it, Berland." Even though his voice was low there was still a commanding quality to it. I was his slave. He could have asked me to perform an animal sacrifice, and I would have.

"Call me by my first name," my voice was minute, unsure if I should request that.

"Bryson," he said before kissing me.

Instinct took over. My arms and legs wrapped around him. My body pressed itself tight against him. My mouth kissed him back with a fiery intensity I didn't even know I possessed.

"Goddamn Bryson!" he said breathing hard. "You sure you're a virgin?"

All I did was smile as I swooped in for more kisses. My hands explored every inch of his. Slowly, I made my way down his body, kissing and licking every inch of him.

252

Pulling his shorts down over his luscious hips his thick hard-on sprung to life like a soldier saluting a general. Gently I ran my finger over it and his full testicles. Gingerly I stuck my tongue out and licked his large mushroom head. A few drops of salty pre-cum leaked out.

"Don't be afraid of it, Bryson," Tim said grabbing the back of my head and holding me in place as he stuffed his penis inside my mouth.

Holding my head in place, he moved his hips back and forth. His penis tickled my tonsils. Clutching his rock hard ass, I stuck my fingers inside his crack and gently rubbed the sensitive glands.

"Fuck yeah. Keep doing that," he moaned out pounding my mouth harder.

I felt the muscles in his ass squeeze. His balls grew tight, and I could feel his cum traveling through his penis. His knees bent as he held my head in place and shot his load into my mouth. His penis shuddered against my tongue as his cum oozed into my taste buds.

"FUUUUUUUUUUUUUUUUUUUUCKKKKKKKKKK!" He moaned. "Don't swallow," he said out of breath. "Get up here."

Hoisting me up, he kissed me. His tongue penetrated my mouth and swirled the cum. We stood there for what felt like eons swapping his cum back and forth as if our mouths were fancy cocktail mixers before swallowing.

"You taste good," I said.

"Your turn," he said.

Before I could react I was upside down in the pile driver position. My legs were wrapped tightly around Tim's neck. He alternated sucking my penis and licking my ass. Both felt great and I couldn't believe I had waited eighteen friggin' years to do this! All too soon, my virgin penis betrayed me, and I came in Tim's mouth. Gently, he sat me down. Lying on the track with my head resting on his shoulder, I gently pinched his dark nipples.

"So is this what you do?" I asked. "Give guys blowjobs on the track?"

"Sometimes," he said.

"Cool hobby," I said. "You ever do anything else with a guy?" I asked, generally curious.

"You mean fuck?" He asked. "No. I've been kind of curious though. Always wondered if ass feels the same as pussy. Tammy won't let me fuck her up her ass."

"You want to fuck me?" I don't know what made me ask that! The words were out before I could stop them.

"You want me to fuck you?" He answered my question with a question.

I nodded. He smiled.

Back in the locker room, lifting my legs over his shoulders, he gently stuck first one finger than a second in my ass and moved them around before sliding his lubed-up penis into me. I wasn't sure I would be able to take all of him, but somehow he was able to get all of him in me. We were still for a while, getting use to the feel of the other before he started pumping his hips.

"You have such a nice body," I moaned.

"So do you," he said kissing me.

"No I don't. I'm a geek."

He laughed. "I think geeks are hot. Why do you think I'm here with you? You know how turned on I am that I get to deflower a geek? I've never taken anyone's virginity before," he said voice taking on a humble quality. "Thank you."

Smiling, I clutched his broad shoulders and kissed him, enjoying the feel of his penis stretching out my asshole. Picking up speed, he pounded me without mercy making me cry out with pleasure.

"You're so tight Bryson! I'm gonna come! I'm gonna come!" He barely got the words out before I felt his hot cum explode inside me.

Collapsing on top of me, he kissed me and slowly pulled out of me. I couldn't believe it! Tim had actually fucked me! He was just as I'd fantasized he'd be: gentle, tender and animalistic.

"So does ass feel like pussy?" I asked.

"No," he said laughing. "It's better. Think I may have to switch teams. Or at least run for both."

I laughed. "That was great," I said.

"Yeah it was," he said smiling and gently stroking my chin.

He kept his arm around me. We walked back out to the field and stayed for hours looking up at the clouds, talking and fucking and sucking. Before long, we were bathed in twilight. The stars twinkled like diamonds. The moon was large and full bathing us in its pale lavender-blue spotlight. That was when I popped Tim's ass cherry! You don't know how great it felt for a skinny guy like me to actually be fucking the hottest guy in school! When I came, I actually had to restrain myself from crying out, "Geek Power!" His virgin ass was so tight I ... Well, the story of the jock's deflowering is really a story for another day.

MAN-CRUSH
By R. W. Clinger

"Matty, I told you not to touch me down there," Stephan Holdman warns, looking over his right shoulder, attempting to draw my fingers and attention away from his tight bottom.

"Three strikes I'm out, right?" I ask, straying from his not-so-professional lesson in stretching quadriceps.

"You're already out. That's your problem. You have no inhibitions when it comes to guys, even straight ones."

Stephan wears the tightest shorts ever; it's inevitable not to take a finger-tour of his hot rump. The hockey jock is totally too hot to keep my hands off. The six-two goalie is bare-chested and stands in front of me with his palms on the back of a kitchen chair in our apartment. I instruct him, "Lift your right leg off the ground, holding your ankle to your buttock with your knee pointed toward the floor. Hold it for twenty seconds."

"I can't do that with your finger touching my asshole. It's a total distraction."

I think about pulling his shorts down to his ankles and shoving my tongue into his bottom for pure fun. What a shock this would be for the straight guy. Instead, I remove my fingers from his bottom, and place one palm on his muscular hip, assisting his balance. "That's old news. Remember, you're the distraction for me."

Stephan drops his leg, sighs heavily, spins around, and we have a face-off. I wonder what hockey move he is going to harm me with, being a bully: back-check, deflect, hook? Instead, he eyes up my blond-white curls, tepid-blue eyes, muscular six-foot frame, and says, "Let's get the blowjob out of the way, so I can learn how to take care of my body."

His lips almost touch my lips. I feel his masculine breath against my face. I disbelieve what the hockey jock says, and reply with: "Excuse me?"

Stephan's hands go to his sides and leash cotton. He pushes the gold-blue shorts down to his ankles, and says, "Blow it, Matty. Get it over with. You know you want to. You're sexually frustrated over me, and we won't get anything done until you take a lick of it."

The wanker is seven inches of uncut tube and decorated with a triangular patch of spiral brown hair. Balls droop in a mouth-watering furry sack behind limp cock. The entire package is accessorized with muscular hips and a narrow treasure trail of brown curls that lead up to a puckered navel on a muscular stomach.

I assume Stephan is joking with me. He's known for a good tease, particularly when it comes to me having an attraction to his body. Dares are not uncommon practice between roommates. Shaking his naked goods in my face is typical. Usually, I don't call his bluff, but today is different. I'm tired of his playful games. Straight or gay, I desire nothing more than our two bodies to mesh, and want to show him a good time. In doing so, I drop to my knees, open my mouth for his thick stick to do a wake-check on my throat. Lips clamp over the tool, sucking ensues, and his meat starts to come to life, swelling within my mouth.

"Matty," Stephan murmurs, "Matty, what are you doing?"

He doesn't knee me like in a hockey game. Defensive angry punches to my skull do not transpire. A rush does not happen, knocking the wind out of me. Slashing and roughing are not his motive. Instead, hockey boy jives with the rhythm: cock riding in my mouth, steady sucking motion, lips sticking to the pole's base, fingers grazing drooping balls, nose buried into brown curls.

I hold his left hip for balance, and take in the numbingly pleasant smell of his semi-sweaty torso of ash soap and wood spice. The seven inches of his dong turns into nine with chaotic bliss. My head moves up and down on the knob in a feisty and dramatic motion; something I have been longing to carry out for the past six months with his body. My fingertips strum his hairy sack, gliding over their soft texture.

"Matty, you can't do this," Stephan whispers above me, thrusting his hips into my face, bucking my throat with his stick. "Honestly, you have to stop." His palms meet the back of my head and he helps with my up and down mouth-action. "Matty, please stop," he whispers, but his hips glide toward me. Fingertips crumple my blond curls as he begins to huff and puff, catapulted to a plain of deep satisfaction. Sweat drips off of his torso and stings my face. And for the next eight minutes, Stephan forces all nine inches of his meat inside my body, pulls out, and forces them inside again.

I taste a squirt of pre-ooze in my mouth: sticky and bittersweet wonderment on the tip of my tongue. The jock is going to cream my insides if I don't pull off and away from his beef. With skill, I follow my own agenda, end his suck-job, but begin something he has never experienced with another guy before. Still positioned on my knees, my palms find the swollen flag between his thick thighs and begin to massage the protein in a north and south motion. Their action increases by the seconds and ...

"Holy shit, Matty ... I'm going to shoot."

I look up and see that Stephan is red-faced and sweaty. His bear-brown eyes are wide pools of tears, and his mouth is a pink-shadowy cave of awe. Observing these

259

details, I also notice that Stephan's torso starts to tremble with orgasm. And like a good tour-guide on this Sunday afternoon in our apartment's kitchen, I instruct, "Don't be shy now, Stephan. Go ahead and spray it on my ..."

Four lines of shooting cream decorate my chest. Firm nipples are coated in the goo. Tight abs lining my stomach are glazed in the white sap. Shoulders are doused in the sticky stuff. I become soaked in his spurt, cream-covered, and sloppy-sticky.

When Stephan pulls me up and off our kitchen floor, I half expect him to push me away and start cussing me out. Instead, he clings my face to his face, provides a world-spinning kiss with me, pulls off and away, and explains, "I think I have a man-crush on you, Matty Baye. What are we going to do about that?"

What we do about our kitchen affair is simple: We don't bring it up. Not for a week. Not for two weeks. Not for a month. Stephan goes to work at Custer Windows during the day, plays hockey with his male pals in the evenings and on the weekends, and our man-sucking-man tryst in our apartment is never discussed. Stephan is straight with straight friends. I'm gay with a load of Tinkerbell pals. Our only connections are splitting the rent, and my shared knowledge of how to stretch the human body, exercise, and eat well. Stephan sometimes teaches me a little bit about hockey terms, which I don't mind. And, I use his rock-hard jock body as eye candy, often walking around the two-bedroom apartment with a boner the size of the Stanley Cup. What are roommates for, right? It seems to work out just perfectly fine for the both of us. Hell, how can we complain?

Something changes in this design, though. Something wild and shocking, and ...

I do a little bartending at Flower's Bar: Pour whiskey, pass a beer, fill nuts. The place is in-and-out pink, and none of Stephan's jock-friends would ever show their faces under the disco ball, let alone in the bathroom. Friday night is one of the busiest nights. The place is wall-to-wall fags: dancing, smoking, drinking, blowing, doing drugs, and whatever else happens while a Lady Ga Ga impersonator sings on the mini-stage. To my surprise, Stephan shows up around midnight, still wearing his hockey jersey from his evening game on the ice.

Dudes flock to him, which he pushes away. A twink tries to nibble on his right ear, but a dragon stare from Stephan scares him off. Two blonds are interested in his bottom, but Stephan threatens to check them if they get too close.

Caught off guard by his impromptu visit, I lean across the bar and bitch at him, "Stop roughing these innocent guys. Make this short and to the point, and get the fuck out of our bar. No straight guys allowed."

Five words escape his beautiful mouth, and they totally blow me away: "I don't think I'm straight."

I call out to my bar-buddy, "Bobby, cover for me, I've got an emergency here!" and toss down my bar towel for the night. Before I know it, I'm walking with Stephan back to our apartment, overwhelmed with confusion, in silence regarding his confession.

Forty minutes later, inside his bedroom, he pops a DVD into the Sony and ... shit! A quarterback is rimming his linebacker buddy on the screen. And Stephan pulls his hockey jersey off, drops it to the floor, unbuttons his jeans, and says in a rather sexy and heartwarming manner, "I want you to do that to me, Matty. You're the only guy I can trust to get the job done right."

Before I can respond, he is already in his birthday suit, half-sitting and half-lying on his bed: legs spread open, fully erect timber pointing at his chin, taut nipples, and his palms behind his head.

What do I have to lose? Stephan doesn't sleep around. He's not a whore and doesn't go from girl to girl. Plus, he's dazzling perfect: scruff on chin and cheeks, fall-into muddy-brown eyes, steel lines on his chest, perfectly rounded pecs covered in a drizzle of man-fur. I'm given a gift by the gay gods in heaven, and decide to take the hockey player up on his rimming offer.

Quickly, I peel out of my bar clothes, crawl onto his queen-size bed, and drag lips over his smooth, inner thighs. I dot the tip of my tongue at his man-opening and ... Stephan turns off the Sony, totally into the beginning stages of our connection. He moans, agreeing to my tongue-to-ass adventure.

My sliver of moistened tongue laps diligently at his hole, pulls quickly away, and enters its smooth core again.

"Matty, you're a pro at this. You do know everything about the body." He cups the back of my head with his palms, and pushes my face into his bottom. Stephan groans with deep satisfaction, enlightened by this new sexual escapade.

I come off for air, substituting an index finger for my tongue, and ...

The jock throws his head back onto the three cotton pillows in utter bliss and begins to moan.

One fingertip in his asshole turns into two, plus I add my tongue, just for the hell of it. I move the three together with a porn-quality skill. I wiggle and lick, wiggle and lick, and ...

"Your cock, Matty .... Use your cock in my ass. I can't wait for it. I want it. I've been thinking about it since your blowjob in the kitchen."

It's news to me, but good news. Someone's been thinking about me. No, not someone. Stephan Holdman.

The hunky super jock, roommate and window maker with the hold-me-up-from-falling-over charm.

I know he keeps lube and condoms in the night stand next to his bed. Who doesn't? I find the pair and ...

The door to our apartment busts open. Footsteps run through the living room toward Stephan's bedroom.

I quickly bolt under the bed with the lube and condom, and Stephan covers up his firm middle with a blanket near his ankles.

The bedroom door flies open, and one of his jock-buddies enters the room. Sergei Kamensky. The hot and steamy Russian enforcer on Stephan's hockey team. Bald and beautiful from head to toe. One hundred percent beef. He says in his thick Russian, "No more secret, Stephan."

"What secret?" Stephan replies, above me on the mattress.

I see the Russian's clothes drop to the floor: dress shirt, T-shirt, belt. I hear Sergei say, "Fuck you. Now. Tonight. No more secret," and hear him climb onto the bed.

What am I supposed to do? Climb out from under the bed and greet the two with my hard, swinging dog between my legs? Jump into the sack with the duo and ensue a threesome? Or, should I stay hidden under the mattress and springs, and listen to the hockey-jocks get it on?

To my surprise, the bald beauty Russian says, "Man under bed ... join us."

I guess the enforcer must have seen me under the bed when he came into the room. Whatever? It is what it is.

263

Stephan calls down to me, "You heard him, Matty. Get up here and join the fun. It's just one big surprise after the next, isn't it?"

Indeed it is. Not that I object. I slide out from under the bed with the lube and condom, and the hardest piece of meat between my legs. Standing over the twosome, my eyes grow wide with excitement at the sight of the six-plus, 220-pound enforcer on his back. Stephan is positioned on his knees between the jock's legs, and his tight, white ass smiles at me. Following a few slurps and sucks to Sergei's pole, Stephan looks over his left shoulder and says to me in a most alluring tone, "What are you waiting for, Matty? Hop on and fuck me. You know I'm ready for you."

And so it is done. It's hockey time, even if I've never played the game before. I jump on the bed, squirt some lube on my pole, roll a condom over my eight inches, and go to town on Stephan as his mouth goes to town on his secret sex-friend Sergei.

My swollen piece of lumber stabs Stephan's bottom, shocking him. The goalie lets out a roar of desirable pain as if he is being butt-ended on the ice during a heated practice. I reach forward and grab onto his hips, ready for my man-ride. Another inch of my jack enters his hole. Inch number three causes the hockey player to grunt, and inch number four prompts the muscle head to back into my erection. Enough is enough with this light cock-tampering though. I plunge the other four inches of my pole into his center, and begin to glide in and out of his never-been-touched-hole with utter delight.

"High stick it," Sergei coaches our mutual friend in his broken Russian."Suck cum out of it."

Stephan takes the instructions like a pro, even with my rod in his ass. The guy is totally into his work: sucking the Russian off and rocking to and fro with my dick jammed into his bottom. In fact, he works the two of us as

264

well as he works ice. Stephan is a champion between us, a Cup winner. He moans and groans and murmurs. He slurps and sucks and gags. He is completely overjoyed with his beef-buffet and my backside spearing. The guy's ass sucks my dong like his mouth sucks Sergei's tool. He twists in front of me, pushes backward, and takes my shaft deeper and deeper into his middle.

What comes over me is cock-vibrating, and something I have never accomplished before in the company of a man. I spank Stephan: lightly with just enough force. My palm opens and meets his bottom with such ease. One gentle spank turns into three. Slashing in and out of his center in a repeated manner, I whisper, "Blow him, Stephan. Get him off."

Our bodies trip together in a trio of connected bliss. Backs arch with synchronized motion. Cocks pulse together, ready to burst with spirals of geyser-spew. Sweat lathers our threesome pores. And rugged and ripped hips move with a sex-induced harmony. Together we become one on the queen-size bed, in sync with a working mouth, two cocks, and Stephan's firm ass. Our motion is heated, driven, and energetic.

But all good things come to an end, of course. The Russian begins our spray-fest, exclaiming under Stephan's mouth-job, "I going to burst."

Stephen comes off the jock's rod, heaving for breath, and I pull out of his rump, tossing the used condom over my right shoulder, twirling it to the floor.

Sergei instructs, "Circle me."

And like pent sex-followers in a dick-blowing flesh cult, Stephan kneels on the Russian's left side, and I kneel on his right side.

"Jack you off," Sergei says in his broken language, and reaches for our swollen thumpers. Immediately, he starts to move his fists to and fro on our sticks, working them with speed. Sergei looks up at the two of us, and coaches, "Blow on me."

Stephan's fall-into eyes connect with mine. He leans forward and kisses me, moaning from Sergei's hand-job. Our tongues connect and we close our eyes, finding a state of aloneness. The kiss is pure magic between us, moving our friendship to a whole new level of likeness. His fingertips find my chest and he begins to pinch my nipples: first the right one, then the left one.

My hips thrust forward and backward, and I can't hold my load in any longer. Sergei's palm on my rod is too much to handle. And Stephan's fingertips gently pinching my nipples are just as mind-blowing. I'm the first one to blow, slap shotting hot sap all over Sergei, decorating his abs, navel, and nipples.

Still kissing Stephan, I mumble, "Fire your wad. I want to watch you."

Stephan huffs with satisfaction. He quickly pulls away from me, plants his palms on his hips, and begins to ride Sergei's palm. Thrust after thrust builds an energetic orgasm. He clamps his teeth together. Every muscle on his torso firms up. Four more thrusts transpire and ...

Stephan finds his shooting angle with skill. White juice arches out of his poker and washes Sergei's abs. Two more arches exit Stephan's stick, lining Serge's skin. The man-liquid clings to the enforcer's bare flesh like syrup. And Stephan releases a sigh of contentment, spent and drained with elation spread over his adorable face.

Seconds later, I suggest to Stephan, "Let's blow the Russian off," and bend over. My lips meet Sergei's stiff pole, and I begin to lick the side of it in a quick, up and down motion.

Stephan joins in on the fun, licking the other side of the Russian's dick. Together we give the enforcer some heavy-duty slurping and spit-lathering action. Our tongues meet and our eyes connect with passion.

Sergei palms our heads, pushing them down when my lips meet Stephan's lips at the uncut head of Sergei's pole. Downward our opened mouths and outstretched tongues fall. Upward our faces rise in a speedy motion. Together, we drive the Russian into a panting and hip-rising action. And together we cause the jock to mumble, "Coming."

Our lips and tongues are replaced with right hands. We finish Sergei off with our busy fists, gliding them up and down on his beef, working him into overdrive. The Russian heaves for breath and bucks our grips. He mumbles, "Coming," again, red-faced and sweaty.

A thick stream of ooze juts out of his post and flies against his ripped torso and mountainous nipples, mixing with our loads. The Russian continues to mumble, "Coming ... coming ... coming," until his wanker is fully drained, until he becomes spent and crumpled on the bed next to us, smiling in absolute pleasure.

Post-sex, we kiss as a trio, laughing. And then the Russian decides to get a shower, leaving me alone with Stephan. I cuddle next to his mass on the bed, taking in his aftermath man-stink, which is a total turn-on for me. I inquire, "What's up with the Russian?"

"Trust me," Stephan huffs, "that was a total surprise for me. We're pretty good friends, but obviously the guy has a man-crush on me."

"That makes two of us," I reply, providing his right nipple with a greedy lick.

"Make that three," Stephan chants, kissing me. Following the tongue-in-mouth kiss, he asks, "You okay with sharing me, Matty?"

"Are you kidding? Sergei is fucking hot. Two hockey players to fuck around with. What more could a physical trainer want?"

"Two cocks are better than one, right?"

"I wouldn't have it any other way."

Stephan laughs, "I thought you would say that," and pulls me off the bed, leading me to our bathroom to shower with Sergei, beginning another sex round among the three of us.

FOOTBALL DADDIES
By Milton Stern

Dan and Bobby had played football together for close to thirty years, from peewee through high school and finally on the same pro team and always on the offensive line. When Dan decided before he turned forty-two that it was time to retire, Bobby came to the same conclusion within minutes. He couldn't imagine playing the game without his best friend around, especially since they had been lovers for the past fifteen years. But, they didn't know what to do in retirement? A lot of football players went into the restaurant business or lent their names to other service industry venues, but Dan and Bobby had no interest in that. Their decision became easier when they heard of a gym that was up for sale in their hometown because the owner had died and his kids had no intention of running it.

They flew down to Elkhart, North Carolina, a small town most maps ignore, and made an offer on the old place. The heirs were more than happy to unload the business and accepted their price without hesitation. Dan and Bobby paid cash and found themselves in the gym business.

Once they found a place to rent until they decided where to live permanently, they began the work of renovating what would become the D&B Fitness Factory. This was one of those old time gyms with benches, free weights, no machines to speak of, and only a couple of stationary bikes serving as cardio equipment. There were mirrors on all the walls and an open shower room that could accommodate eight people at a time.

The work began with getting rid of all the old equipment, so they donated it to an organization that sends fitness gear to developing countries. They ordered all new benches, rubber coated plates, a few basic machines and a couple of treadmills and arc trainers. Their goal was to keep the gym as 'old-school' as possible. They figured if they tried to go fancy, they would not be able to compete with the 'pretty boy' club in the next town.

Elkhart may have been a small town, but football was huge there. Dan and Bobby weren't the only former residents to go pro. Many of their former teammates bought property near the coast, which was only a thirty minute drive from where they were, and once they opened for business, the D&B Fitness Factory filled up every day with quite a few muscle daddies.

Dan and Bobby were all too happy to offer a gym their fellow gray hairs could enjoy. Dan stood over six feet and weighed over 250 pounds of solid muscle with a 50-inch chest, 19-inch arms and maintaining a 36-inch waist, all covered in salt and pepper fur from his head to his feet. Bobby was smooth, but no less impressive with a shaved head to match. He stood barely five-ten, weighed almost 225 pounds, but had just as much muscle as Dan with an even broader chest and bigger biceps, but he carried a few inches around his belly. He had one of those tight bellies that many a boy finds sexy. Dan loved Bobby's belly and would come on it every chance he could get. They were both also hung very nicely and circumcised with big round balls, making for a beautiful sight in the bedroom.

The gym was doing very well as they had tapped into a market that the mega-gyms were ignoring. It also helped that they did not require that their members wear shirts, only proper footwear and shorts as long as they cleaned off the equipment after each use. Dan and Bobby did this mostly for their own entertainment since they both enjoyed watching big men get all sweaty and pumped. Even with the lenient rules, the place was kept immaculate, especially the shower room, which was no small feat considering some of the action, rumored to be occurring in there, especially right before the 10:00 pm closing time.

Dan and Bobby had not engaged in any of the antics but had witnessed a few while they were working. They had hired a college senior, who was getting a degree as a physical therapist, to work the evening hours, so they could have a life outside the business, and he was a very hard worker. Miles was also an offensive lineman in high school, who decided not to play college ball for reasons he never explained, so Bobby and Dan took a special liking to him. At twenty-two years old, Miles was already as big as many of the pros, standing at over six-foot-four and over 260 pounds with a solid frame holding a 52-inch chest and 20-inch arms. He was not only big and muscular, but he was devastatingly handsome as well with dark features, curly black hair and covered in just a touch of curly black fur. When he smiled, men and women melted regardless of their sexual inclinations.

Dan joked that he didn't care how competent he was; Miles had the job the second he applied. What made him even more appealing was his lack of attitude or ego. Miles was a damn hard worker and kept the gym spotless and in order. He never engaged in 'activities,' nor did he do anything inappropriate. He was quiet and respectful with a pleasant demeanor. He only made one request. Miles wanted to be able to work out after the gym closed for the evening since this would not interfere with his studies. Dan and Bobby suspected Miles was a bit of a loner, for he never received personal calls, was seen texting or had any buddies come by the gym to visit. They wanted to invite him over for dinner, but somehow never got around to it. What they did learn was that his parents died when he was very young and that he was raised by his grandmother, who recently died. He had no other family and lived in the apartment where he was raised.

Dan and Bobby would usually workout mid-day when the gym was the least busy, but this became a hassle as the business of running a business takes more time than people realize, so they decided to try working out at 4:00 am before they opened. This lasted only a couple of days because getting up at 3:00 am was nearly impossible, too. That was when Dan suggested they follow Miles's lead and workout after hours. This would work since they hired Bobby's nephew to open for them during the week, and they could come in around 7:00 am. Bobby's nephew was competent but not worth the trouble of describing since he spent most of his time at work surfing the net and texting his girlfriend. He was just there to occupy space until Dan and Bobby came in. Miles left the place in such order that there was nothing to do in the mornings, and Bobby told Miles that he knew his nephew was useless, but he needed him for those two hours, so he and Dan could get some rest. Miles never complained. And, Dan and Bobby would keep the place in order while they worked and tended to the business as well.

Around 10:30 pm, Dan and Bobby showed up on the first night they decided to try their new workout schedule. The gym was closed, and the blinds were drawn, but they could see Miles shadow as he worked out inside. They told Miles they would be coming in to work out, so that he wouldn't be startled when the door opened.

Dan and Bobby walked in just as Miles lay down on a bench to perform dumbbell presses with 110-pound weights. They both stopped in their tracks at the sight before them. Wearing nothing but a pair of black 2xist briefs that did little to hide his candy and a pair of New Balance cross trainers, he was pushing the weights up, and his chest was glistening and pumped.

He finished his set and sat up on the bench. "Hey, when you didn't show up at closing, I decided to get comfortable. I'll go get my shorts," Miles said as he greeted them.

"Don't ...," Dan almost shouted.

"... worry about us," Bobby interrupted. "Stay comfortable."

"Are you sure?" Miles asked as he stood up, revealing his body to them for the first time.

"I didn't realize how hot it gets in here with the AC off. Why didn't you reprogram it to stay on for an hour after closing?" Bobby asked.

"I didn't think I had the authority," Miles the ever-dutiful employee responded. "Besides, I prefer it warm when I work out."

Dan and Bobby walked toward the locker room to put away their gym bags, and Miles dropped to the floor to do a set of push-ups. They each glanced at his perfect, big, muscular butt as it went up and down.

In the locker room, Dan took off his shirt as Bobby did the same. "Should we strip down as well?" Dan whispered.

"I might pop wood," Bobby said with a smile. "But, what the hell?!?"

They each stripped down, Dan to a pair of white Calvin Klein briefs, and Bobby to a pair of black trunk briefs of the same brand. They exited the locker room and joined Miles in the gym. Miles went about his chest workout as if everything was normal, and Dan and Bobby worked legs.

Occasionally, they would smile at each other, but Miles was very serious about his workouts, as were Dan and Bobby, and after the initial excitement of being half

273

naked with the college senior wore off, all were grunting and sweating their asses off.

Miles was attempting to do a set of incline dumbbell presses with 110-pound weights, but was struggling to lift them into position to begin his set. Dan noticed this and offered to help him.

"Thanks, maybe I should begin with the inclines. I can never lift them up this far into my workout," Miles said as Dan walked over. Bobby followed.

"Lie back, and Bobby and I'll hand them to you."

"I'll give you a spot, once you get started," Bobby added.

Miles lay back, and Dan and Bobby on either side of him lifted up the dumbbells and waited until Miles was holding them firmly. Bobby then positioned himself behind Miles to spot him. He managed five reps before he needed assistance, and Bobby helped him with two more.

Once he was done with the set, Miles thanked them, but Bobby remained crouched behind the bench. Dan looked at him, and Bobby motioned downward with his eyes, for he was sporting a hard-on that could not be hidden.

"Let us know when you are ready for another set," Dan said and winked at Bobby.

Miles lay down on the bench again, and was ready in thirty seconds. The kid really did an intense workout.

They helped him get a grip on the dumbbells again, and Bobby hoped Miles didn't see the bulge in his trunk briefs.

Miles did this set and another, and at that point, Bobby's underwear was soaked with precum. He quickly went to the locker room to fetch another pair he hoped he remembered to put in his gym bag. There was a pair, and by the time he had removed the soaked pair and wiped off his dick, he was no longer as hard, but still a little firm. He changed into a matching pair of black trunk briefs, which he was relieved he packed, for he would have to explain the change in wardrobe.

He exited the locker room, and the sight he saw was about to ruin another pair of underwear. Dan was doing a set of squats, and Miles was spotting him from behind. Bobby stood there awestruck at the sight before him, and his dick was now out of control, hard as a rock and leaking like a faucet. When Dan struggled for a few more reps, Miles leaned in closely to help. Two reps later, the set was done.

Miles stepped back, and Dan stepped away from the rack, and he was now sporting a rager equal to Bobby's. He looked over at Bobby, who looked over at Miles, who looked at both of them and smiled.

"I get hard when I work out, too," Miles said. And when they looked down, they noticed his underwear was beginning to stretch quite a bit. He then dropped down and did another set of push-ups, while Dan and Bobby watched.

Dan looked at Bobby and shrugged, and Bobby shrugged back. Miles then finished his set and declared his workout was done, and he was going to take a shower. Meanwhile, the bulge in his briefs was bigger than before and the head of his dick was sticking out of the waistband. Miles walked past Bobby and into the locker room. Within seconds, the sound of a shower being turned on was heard, and Bobby turned to follow him.

"Are we done working out?" Dan asked as he followed Bobby.

Bobby never answered. He stepped out of his newly precummed briefs and into the shower room where Miles was using the middle-most showerhead. Dan followed suit. Bobby chose the shower to the right of Miles and Dan decided to occupy the one on the left. They watched as Miles soaped himself up and were mesmerized by his pumped, heavily muscled and lathered body and his enormous circumcised cock that stood out and up. Dan and Bobby's big dicks were just as hard.

Dan soaped himself up waiting for Bobby to take the lead if anything were going to happen. And, take the lead, Bobby did. He lathered up his hand, reached down, and began stroking Miles's dick, and he was met with no resistance. Dan then leaned in and kissed Bobby full on the mouth, and their tongues wrestled as Miles reached down and stroked both their cocks. Within seconds, Bobby was ready to pop, so he grabbed Miles's hand to stop the momentum, but Miles proved to be quite strong. That strength was all it took, and Bobby was shouting and shooting a load all over Miles's hand and leg.

Not even a second after that, Dan added to the spunk on Miles and shouted his pleasure as well. The hands of a physical therapist were obviously magic. Dan planted his mouth back on Miles and Bobby continued to stroke the enormous cock until it shot a load all over the shower wall – a load so impressive that Dan and Bobby almost applauded.

Once he caught his breath, Miles declared, "I've never touched a man before. I have wanted to do that with you guys since the day you hired me."

"You never touched a man?" Bobby asked with surprise.

"Where did you learn to stroke like that?" Dan asked.

"I guess from playing with myself," Miles said as he resumed soaping himself up.

Bobby stopped him, and Dan joined Bobby as they lathered up Miles, taking turns kissing him and stroking

276

him until he shot another load – this time on the shower floor.

# # # # #

Dan and Bobby soon found a 19th Century home that suited them perfectly and settle in nicely. Miles graduated from college and landed a job at a local hospital as a physical therapist.

Does Miles still work at the gym part-time? You bet he does, and he still works out in his underwear after closing every night along with Dan and Bobby. But now, they sometimes shower at the gym or the three of them go home afterward to shower, where they live in a poly-amorous relationship that has 'worked out' quite well.

Teammates for life!

ABOUT THE AUTHORS

CLIFF MORTEN is German, a teacher of art, and a licensed guide for free climbing.

DERRICK DELLA GIORGIA was born in Italy and currently lives between Manhattan and Rome. His work has been published in several anthologies and literary magazines: "Courtesy of the Hotel" in *Island Boys* (Alyson Books), "Couch with a View" in *Cruising for Bad Boys* (STARbooks Press), "A Secret Worth Keeping" in *Pretty Boys & Roughnecks* (STARbooks Press), "Pyramids in Rome" in *Best Gay Love Stories 2010* (Alyson Books), "Antimatter Matt" in *Unmasked II: More Erotic Tales of Gay Superheroes* (STARbooks Press), "Santa's Red Furry Briefs" in *Unwrapped: Erotic Holiday Tales* (STARbooks Press), "Panoply" on Six Sentences, "Heart Tartare" on writers'DOJO, "How Did You Meet Philippe Hcnirt?" in *Boys Getting Ahead* (STARbooks Press), "Number 023 of the 200 Made" in *Biker Boys: Gay Erotic Stories* (Cleis Press). Visit him at www.derrickdellagiorgia.com.

DONALD WEBB has been writing for a number of years, and he's had stories published in *Obsessions*, *Mandate*, *Honcho*, and *Torso*. He is currently editing a completed mystery novel.

GARLAND ran long distance in high school and always spent time in the locker room discovering who the real MVPs of the team were. Garland is currently living in North Hollywood, California, where he works as an actor and writer. His short stories have appeared in the anthologies *Best Gay Love Stories: Summer Flings*, *Frat Sex II*, *The Mammoth Book of Erotic Confessions*, *The Mammoth Book of the Kama Sutra*, *SexTime: Erotic Stories of Time Travel*, and the forthcoming *The Moron's Guide to the*

Inevitable Zombocolypse. Garland is also currently working on a paranormal-erotic TV series he hopes to pitch to Cinemax as well as getting into writing scripts for adult studios. Garland can be contacted via www.myspace.com/hiphopjoe or JFilip4675@aol.com.

Published in dozens of gay erotic anthologies, **JAY STARRE** grinds out fiction from his home in Vancouver, Canada. His short stories can be found in STARbooks titles like *Love in a Lock-Up, Don't Ask, Don't Tie Me Up, Unmasked: Erotic Tales of Gay Superheroes, Boys Caught in the Act, Pretty Boys and Roughnecks* and *Service With a Smile.* His steamy gay novels, *Erotic Tales of the Knights Templar* and *Lusty Adventures of the Knossos Prince*, are also published by STARbooks Press.

Originally from Vancouver, BC, **JUSTIN SHEPHERD** now lives and works in New York City. Road cycling is one of his life's passions, along with modern art, male-themed photography, gay causes and Italian coffee, to name only a few. He enjoys writing and sees it as a way of bringing together many diverse interests and exploring some of life's mysteries.

KALE NAYLOR is an Atlanta writer whose work has appeared in a number of LGBT magazines and anthologies. His piece, *The Legacy of Caliban*, was featured in STARbooks popular *Unmasked II: More Erotic Tales of Gay Superheroes* anthology. An All-American frat boy, many of Naylor's stories are based on his real life misadventures. That is, the stories that won't get him in trouble with the law are the only ones he's admitting to.

South African **LEW BULL** recently had his fifth novel published, entitled *Shadows*. This novel adds to his collection of mystery stories titled, *Power Buddies, Wet, Wild & Willing, The Bonds of Friendship*, and Caribbean Cruising. Added to these is his recently published anthology of exotic cocktail recipes accompanied by equally erotic stories entitled, *Cocktales*. Other recent anthologies that contain his work include, *Cruise Lines, Taken By Force, Boys Will Be Boys, Don't Ask, Don't Tie Me Up, Service with a Smile, Pretty Boys & Roughnecks, Special Forces,* and *SexTime.*

LOGAN ZACHARY lives in Minneapolis, where he is an avid reader, writer, and book collector. His stories can be found in *Hard Hats, Taken by Force, Boys Caught in the Act, Ride Me Cowboy, Service with a Smile, Surfer Boys, Ultimate Gay Erotica 2009, Time Travel Sex, Queer Dimensions, Best Gay Erotica 2009, Unwrapped, Unmasked II, Biker Boys,* and *Boys Getting Ahead.* He can be reached at LoganZachary2002@yahoo.com.

MICHAEL BRACKEN's short fiction has been published or is forthcoming in *Best Gay Romance 2010, Boys Getting Ahead, Country Boys, Flesh & Blood: Guilty as Sin, Freshmen, Hot Blood: Strange Bedfellows, The Mammoth Book of Best New Erotica 4, Men, Ultimate Gay Erotica 2006,* and in many other anthologies and periodicals.

With almost a quarter-century experience in the publishing industry, **MILTON STERN** has written several short stories for the Eric Summers anthologies, including, *Unmasked: Erotic Tales of Gay Superheroes, Don't Ask, Don't Tie Me Up, Ride Me Cowboy, Service with a Smile, Unwrapped – Erotic Holiday Tales,* and *Unmasked II: More Erotic Tales of Gay Superheroes.* In 2011, STARbooks will release his first anthology collection: *Muscles, Men and Mayhem.* He is also the creator of "Kosher Man!" Milton is the author of several books, including *Harriet Lane, America's First Lady; On Tuesdays, They Played Mah Jongg;* and *Michael's Secrets.* Residing in Rockville, MD, Stern is also an active volunteer with the Leukemia and Lymphoma Society, The Washington Animal Rescue League, Straight Eights LCCI, Gay Antique Car Club, and Montgomery Men. Milton also played center from little league to high school, including a few seasons with Eric

Summers! You can learn more about Milton at www.miltonstern.com.

R. TALENT is the bastard seed that STARbooks Press thought they wiped away on the cum towel. He has been published in such anthologies as *Love in a Lock-Up*, *Don't Ask, Don't Tie Me Up*, and *Ride Me Cowboy*. He can be reached for comment or conversation at rtalent@rocketmail.com.

R. W. CLINGER's gay erotic fiction has appeared in the *Friction* series, *Men Magazine*, and *Freshmen*. His novels with STARbooks Press include *The Pool Boy* and *Soft on the Eyes*. He is currently at work on a new novel titled *Splash Boys*.

RJ BRADSHAW lives in Saskatoon, Saskatchewan, where he founded a romantic greeting card company to showcase this poetry. His short fiction has been published in Queered Fiction's *Queer Wolf* and Queer Dimensions anthologies.

ROB ROSEN, author of the novels *Sparkle: The Queerest Book You'll Ever Love* and *Divas Las Vegas*, has been published, to date, in more than eighty anthologies, most notably the STARbooks Press collections: *Ride Me Cowboy*, *Service with a Smile*, *Unmasked II: More Erotic Tales of Gay Superheroes*, *Cruising for Bad Boys*, *SexTime*, *Pretty Boys and Roughnecks*, and *Boys Getting Ahead*. Please visit him at www.therobrosen.com or email him at robrosen@therobrosen.com.

SHANE ALLISON's first volume of poetry, *Slut Machine* is forthcoming from Rebel Satori Press.

STEPHEN OSBORNE has had stories published in dozens of anthologies, including *Pretty Boys and Roughnecks*, *Unwrapped*, *Best Gay Love Stories 2010*, *Queer Wolf*, and *Service with a Smile*. He is also the author of *South Bend Ghosts and Other Northern Indiana Haunts*. He lives in Indianapolis with Jadzia the Wonder Dog where

282

he denies the rumors that he likes to make out with straight guys at parties.

WAYNE MANSFIELD lives in Perth, Western Australia. His erotica has appeared in STARbooks collections, *Boys Caught in the Act*, *Pretty Boys and Roughnecks*, *Nerdvana* and *SexTime,* and he is the author of *Highway Patrol* – one of the first short stories available in paperback. He is currently working on a collection of his vampire erotica.

THE EDITOR

ERIC SUMMERS resides in West Palm Beach with his partner, Mickey Erlach. This is his eleventh anthology for STARbooks Press. He played on the same football team as one of our contributors for a couple of seasons, and they continue to play on the same team with Mickey as their coach.

earing any underwear. "Excuse me," I said, having a hard time look

linded by that bulge in his crotch, "but don't I know you?" "Maybe

ind of t   bout a

with Ray   God, y

t loser?   in?" h

aid. "Lik   s stron

ce body   e on G

lly, he l   s I ever

u up to t   any ide

istaking   e sam

n, I coul   ery lor

ood raci   ie swe

ing with   e in st

we go c   behin

ill see u   in pul

ed?" he   vent tc

rivacy.   grabb

hard. I

k, traci   t, so f

ed it, ha

with my   bbing c

bbing, I   n cock

he sound of unzipping filled the small space. I don't know who's h

, but before I knew it, I had his rod in my hand, and mine was in hi

t to do?" he asked, his tone challenging. I knew exactly, and sank

www.ingramcontent.com/pod-product-compliance
Lightning Source LLC
Chambersburg PA
CBHW051527260626
47170CB00003B/824

* 9 7 8 1 9 3 4 1 8 7 7 0 8 *